Burroughs c.2
The bandit of Hell's Bend..

DATE DUE			
JUL 1 1981	OCT 4 1991		
JUL 6 1981	OCT 21 1991		
JUL 14 1981	FEB 18 '92		
JUL 22 1981	MAY 27 '92		
JUL 28 1981	AUG 17 '92		
AUG 31 1981	MAY 19 '94		
DEC 28 1981			
JAN 11 1982			
JAN 20 1982			
MAY 22 '84			
FEB 19 '85			
APR 11 '85			

The Bandit of Hell's Bend

The Gregg Press Western Fiction Series

Priscilla Oaks, Editor

The Bandit of Hell's Bend

Edgar Rice Burroughs

with a new introduction by

Robert E. Morsberger

Gregg Press

A division of G. K. Hall & Co., Boston, 1979

With the exception of the Introduction, this is a complete photographic reprint of a work first published in New York by Grosset & Dunlap in 1925. The trim size of the original hardcover edition was 5 by 7½ inches.

Frontmatter designed by Designworks, Inc. of Cambridge, Massachusetts.

Printed on permanent/durable acid-free paper and bound in the United States of America.

Republished in 1979 by Gregg Press, A Division of G.K. Hall & Co., 70 Lincoln St., Boston, Massachusetts 02111

First Printing, September 1979

Library of Congress Catalging in Publication Data
Burroughs, Edgar Rice, 1875–1950.
The bandit of Hell's Bend.

(The Gregg Press western fiction series)
Reprint of the ed. published by Grosset & Dunlap, New York.
Includes bibliographical references.
I. Title. II. Series: Gregg Press western fiction series.
PZ3.B944Ban 1979 [PS3503.U687] 813'.5'2 79-16673
ISBN 0-8398-2577-3

Introduction

Of Edgar Rice Burroughs' approximately 70 novels, only four are Westerns. The works which made his reputation and which caused Ray Bradbury to call him to most influential writer of the 20th century are science fiction and fantasy novels—the series of books about Tarzan, Barsoom (Mars), Amtor (Venus), and Pellucidar. Yet Burroughs was better equipped to write Westerns than such novelists as Zane Grey and Clarence Mulford, who worked exclusively in that genre. Grey was an Ohioan and Mulford a New Yorker, neither of whom saw the West until after they became established as novelists, whereas Burroughs knew the old West first hand and had experience both as a working cowboy and as a cavalryman.

In fact, his first novel opens in Arizona in 1866, as Captain John Carter of Virginia, formerly of the Confederate cavalry, is prospecting for gold. Carter is trapped in a cave by hostile Apaches who have killed his partner. But instead of continuing a Western tale, Burroughs transports his hero's spirit out of his body and sends it across the immensities of space to the red planet Mars. Thus Burroughs was launched into a career as a writer of speculative rather than realistic fiction. And once he had started his major series of novels, it was easier to write sequels (especially as publishers and readers were eager for them) than to shift into a different direction.

It was not until 1923 that Burroughs began his first Western, and then only at the urging of Sir Algernon Methuen, his British publisher, whose request for a "wild west" story made Burroughs think "the English reader would want the motion picture type of cowboy, which exists only in the pictures." Burroughs responded with reservations, saying such a book "might have little or no value here, since the readers on this side seem to prefer my highly imaginative stuff."[1] When Sir Algernon made no financial commitment, Burroughs asked Robert Davis, fiction editor of the Munsey magazines, for his advice. Davis answered, "You seem to be pretty well equipped to handle rough men, wild animals, and coarse country. I would print a western story from you in a minute. Let 'er go."[2] Accordingly, Burroughs began the project, but (as he informed Curtis Brown) "with little likelihood of its being very enthusiastically received by my American publishers. . . ."[3]

Burroughs' original genius lay in conjuring up imaginary worlds—the outward trappings of the historic West. Having known this West first hand, Burroughs was determined to present it as realistically as possible, both in background, character, and colloquial dialogue, though he admitted that ranch life was "rather prosaic" and that "for English consumption" it would "have to be speeded up a bit. . . ."[4] Burroughs had, in fact, ventured occasionally into fiction with an attempt at social realism—*The Girl From Farris's (1965), The Efficiency Expert (1966),* and *The Girl From Hollywood (1923).* The latter, written the year before Burroughs received the communication from Metheun, is, in fact, a Western in part, for it contrasts the corruption of the motion picture industry at the time of the drug addiction of Olive Thomas and Wallace Reid, the sex scandals of Mary Miles Minter and Mabel Normand, the murder of William Desmond Taylor, and the Fatty Arbuckle scandal with the wholesome outdoor life on a ranch in the San Fernando Valley, where the heroine becomes cured of heroin addiction and helps the hero outmaneuver a band of smugglers operating in the foothills. But this is the West of Tarzana, when it was still unspoiled and rancho country and had not become part of megalopolitan Los Angeles. For his new project, though he indicated that it was not to be a historical novel, he went back to Arizona in the 1880s and drew upon the memories of his youth.

Burroughs was born in Chicago in 1875 and grew up in the Middle West. His father owned and operated the American Battery Company in Chicago, and when one of his sons developed weak lungs from inhaling battery fumes, the father bought part interest in a cattle ranch in Southern Idaho and sent the patient there to recover his health. Harry Burroughs, the battery fumes victim, and his brother George were to manage the Burroughs interests at Sweetser & Burroughs, Dealers in Livestock. Since both of the brothers were Yale graduates, they named the post office Yale, Idaho, and called the ranch the Bar Y, in honor of their alma mater. It was located in the southern part of the state, about 30 miles from American falls, along the lower Raft River. There, in 1891, Burroughs senior sent their younger brother Edgar, in the hope of instilling some discipline into the reluctant and rebellious schoolboy. Burroughs was 15 years old in the spring of 1891, and knew so little about the West that as a schoolboy he drew a picture of an American Indian riding an elephant. But he learned fast. Though he had never ridden a horse before, and had had only an occasional pony ride in Chicago, he rapidly became an expert horseman who frequently rode 60 miles round trip in a day to carry the mail to American Falls. He took part in the spring roundup and thoroughly enjoyed himself. As he recalled for an article in *Amazing Stories* in June of 1941, "Somewhere along the line I went to Idaho and punched cows. I greatly enjoyed the experience, as there were no bathtubs in Idaho at that time. I recall having gone as long as three weeks on a roundup without taking off my boots and Stetson."

Eminent historian Frederick Jackson Turner had declared 1890 as the date for the closing of the frontier, but the message had not reached Idaho a few months later, when Burroughs arrived there in the spring of 1891. Range wars were still being carried on, and Burroughs recalled that one man with whom he rode during the spring roundup was "a very likeable murderer" who had beaten to the draw a man hired to kill him.[5] He also met several characters who were to reappear in his novel. In a note of April 17, 1925, to the copyeditor of the hardcover edition, Burroughs stated that several characters were based upon people he had known in Idaho: "Gum Smith the sheriff, and Wildcat Bob are drawn with more or less fidelity to life, though they are paraded under assumed names." The actual sheriff was one Gum Brown, of whom Burroughs recollected, "Whenever anyone had to be arrested or a posse was formed, Gum would go around the saloon and point to the cowboys saying, 'I deputize yo; I deputize yo,' and nobody would pay any attention to him. It was a standing joke in Albion."[6] Bill Gatlin, the stagecoach driver with his tall tales, was also taken from life. Burroughs also remembered a young cowboy named Texas Pete, who worked several weeks at the ranch clearing out sagebrush for $.75 an acre, from which he had to pay for room and board, so that when he quit several weeks later, his total take was "six bits," which he promptly lost to Burroughs in a crap game. Burroughs commented about him, "He had the reputation of being a bad man, but there was nothing bad about him."[7] But the sheriff was after Pete for some petty offense; and when Pete tried to escape across the Snake River in a rowboat, the sheriff shot and killed him. The Texas Pete of the novel is the hero's loyal sidekick, the balladeer of an endless piece of comic doggerel. The description of Pete as "a thing of beauty and a joy forever," with silver inlaid Mexican spurs that dragged the ground and had dumbbells attached to them is a self-portrait of Burroughs, who wrote of himself (in *Amazing Stories*, June, 1941), "I wore Mexican spurs inlaid with silver; they had enormous rowels and were equipped with dumbbells. When I walked across a floor, rowels dragged behind and the dumbbells clattered; you could have heard me coming for a city block." Despite his comic self-portrait, he became a superb rider and prided himself on being able "to ride anything that wears hair."[8]

Burroughs' first Western adventure was of short duration, for his father summoned him home in September, 1891 and enrolled him in the Phillips Academy, where he was a misfit. After several frustrating months, his father withdrew him and enrolled him in the Michigan Military Academy, where he continued to be restless and rebellious at first but where he furthered his riding skills in the Academy's cavalry platoon. Furthermore, the new commandant of the school, Captain Charles King, had written a number of novels about army life in the West. Burroughs read many of these, continued to buy them after graduation, and called them "the best army stories ever written."[9] Perhaps they inspired his next move, for upon graduation, having failed the West Point entrance examination (a congressman from Idaho had nominated him), he enlisted as a private in the regular Army in May, 1896, and was posted to Fort Grant in the Arizona Territory, where he was assigned to Troop B, 7th Regiment, U.S. Cavalry. Most of the men in the regiment that Custer had once commanded were veterans of the Indian wars. Though the wars had been over now for ten years, there were still minor skirmishes with outlaw Apaches who had not been subdued when Geronimo surrendered in 1886. In addition, an outlaw named "Black Jack" Tom Ketchum was raiding nearby towns. Despite some expeditions in search of another outlaw named the Apache Kid, who was terrorizing the region, Burroughs did not find in Arizona the adventure or romance he had hoped for. Instead, life at the remote, bleak, and dusty army post consisted mostly of monotonous road work. Frustrated and homesick, Burroughs tried to arrange a transfer back to Illinois. He was unsuccessful but was discharged altogether on March 23, 1897, when he was diagnosed as disabled by an irregular heartbeat.

Considering that his positive experiences with the West had been in Idaho, and his ten months in Arizona had been almost entirely disappointing, it is curious that all of Burroughs' Western novels take place in Arizona, which aside from just enough danger to give it an edge of excitement, appears positively idyllic in *The Bandit of Hell's Bend* and *The Deputy Sheriff of Comanche County (1940)*. Perhaps the reason is that the Southwest has taken on more associations of adventure, so that a majority of Western movies take place there, and hardly any are located in Idaho, Oregon, Washington, and northern California.

Burroughs returned to the American Battery Company for a year but then headed West again to join his brothers in Idaho. Unfortunately, they had been losing money and could not offer him a steady job. The Spanish-American War was breaking out, and despite his discharge for disability, Burroughs wrote to Colonel Theodore Roosevelt, requesting a position in the Rough Riders; but Roosevelt replied that he was swamped with volunteers and could not take one from so far away as Idaho. With no better prospects, Burroughs borrowed some money and opened a stationery store in Pocatello. Apparently, Pocatellans were not reliable correspondents, for the store failed; and after helping again with the spring roundup, Burroughs retreated once more to the American Battery Company. His brothers, in the interim, gave up the ranch and formed the Sweetser-Burroughs Mining Company. By 1903, Burroughs had had enough of business and battery fumes and headed once more for Idaho, this time accompanied by his wife Emma, whom he had married in 1900, and a collie dog. Burroughs and his brothers dredged for gold along the Salmon and Snake Rivers in western Idaho and eastern Oregon but had increasingly bad luck. This operation also failed, and Burroughs went to Salt Lake City, where he worked for a few months as railway policeman at the Union Pacific yards. This was a desperation move; finally defeated in his attempt to make a fortune or even a living in the West, Burroughs returned to Chicago in 1905 and settled into a series of frustrating office jobs, from which he did not escape until 1912, when his first ventures into adventure fiction set him on the road to financial independence. In 1919, a successful and affluent novelist, he moved his family to the San Fernando Valley and made a permanent home on a 540 acre rancho that became the nucleus of what is now the town of Tarzana.

Perhaps his return to the West made him responsive to Sir Algernon Methuen's request for a Western novel (in *The Girl from Hollywood,* thc hcad of the Pennington family says that his home state of Virginia is like a mother but that California is a sweetheart), or perhaps he was aroused by memories of his adventures in Idaho and Arizona. At any rate, he wrote rapidly, completing the 81,000 word manuscript between March 30 and May 24, 1923. Robert Davis of Munsey's, who had encouraged him to write it, replied with three pages of criticism in which he called the story conventional and lamented Burroughs' not "slamming a few novelties into the good old powder-burned frontier," but he accepted it nevertheless and published the novel in *Argosy All-Story Weekly* in six installments from September 13 to October 18, 1924.[10] McClurg brought out a hardcover edition on June 4, 1925; and Methuen, which had initiated the project, dawdled until January 28, 1926 in bringing out a British edition.

The story, as Davis noted, is conventional enough: a pair of Eastern financiers and a corrupt foreman team up to swindle the orphaned Diana Henders out of her ranch and gold mine. She is saved by the hero, Bull, whom the foreman has tried to frame as the stage-robbing and murdering bandit of Hell's Bend. This plot is as old as 19th-century melodrama about the poor girl who can't pay the rent and as rehashed as the film *Oklahoma Crude (1973)* in which the nasty oilmen try to rob an orphan girl's solitary oil well. But literature is full of twice told tales; what matters is not so much the story as the manner of its telling.

Unlike the breathless pace of his Tarzan and science fiction novels, with one cliff-hanging episode piled upon another, Burroughs relaxes and takes his time with the story, concentrating more on character, atmosphere, and frontier humor than on action. There is enough action to enliven the narrative—several stagecoach holdups, two fights with the Apaches, and the climactic abduction of the heroine (a standard Burroughs plot device) and shoot-out—but these episodes are brief. The novel depends more upon suspense than upon action—the mystery of who is the bandit of Hell's Bend, Colby's plotting against Bull, and the scheme by Corson and Wainwright to defraud the heroine—and the reader's interest is held less through the plotting than through the characters.

For a change, Burroughs' leading character is not the hero but the heroine, Diana Henders; and for a while the author considered calling the novel *Diana of the Bar Y*. She is neither a clinging vine nor a conventional dainty damsel who swoons in moments of crisis like most of James Fenimore Cooper's insipid heroines but rather refreshingly self-reliant, one of Burroughs' most attractively independent heroines. (Feminists might note that many of Burroughs' heroines are energetically independent: John Carter's daughter Tara of Helium is a courageous fighter worthy of her father the Warlord of Mars, Witchita Billings of *The War Chief* [1927; Gregg Press edition, 1978] and *Apache Devil* [1933; Gregg Press edition, 1978] is a rugged frontier girl, and Shannon Burke of *The Mucker* [1921] even carves up villains with a samurai sword.) Diana has grown up on an Arizona ranch and has learned to ride, shoot, and run a ranch as well as any man, and better than most. From her parents she has acquired the education and refinement of a lady. Though she sometimes misses the culture and society of educated people that she associates with the East, when her father is killed by Apaches she decides against selling out and determines to remain in Arizona and run the ranch herself, though she is only 19 years old. All the men are in love with her, but the ranchhands hold her in awe: "Men did not curse in Diana's presence, nor did they throw an arm across her slim shoulders, or slap her upon the back in good fellowship, and yet they all worshipped her, and most of them had been violently in love with her. Something within her, inherently fine and noble, kept them at a distance, or rather in their places. . . . The men often spoke of her as a thoroughbred, sensing perhaps, the fine breeding that made her what she was." Yet Diana is no snob, but rather a thorough democrat who associates with the men in a relaxed and friendly way and is almost "one of the boys."

Only the new foreman, Colby, and a wealthy Easterner, Jefferson Wainright, Jr., have the nerve to woo her. She is in no hurry to marry but thinks she may eventually wed one of them. Wainright, however, proves himself a coward, deserting the Henderses and Colby when the Apaches attack. When he later proposes, Diana rejects him, preferring the crude but gentle men of Arizona: "Rough, uncouth they often were; worn and soiled and careless their apparel; afraid of nothing, man, beast or the devil; risking their lives joyously; joking with death; and yet they had been as gentle as women when they took her back to camp . . ."

Burroughs spent a good deal of time, both in *The Bandit of Hell's Bend* and *The Deputy Sheriff of Comanche County,* contrasting Eastern culture with Western self-reliance, to the invariable advantage of the latter. Burroughs' Easterners are usually arrogant and inconsiderate snobs. Pseudoaristocrats with more money than character, they consider the Western ranchhands to be immeasurably beneath them, and they shrink with squeamish revulsion from the plain and sometimes crude Western style of living. Young Wainright first appears as a pleasant and affable man of the world, and Diana is attracted to him; but he lacks the grit, substance, humor, and integrity of her ungrammatical cowhands. The latter are vastly amused by his wearing a dude's extravagant Western attire. "By gollies, he looks like a Christmas tree. . . . All they forgot was the candles," comments Texas Pete. The fact that Wainright is a Harvard graduate prompts the following sarcasm:

> "Dog-gone his hide!" exclaimed Texas Pete.
> "Whose?" inquired Shorty.
> "My ol' man's. If he hadn't gone an' got hung he might 'a' sent me to Havaad. What chanct has a feller got ain one o' them paper-collared, cracker-fed dudes anyway!"

Even Colby, the villain, dislikes Wainright, observing, "He may be pretty slick at them parlor tricks, but they ain't many parlors in Arizona."

When the elder Wainright threatens Diana, Bull drives him off the ranch, saying to Diana, "I ain't a-aimin' to hurt him. . . . I'm just a-aimin' to eddicate him. Them corn-fed Easterners ain't got no eddication nohow. What they need is someone to larn 'em manners."

Corson, another Eastern financier, insults Wong, the Chinese cook; and when Diana defends Wong, he says superciliously,

> Call the Chink in . . . and I'll give him a lesson now—you might learn something yourself. Way out here, so far from New York, you don't get much chance, of course. There's really nothing like the refining influences of the East to take the rough edges off of people."

Diana later calls Corson "one of those arrogant, conceited, provincial New Yorkers."

Accompanying Corson and in league with him to defraud Diana of her inheritance is Lillian Manill. When Texas Pete sees her riding habit, he remarks, "It wouldn't never be safe fer me to go to New York. I'd shore laught myself to death." Lillian acts the role of the dainty society maiden, but it is a pretense. She vamps Diana's foreman, Colby, to get him on her side, though she plans to dump him and marry Corson after she has the ranch. The scenes between her and Colby are surprisingly sensual for a 1920s Western. One night Bull notices her come out of her room, dressed in a "diaphanous negligee. Bull saw Colby seize the girl, strain her to him and cover her lips with kisses. Then the girl drew her lover into the room and closed the door." Colby realizes the sordidness of his affair with her but cannot resist her; "He knew now that he wanted Diana Henders for herself and Lillian Manill for her money and for that coarse, feminine attraction that certain types of women have for coarse men." (Robert Davis of *Argosy All-Star Weekly* objected to this sexual frankness; on June 14, 1923, he wrote to Burroughs, "Shame on you, Edgar. You've got to stop this. You've got to stop it short outside.")[11]

Western movies and fiction often take a populist position, pitting crude but honest Western working people against greedy businessmen (often but not always upper-class dandies) out to take over the town or the range. The senior Wainright falls into this category, but his son defends his ruthlessness with the statement, "You surely cannot blame him for wanting to drive as good a bargain as possible—he is, first and last, a business man."

Burroughs' hero and chief villain are unconventional portraits. Throughout, the protagonist is known only as Bull; we never learn his first and family names. His background is unknown; he seems to have no family and to come from nowhere. A tall, dark man, he has a scarred jaw, the high cheekbones of an Indian, and a grim and even sinister expression. He is undemonstrative, reserved, solitary, taciturn to a fault. Suspicious of his solitude, thinking that a man who talks little has something to hide, most of the men dislike him. A bit like Billy Byrne, the hero of Burroughs' *The Mucker,* Bull is a diamond in the rough. Towards Diana, he is reticent, shy, but respectful; she trusts his integrity, finds him a man she can lean on, and slowly, despite herself, falls in love with him. Unlike the frontier heroes of sentimental romance, who were required by convention to speak polished English, Bull uses crude grammar and has no cultural endowments beyond those of a working cowhand: ". . . he was not a man who read much, nor cared to read, even had there been anything to read, which there was not. . . . His literary requirements were few," confined to the headlines and livestock market reports. Typical of his grammar is

"I wonder what was eatin' them fellers . . . . No one only Wildcat Bob even spoke to me, an' Mack seemed gosh-almighty sore about somethin'. Well, they ain't none of 'em got their brand on me. If I did shoot up Gum Smith's joint it ain't no hair offen none of them."

Though Diana's father (an Oxford graduate) has taught her to love music, literature, and the arts, she does not find Bull beneath her:

> He was just a common cowhand, unlettered, rough, and occasionally uncouth, but of these things she did not think for she had known no other sort, except her father and an occasional visitor from the East, since childhood. Had she cared for him she would not have been ashamed.

Thus Burroughs' Western novels have an egalitarianism missing from the Tarzan and interplanetary novels, which have a distinctly aristocratic bias. Tarzan, after all, is Lord Greystoke, a peer of the British empire; and John Carter is a Virginia gentleman, an ex-Confederate officer, who becomes a Martian nobleman and warlord and marries the Princess of Barsoom. Science fiction and fantasy literature often have a neofeudalism, featuring kings, dukes, counts, and princesses (rarely queens), castles, monarchies and empires; they are costume epics set (usually) in the future rather than the past but, like historical fiction, an escape from the drab present. Most Westerns too are period and costume pieces, but the costumes are those of working people of the old West, where the only aristocracy was that of merit. Thus Diana finds of Bull:

> There was something about the man that demanded obedience even if he was no longer foreman. It was always that way with Bull. Wherever he was he was the leader. Even though men mistrusted, or disliked him, and many did, they involuntarily obeyed him. Possibly because he was a strong man who thought quickly and accurately and was almost invariably right in his decision—it was certainly not because a large proportion of them loved him, for they did not. There was that something lacking in Bull—that quality which attracted the love of his fellows.

Playing upon that lack, Colby persuades most of the ranch and townspeople and almost persuades Diana that Bull is the masked bandit who has been robbing gold shipments from the stagecoach at Hell's Bend. All the evidence against Bull is purely circumstantial, but the townspeople get worked up to the point where they are ready to lynch him. Burroughs handles point of view skillfully; he gives the reader no more evidence than Diana has of Bull's innocence. If the reader trusts Bull, it is only because of the testimony of his several friends and Diana's instinctive feeling that he could not be the criminal. Burroughs frequently enters Diana's thoughts but never lets us into Bull's mind until near the end.

However, the reader may deduce Bull's innocence from seeing the scheming of the villain, Hal Colby. Though as ungrammatical as Bull, Colby is remarkably handsome, suave, even debonaire—a seemingly more likely candidate for hero than the sinister-looking Bull. Bull's one weakness is a fondness for and an inability to hold liquor, and Colby takes advantage of this to get him drunk and fired from his job as foreman. Colby inherits the position and is thus able to see much more of Diana and to court her. When opportunity arises, he smears Bull's character to her while trying to win her. He succeeds reasonably well at first; she likes and trusts him, for despite his treachery to Bull, he is a plausible scoundrel, rather amiable, even admirable in some ways. He is a competent puncher and foreman and helps rescue Diana from the Apaches. Colby begins as an agreeable character who gradually becomes more and more corrupt, an interesting study in damnation. Aside from his treachery to Bull, he remains decent until fairly far along; as he gradually deteriorates, his amiability turns to viciousness.

Not only are the principals well portrayed, but *The Bandit of Hell's Bend* has a colorful gallery of supporting characters, who provide most of the novel's considerable humor. Despite Bull's unpopularity (it is not clear why most people fear and some hate Bull, for he is patient, speaks ill of no one and harms no one except the villains), he has a number of devoted supporters, all of them comical. Texas Pete, Idaho, and Shorty are his buddies on the ranch, and there is a lot of good-natured banter among them. They are rambunctious roughnecks, ridiculing Eastern dudes and scrapping for a fight. Pete is the composer and reciter of an interminable ballad in the comic style of Robert W. Service; it makes up about half of the opening chapter, and thereafter, from time to time, "by gollies," he recalls another verse or two, all of them ludicrous melodrama. These verses are comparable in quality to Service's except that they never come to a climax. Burroughs wrote them himself, observing, "It was easier to compose them than to hunt up others and then get permission from the copyright owners to use them."[12] When some of his buddies express exasperation at his endless versifying, Pete retorts,

> "The trouble with you uneddicated cow-punchers is thet you are too all-fired ignorant to appreciate my efforts to elivate you-all by means of good poetry. It shore is hell to be the only lit'ry gent in a bunch of rough-necks."

Perhaps, but Burroughs observes dryly that "Dr. Johnson would have found nothing in Pete's conversational attainments to have aroused his envy." With deadpan burlesque, Burroughs writes that "Texas Pete never rode other than in a swirl of dust, unless it happened to be raining, then he rode in a shower of mud."

A good deal of *The Bandit of Hell's Bend*'s authenticity and amiability consists in its pervasive use of frontier humor. Humor is not a quality usually associated with Burroughs. There is some strained comedy in *Tarzan of the Apes* (1914) at the expense of Jane's pedantic father, Professor Archimedes Q. Porter, who speaks entirely in polysyllabic circumlocutions, and *Tarzan and the Lion Man* (1923) is largely tongue-in-cheek, but usually Burroughs' tales of adventure are too full of death-defying heroism to take time out for comedy. There was, however, a rich vein of humor in Burroughs. For a while, he longed to be a cartoonist, and his drawings and sketches are often highly amusing. His niece, Mrs. Evelyn McKenzie, recalled "his irrepressible sense of humor."[13]

Besides the comical cowpokes, there are four other humorous characters. Gum Smith, the corrupt, cowardly, and incompetent sheriff, speaks with a ludicrous Southern accent and repeatedly insists, "Ah wants yo'-all to remember that Ah'm sheriff here . . . an' when Ah depatizes yo'-all it's plum legal, an' yo'-all gotta do what Ah tell yo' to." A foil to him is Wildcat Bob, an ancient rip-snorting would-be gunman. Bob is a Western *miles gloriosus,* an aged swaggerer who is actually timid despite his constantly brandishing a pair of six-guns. He is rather like Scratchy Wilson in Stephen Crane's "The Bride Comes to Yellow Sky." As Mary Donovan says of him, he is "Actin' like a wild broth ov a b'y, an' him sivinty if he's a day."

The two of them make a comical couple. She is a tough Irish widow with a thick and plausible brogue, who is proprietress of the local hotel. Though she complains, "Sure, an' its a disgrace, it is, that a poor widdy-lady can't travel in pace without the loikes o' ye takin' advantage of her weak an' unprotected state," she is akin to the Wife of Bath. When she gets riled up, no one around her stands a chance. She and Bob are among Bull's few supporters. Wildcat Bob courts her, and she is ready to accept him, but in a comic Chekhovian scene, he can't get up the nerve to propose; the conversation is only about the weather, and after drinking too much, both stumble off to their separate beds. The fourth source of humor is the stage driver, Bill Gatlin, who spins tall tales worthy of Mark Twain. Once, says he, a horse "drug me fer three days *an'* nights, an' all I hed to eat was when he drug me through a strawberry patch an' all I hed to drink was when he drug me through a river." There is a good deal more subtle humor from the heroine, Diana Henders, who excells at more literate forms of repartee. The dialogue is colloquial throughout, and Burroughs' vigorous use of the vernacular provides a stylistic energy and verisimilitude often lacking in the more formal, stately, and sometimes strained prose of his science fiction adventures.

A word needs to be added about the Apaches and Mexicans. In *The Bandit of Hell's Bend,* the Apaches make several brief appearances as hostile savages. The ranch house is built like a fort against raids, which may come any time. Early on, Bull has to rescue Gregorio from the Apaches, and later a raiding party kills Diana's father. The Indians are the lurking, anonymous enemy, as we see the Apaches only from the point of view of the beleaguered ranchers. This was far from Burroughs' last word on the subject, for in two novels, *The War Chief* and *Apache Devil,* he makes an eloquent statement for the Indian side. At a time when the conventional portrait of the Apaches was as cruel savages, Burroughs championed them, telling the last years of the Apaches wars from the Indian point of view, presenting Geronimo as a sympathetic and heroic figure, and chronicling the deceit, betrayal, greed, and brutality with which the whites conquered Apacheria. Likewise, the villainous Anglos in *The Bandit of Hell's Bend* refer to the Mexican outlaw, Gregorio, as a "greaser," but that should not be taken as Burroughs' view. Gregorio turns out to be loyal to Bull and more honest than the criminals who revile him. Again, in the Apache novels, Burroughs repeatedly praises the Mexicans for their courage in the Indian wars.

Burroughs' Westerns have an honesty as well as authenticity that makes them a genuine contribution to the genre. Though he will remain known primarily for the romantic fantasy of his imaginary worlds, his Westerns are valuable for their realism, based upon the author's first hand experiences in the West during the final years of the frontier.

Robert E. Morsberger
California State Polytechnic University
Pomona, California

REFERENCES

1. Irwin Porges, *Edgar Rice Burroughs, The Man Who Created Tarzan* (Provo, Utah: Brigham Young University Press, 1975), p. 400.
2. Porges, p. 400
3. Edgar Rice Burroughs, letter to Curtis Brown, March 31, 1923.
4. Burroughs' letter to Brown.
5. Porges, p. 23.
6. Spokane, Washington *Spokesman-Review,* May 17, 1935.
7. The *Spokesman-Review.*
8. *The Book News Monthly,* August, 1918.
9. New York *Sunday World,* October 27, 1929.
10. Porges, p. 402.
11. Porges, p. 402.
12. Edgar Rice Burroughs, letter to Mary A. Conklin, February 11, 1932.
13. Robert W. Fenton, *The Big Swingers* (Englewood Cliffs, N. J. : Prentice-Hall, 1967), p. 29.

The Bandit of Hell's Bend

CONTENTS

The Bandit of Hell's Bend

CHAPTER I

TOUGH LUCK

A HALF dozen men sprawled comfortably in back-tilted chairs against the side of the Bar Y bunk-house at the home ranch. They were young men, lithe of limb, tanned of face and clear of eye. Their skins shone from recent ablutions and their slicked hair was still damp, for they had but just come from the evening meal, and meals at the home ranch required a toilet.

One of them was singing.

"In the shade of a tree we two sat, him an' me,
Where the Haegler Hills slope to the Raft
While our ponies browsed 'round, reins a-draggin' the
ground;
Then he looks at me funny an' laft."

"Most any one would," interrupted a listener.

"Shut up," admonished another, "I ain't only heered this three hundred an' sixty-five times in the las' year. Do you think I want to miss anything?"

Unabashed, the sweet singer continued.

"'Do you see thet there town?' he inquires, pintin' down
To some shacks sprawlin' 'round in the heat.
I opined thet I did an' he shifted his quid
After drowndin' a tumble-bug neat.
Then he looks at me square. 'There's a guy waitin' there
Thet the sheep-men have hired to git me.
Are you game to come down to thet jerk-water town
Jest to see what in Hell you will see?'"

One of the group rose and stretched, yawning. He was a tall, dark man. Perhaps in his expression there was something a bit sinister. He seldom smiled and, when not in liquor, rarely spoke.

He was foreman—had been foreman for over a year, and, except for a couple of sprees, during which he had playfully and harmlessly shot up the adjoining town, he had been a good foreman, for he was a thorough horseman, knew the range, understood cattle, was a hard worker and knew how to get work out of others.

It had been six months since he had been drunk, though he had taken a drink now and then if one of the boys chanced to bring a flask back from town. His abstinence might have been accounted for by the fact that Elias Henders, his boss, had threatened to break him the next time he fell from grace.

"You see, Bull," the old man had said, "we're the biggest outfit in this part of the country an' it don't look good to see the foreman of the Bar Y shootin' up the town like some kid tender-foot that's been slapped in the face with a bar-rag. You gotta quit it, Bull; I ain't a-goin' to tell you again."

And Bull knew the old man wouldn't tell him again, so he had stayed good for six long months. Perhaps it was not entirely a desire to cling to the foreman's job that kept him in the straight and narrow path. Perhaps Diana Henders' opinion had had more weight with him than that of her father.

"I'm ashamed of you, Bull," she had said, and she refused to ride with him for more than a week. That had been bad enough, but as if to make it worse she had ridden several times with a new hand who had drifted in from the north a short time before and been taken on by Bull to fill a vacancy.

At first Bull had not liked the new man. "He's too damned pretty to be a puncher," one of the older hands had remarked, and it is possible that the newcomer's rather extreme good looks had antagonized them all a little at first, but he had proven a good man and so the others had come to accept Hal Colby in spite of his wealth of waving black hair, his perfect profile, gleaming teeth and laughing eyes.

"So I told him I'd go, fer I liked thet there bo,
And I'd see thet the shootin' was fair;
But says he: 'It is just to see who starts it fust
Thet I wants anyone to be there.'"

"I'm going to turn in," remarked Bull.

Hal Colby rose. "Same here," he said, and followed the foreman into the bunk-house. A moment later he turned where he stood beside his bunk and looked at Bull who was sitting on the edge of his, removing his spurs. The handsome lips were curved in a pleasant smile. "Lookee here, Bull!" he whispered, and as the other turned toward him he reached a hand beneath the bag of clothes that constituted his pillow and drew forth a pint flask. "Wet your whistle?" he inquired.

"Don't care if I do," replied the foreman, crossing the room to Colby's bunk.

Through the open window floated the drawling notes of Texas Pete's perennial rhapsody.

"When the jedge says: 'Who drew his gun fust, him
or you?'
Then I wants a straight guy on my side,
Fer thet poor puddin' head, why, he's already dead
With a forty-five hole in his hide."

"Here's lookin' at you!" said Bull.

"Drink hearty," replied Colby.

"'Taint so bad at that," remarked the foreman, wiping his lips on the cuff of his shirt and handing the flask back to the other.

"Not so worse for rot-gut," agreed Colby. "Have another!"

The foreman shook his head.

"'T won't hurt you any," Colby assured him. "It's pretty good stuff."

Sang Texas Pete:

"And thet wasn't jest jaw — when it come to a draw
This here guy was like lightnin' turned loose.
Then we rolls us a smoke an' not neither one spoke
'Til he said: 'Climb aboard your cayuse.'
Then we reined down the hill each a-puffin' his pill
To the town 'neath its shimmer o' heat
An' heads up to the shack that's a-leanin' its back
'Gainst the side o' The Cowboys' Retreat."

Bull took another drink — a longer one this time, and, rolling a cigarette, sat down on the edge of Colby's bunk and commenced to talk — whiskey always broke the bonds of his taciturnity. His voice was low and not unpleasant.

He spoke of the day's work and the plans for tomorrow and Hal Colby encouraged him. Perhaps he liked him; perhaps, like others, he felt that it paid to be on friendly terms with the foreman.

While from outside:

"It is Slewfoot's Good Luck where they hand you out
chuck
Thet is mostly sow-belly an' beans.
Says he: 'Bub, let's us feed — I'm a-feelin' the need
O' more substance than air in my jeans.'
So ol' Slewfoot was there, all red freckles an' hair,
An' we lined our insides with his grub.
Says Bill, then: 'Show your gait — let's be pullin'
our freight,
Fer I'm rarin' to go,' says he, 'Bub.'"

Inside the bunk-house Bull rose to his feet. "That's damn good stuff, Hal," he said. The two had emptied the flask.

"Wait a minute," said the other, "I got another flask," and reached again beneath his bag.

"No," demurred the foreman, "I guess I got enough."

"Oh, hell, you ain't had none yet," insisted Colby.

The song of Texas Pete suffered many interruptions due to various arguments in which he felt compelled to take sides, but whenever there was a lull in the conversation he resumed his efforts to which no one paid any attention further than as they elicited an occasional word of banter.

The sweet singer never stopped except at the end of a stanza, and no matter how long the interruption, even though days might elapse, he always began again with the succeeding stanza, without the slightest hesitation or repetition. And so now, as Bull and Colby drank, he sang on.

"'Now we'll sashay next door to thet hard-licker store
Where his nibs is most likely to be
An' then you goes in first an' starts drowdin' your thirst;
But a-keepin' your eyes peeled fer me.'"

Bull, the foreman, rose to his feet. He stood as steady as a rock, but Colby saw that he was drunk. After six months' of almost total abstinence he had just consumed considerably more than a pint of cheap and fiery whiskey in less than a half hour.

"Goin' to bed?" asked Colby.

"Bed, hell," replied the other. "I'm goin' to town—it's my night to howl. Comin'?"

"No," said Colby. "I think I'll turn in. Have a good time."

"I sure will." The foreman walked to his bunk and strapped his guns about his hips, resumed the single spur he had removed, tied a fresh black silk handkerchief about his neck, clapped his sombrero over his shock of straight black hair and strode out of the bunk-house.

> "'Fcr I wants you to see thet it's him draws on me
> So the jedge he cain't make me the goat.'
> So I heads fer that dump an' a queer little lump
> Starts a-wrigglin' aroun' in my throat."

"Say, where in hell's Bull goin' this time o' night?" Pete interrupted himself.

"He's headin' fer the horse c'rel," stated another.

"Acts like he was full," said a third. "Didje hear him hummin' a tune as he went out? That's always a sign with him. The stuff sort o' addles up his brains, like Pete's always is, an' makes him sing."

> "Fer I wants you to know thet I likes thet there bo
> An' I'd seen more than one good one kilt,
> Fer you cain't never tell, leastways this side o' Hell,
> When there's shootin' whose blood will be spilt."

"There he goes now," said one of the men as the figure of a rider shown dimly in the starlight loping easily away toward the south, "an' he's goin' toward town."

"I wonder," said Texas Pete, "if he knows the old man is in town tonight.

"Jest inside o' the door with one foot on the floor
An' the other hist up on the rail
Stands a big, raw-boned guy with the orn'riest eye
Thet I ever seen outen a jail."

"By gollies, I'm goin' after Bull. I doan b'lieve he-all knows thet the ol' man's in town," and leaping to his feet he walked off toward the horse corral, still singing:

"An' beside him a girl, thet sure looked like a pearl
Thet the Bible guy cast before swine,
Was a-pleadin' with him, her eyes teary an' dim,
As I high-sign the bar-keep fer mine."

He caught up one of the loose horses in the corral, rammed a great, silver-mounted spade bit between its jaws, threw a heavy, carved saddle upon the animal's back, stepped one foot into a trailing, tapaderaed stirrup and was off in a swirl of dust. Texas Pete never rode other than in a swirl of dust, unless it happened to be raining, then he rode in a shower of mud.

His speed tonight was, therefore, not necessarily an indication of haste. He would have ridden at the same pace to either a funeral or a wedding, or home from either.

But any who knew Texas Pete could have guessed that he was in considerable haste, for he rode without his woolly, sheepskin chaps—one of the prides of his existence. If he had been in too much of a hurry to don them he must have been in a great hurry, indeed.

Texas Pete might be without a job, with not more than two-bits between himself and starvation, but he was never without a fine pair of sheepskin chaps, a silver encrusted bit, a heavy bridle garnished with the same precious metal, an ornate saddle of hand carved leather and silver conchas, a Stetson, two good six-guns with their belt and holsters and a vivid silk neckerchief.

Possibly his pony cost no more than ten dollars, his boots were worn and his trousers blue denim overalls, greasy and frayed, yet Texas Pete otherwise was a thing of beauty and a joy forever. The rowels of his silver-inlaid Mexican spurs dragged the ground when he walked and the dumb-bells depending from their hubs tinkled merrily a gay accompaniment to his boyish heart beating beneath ragged underclothing.

Texas Pete galloped along the dusty road toward the small cattle-town that served the simple needs of that frontier community with its general store, its restaurant, its Chinese laundry, blacksmith shop, hotel, newspaper office and five saloons, and as he galloped he sang:

"Then the door swings agin an' my pal he steps in
An' the light in his eye it was bad,
An' the raw-boned guy wheels an' the girl there she squeals:
'O, fer gawd's sake don't shoot, Bill, it's dad!'"

A mile ahead of Pete another pony tore through the dust toward town — a blazed face chestnut with two white hind feet — Blazes, the pride of the foreman's heart.

In the deep saddle, centaurlike, sat the horseman.

Hendersville tinkled softly in the quiet of early evening. Later, gaining momentum, it would speed up a bit under his own power. At present it reposed in the partial lethargy of digestive functionings — it was barely first drink time after supper. Its tinkling was the tinkling of spurs, chips and only very occasional glassware.

Suddenly its repose was shattered by a wild whoop from without, the clatter of swift hoofs and the rapid crack, crack, crack of a six-gun. Gum Smith, sheriff, rose from behind the faro layout and cocked an attentive ear.

Gum guided the destinies of the most lucrative thirst emporium in Hendersville. Being sheriff flattered his vanity and attracted business, but it had its drawbacks; the noises from without sounded like one of them and Gum was pained.

It was at times such as this that he almost wished that someone else was sheriff, but a quick glance at the shiny badge pinned to the left hand pocket of his vest reassured him quickly on that point and he glanced swiftly about the room at its other occupants and sighed in relief — there were at least a dozen husky young punchers there.

Across the street, in the office of the Hendersville *Tribune,* Elias Henders sat visiting with Ye Editor. As the shouting and the shots broke the quiet of the evening the two men looked up and outward toward the street.

"Boys will be boys," remarked the editor.

A bullet crashed through the glass at the top of the window. With a single movement the editor extinguished the lamp that burned on the desk before them, and both men, with a celerity that spoke habit, crouched quickly behind that piece of furniture.

"Sometimes they're damn careless, though," replied Elias Henders.

Down the road Texas Pete galloped and sang:

"For the thing she had saw was Bill reach for to draw
When the guy she called dad drawed on Bill.
In the door was my pal with his eyes on the gal
An' his hand on his gun — standin' still."

From the distance ahead came, thinly, the sound of shots.

"By gollies!" exclaimed Texas Pete, "the darned son-of-a-gun!"

The men lolling about the barroom of *Gum's Place — Liquors and Cigars* — looked up at the sound of the shots and grinned. An instant later a horse's unshod hoofs pounded on the rough boards of the covered "porch" in front of Gum's Place, the swinging doors burst in and Blazes was brought to his haunches in the center of the floor with a wild whoop from his rider, who waved a smoking gun above his head.

Bull, the Bar Y foreman, let his gaze run quickly

about the room. When his steel grey eyes alighted upon the sheriff they remained there. Gum Smith appeared to wilt behind the faro table. He shook a wavering finger at the Bar Y foreman.

"Yo' all's undah arrest," he piped in a high, thin voice, and turning toward the men seated about the neighboring tables he pointed first at one and then at another. "Ah depatize yo! Ah depatize yo! Ah depatize yo!" he announced to each as he covered them in turn with his swiftly moving index finger. "Seize him, men!" No one moved. Gum Smith waxed excited. "Seize him, yo'-all! Ah'm sheriff o' this yere county. Ef Ah depatize yo'-all yo'-all's got to be depatized."

"My mother was a wild cat,
My father was a bear,"

announced Bull,

"I picks my teeth with barb-wire
With cactus combs my hair."

and I craves drink—pronto!"

"Yo'-all's undah arrest! Seize him, men!" shrilled Gum.

Bull fired into the floor at the foot of the faro table and Gum Smith disappeared behind it. The men all laughed. Bull turned his attention toward the bar-keep and fired into the back bar. The bar-keep grinned.

"Be keerful, Bull," he admonished, "I got a bad

heart. My doctor tells me as how I should avoid excitement."

The front doors swung in again and Bull wheeled with ready six-gun to cover the newcomer, but at sight of the man who entered the room the muzzle of his gun dropped and he was sobered in the instant.

"Oh!" said Elias Henders, "so it's you agin, Bull, eh?"

The two men stood looking at one another in silence for a moment. What was passing in their minds no one might have guessed. It was the older man who spoke again first.

"I reckon I'll not be needin' you any more, Bull," he said, and then, after a moment's reflection, "unless you want a job as a hand—after you sober up."

He turned and left the building and as he stepped down into the dust of the road Texas Pete swung from his pony and brushed past him.

Inside, Bull sat his horse at one side of the large room, near the bar. Behind him Gum Smith was slowly emerging from the concealment of the faro table. When he saw the man he feared sitting with his back toward him, a crafty look came into the eyes of the sheriff. He glanced quickly about the room. The men were all looking at Bull. No one seemed to be noticing Gum.

He drew his gun and levelled it at the back of the ex-foreman of the Bar Y. Instantly there was a flash from the doorway, the crack of a shot, and the sheriff's gun dropped from his hand. All eyes turned in the direction of the entrance. There stood Texas Pete, his shooting iron smoking in his hand.

"You damn pole-cat!" he exclaimed, his eyes on Gum. "Come on, Bull; this ain't no place for quiet young fellers like us."

Bull wheeled Blazes and rode slowly through the doorway, with never a glance toward the sheriff; nor could he better have shown his utter contempt for the man. There had always been bad blood between them. Smith had been elected by the lawless element of the community and at the time of the campaign Bull had worked diligently for the opposing candidate who had been backed by the better element, consisting largely of the cattle owners, headed by Elias Henders.

What Bull's position would have been had he not been foreman for Henders at the time was rather an open question among the voters of Hendersville, but the fact remained that he had been foreman and that he had worked to such good purpose for the candidate of the reform element that he had not only almost succeeded in electing him, but had so exposed the rottenness of the gang back of Smith's candidacy that their power was generally considered to be on the wane.

"It'll be Bull for sheriff next election," was considered a safe prophecy and even a foregone conclusion, by some.

Gum Smith picked up his gun and examined it. Texas Pete's shot had struck the barrel just in front of the cylinder. The man looked angrily around at the other occupants of the room.

"Ah wants yo'-all to remember that Ah'm sheriff here," he cried, "an' when Ah depatizes yo'-all it's plum legal, an' yo'-all gotta do what Ah tell yo' to."

"Oh, shut up, Gum," admonished one of the men.

Outside, Texas Pete had mounted his pony and was moving along slowly stirrup to stirrup with Bull, who was now apparently as sober as though he had never had a drink in his life.

"It's a good thing fer us he didn't have his gang there tonight," remarked Pete.

Bull shrugged, but said nothing in reply. Texas Pete resigned himself to song.

"Then thet damned raw-boned guy with the ornery eye
Up an' shoots my pal dead in the door;
But I'm here to opine with this bazoo o' mine
Thet he won't shoot no hombres no more."

"What was you doin' up to town, Texas?" inquired Bull.

"O, I jest thought as how I'd ride up an' see what was doin'—thought maybe you didn't know the old man was there tonight—reckon I was a bit late, eh?"

"Yes. Thanks, just the same—I won't ferget it."

"Tough luck."

"How'd you know the old man was goin' to be in town tonight?"

"Why, I reckon as how everybody exceptin' you knew it, Bull."

"Did Colby know it?"

"Why, I recken as how he must of."

They rode on for some time in silence, which Texas finally broke.

"Jest a moment, an' where they'd been five o' us there,
We hed suddenly dwindled to three.
The bar-keep, he was one — the darned son-of-a-gun —
An' the others, a orphan an' me."

When Bull and Texas entered the bunk-house most of the men were asleep, but Hal Colby rolled over on his bunk and smiled at Bull as the latter lighted a lamp.

"Have a good time, Bull?" he inquired.

"The old man was there," said Bull, "an' I ain't foreman no more."

"Tough luck," sympathized Colby.

CHAPTER II

THE HOLDUP

AFTER breakfast the following morning the men were saddling-up listlessly for the day's work. There was no foreman now and they were hanging about waiting for the boss. Bull sat on the top rail of the corral, idle. He was out of a job. His fellows paid little or no attention to him, but whether from motives of consideration for his feelings, or because they were not interested in him or his troubles a casual observer could not have deduced from their manner.

Unquestionably he had friends among them, but he was a taciturn man and, like all such, did not make friends quickly. Undemonstrative himself, he aroused no show of demonstration in others. His straight black hair, and rather high cheek bones, coupled with a tanned skin, gave him something the appearance of an Indian, a similarity that was further heightened by his natural reserve, while a long, red scar across his jaw accentuated a suggestion of grimness that his countenance possessed in repose.

Texas Pete, saddling his pony directly below him in the corral, was starting the day with a new song.

"I stood at the bar, at The Spread Eagle Bar,
A-drinkin' a drink whilst I smoked a seegar——

"Quittin', Bull?" he inquired, looking up at the ex-foreman.

"Reckon so," came the reply.

"When in walks a gent thet I ain't never see
An' he lets out a beller an' then says, says he:——"

Texas Pete swung easily into his saddle.

"Reckon as how I'll be pullin' my freight, too," he announced. "I been aimin' to do thet for quite a spell. Where'll we head fer?"

Bull's eyes wandered to the front of the ranch house, and as they did so they beheld "the old man" emerging from the office. Behind him came his daughter Diana and Hal Colby. The latter were laughing and talking gaily. Bull could not but notice how close the man leaned toward the girl's face. What an easy way Colby had with people—especially women.

"Well," demanded Texas Pete, "if you're comin' why don't you saddle up?"

"Reckon I've changed my mind."

Texas Pete glanced toward the ranch house, following the direction of the other's eyes, and shrugged his shoulders.

"O, well," he said, "this ain't a bad place. Reckon as how I'll stay on, too, fer a spell."

Elias Henders and Hal Colby were walking slowly in the direction of the horse corral. The girl had turned and reëntered the house. The two men entered the corral and as they did so Bull descended from the fence and approached Henders.

"You don't happen to need no hands, do you?" he asked the older man.

"I can use you, Bull," replied Henders with a faint smile. "Thirty-five a month and found."

The former foreman nodded in acceptance of the terms and, walking toward the bunch of horses huddled at one side of the corral, whistled. Instantly Blazes' head came up above those of the other animals. With up-pricked ears he regarded his owner for a moment, and then, shouldering his way through the bunch, he walked directly to him.

Elias Henders stopped in the center of the corral and attracted the attention of the men. "Colby here," he announced, "is the new foreman."

That was all. There was a moment's embarrassed silence and then the men resumed their preparations for the work of the day, or, if they were ready, lolled in their saddles rolling cigarettes. Colby went among them assigning the various duties for the day—pretty much routine work with which all were familiar.

"And you, Bull," he said when he reached the ex-foreman, "I wish you'd ride up to the head of Cottonwood Canyon and see if you can see anything of that bunch of Crazy J cows—I ain't seen nothin' of 'em for a week or more."

It was the longest, hardest assignment of the day,

but if Bull was dissatisfied with it he gave no indication. As a matter of fact he probably was content, for he was a hard rider and he liked to be off alone. A trait that had always been a matter for comment and some conjecture.

More than one had asked himself or a neighbor what Bull found to do that took him off by himself so often. There are those who cannot conceive that a man can find pleasure in his own company, or in that of a good horse and the open.

The mouth of Cottonwood Canyon lay a good twenty miles from the ranch and the head of it five miles of rough going farther. It was ten o'clock when Bull suddenly drew rein beside the lone cottonwood that marked the entrance to the canyon and gave it its name.

He sat motionless, listening intently. Faintly, from far up the canyon, came the staccato of rifle shots. How far it was difficult to judge, for the walls of a winding canyon quickly absorb sound. Once convinced of the direction of their origin, however, the man urged his pony into a gallop, turning his head up the canyon.

As the last of the cow hands loped away from the ranch upon the business of the day Elias Henders turned back toward the office, while Hal Colby caught up two ponies which he saddled and bridled, humming meanwhile a gay little tune. Mounting one, he rode toward the ranch house, leading the other, just as Diana Henders emerged from the interior, making it apparent for whom the led horse was intended.

Taking the reins from Colby, the girl swung into the saddle like a man, and she sat her horse like a man, too, and yet, though she could ride with the best of them, and shoot with the best of them, there was nothing coarse or common about her. Some of the older hands had known her since childhood, yet even that fact, coupled with the proverbial freedom of the eighties in Arizona, never permitted them the same freedom with Diana Henders that most of the few girls in that wild country either overlooked or accepted as a matter of course.

Men did not curse in Diana's presence, nor did they throw an arm across her slim shoulders, or slap her upon the back in good fellowship, and yet they all worshipped her, and most of them had been violently in love with her. Something within her, inherently fine and noble, kept them at a distance, or rather in their places, for only those men who were hopelessly bashful ever remained at a distance from Diana where there was the slightest chance to be near her.

The men often spoke of her as a thoroughbred, sensing, perhaps, the fine breeding that made her what she was. Elias Henders was one of the Henders of Kentucky, and, like all the males of his line for generations, held a degree from Oxford, which he had entered after graduation from the beloved alma mater of his native state, for the very excellent reason that old Sir John Henders, who had established the American branch of the family, had been an Oxford man and had seen his son and his grandson follow his footsteps.

Twenty-five years before Elias Henders had come west with John Manill, a class-mate and neighbor of Kentucky, and the two young men had entered the cattle business. Their combined capital managed to keep them from the embarrassments and annoyances of a sheriff's sale for some three years, but what with raiding Apaches, poor rail facilities and a distant market, coupled with inexperience, they were at last upon the very brink of bankruptcy when Henders discovered gold on their property. Two years later they were rich men.

Henders returned to Kentucky and married Manill's sister, and shortly afterwards moved to New York, as it was decided that the best interests of the partnership required an eastern representative. Manill remained in Arizona.

Diana Henders was born in New York City, and when she was about five years old her mother contracted tuberculosis of the lungs. Physicians advising a dry climate, Henders and Manill changed places, Henders taking his family to Arizona and Manill removing to New York with his wife and little daughter. He had married beneath him and unhappily with the result that being both a proud and rather reserved man he had confided nothing to his sister, the wife of his partner and best friend.

When Diana was fifteen her mother had died, and the girl, refusing to leave her father, had abandoned the idea of finishing her education in an eastern college, and Elias Henders, loath to give her up, had acquiesced in her decision. Qualified by education as he was to instruct her, Diana's training had been carried on under the tutorage of her father, so that at nineteen, though essentially a frontier girl unversed in many of the finer artificialities of social usage, she was yet a young woman of culture and refinement. Her music, which was the delight of her father, she owed to the careful training of her mother as well as to the possession of a grand piano that had come over Raton Pass behind an ox team in the seventies.

Her father, her books, her music and her horses constituted the life of this young girl; her social companions the young vaqueros who rode for her father, and without at least one of whom she was not permitted to ride abroad, since the Apaches were still a menace in the Arizona of that day.

And so it was that this morning she rode out with the new foreman. They walked their horses in silence for a few minutes, the man's stirrup just behind that of the girl, where he might let his eyes rest upon her profile without detection. The heavy lashed eye, the short, straight nose, the patrician mouth and chin held the adoring gaze of the young foreman in mute worship; but it was he who, at length, broke the silence.

"You ain't congratulated me yet, Di," he said, "or maybe you didn't know?"

"Yes, I knew," she replied, "and I do congratulate you; but I cannot forget that your fortune means another man's sorrow."

"It's his own fault. A man that can't keep sober can't be trusted with a job like this."

"He was a good foreman."

"Maybe so—I ain't sayin' nothin' about a man that's down. It seems to me you set a lot of store by him, though; and what do you know about him? You can't be too careful, Di. There's lots of bad 'uns in these parts and when a feller never talks none, like him, its probably because he's got something on his mind he don't want to talk about."

"I thought he was your friend," said the girl.

Colby flushed. "He is my friend. I set a lot of store by Bull; but it's you I'm thinkin' of—not him or me. I wouldn't want nothin' to happen that you'd have to be sorry about."

"I don't understand you, Hal."

He flecked the leg of his chaps with the lash of his quirt. "Oh, pshaw, Di," he parried, "I don't want to say nothin' about a friend. I only want to put you on your guard, that's all. You know there ain't nothin' I wouldn't do for you—no, not even if it cost me all the friends I got."

He passed his reins to his right hand and reaching across laid his left across one of hers, which she quickly withdrew.

"Please don't," she begged.

"I love you, Di," he blurted suddenly.

The girl laughed gaily, though not in derision. "All the men think they do. It's because I'm the only girl within miles and miles."

"You're the only girl in the world—for me."

She turned and looked at him quizzically. He was very handsome. That and his boyish, laughing manner had attracted her to him from the first. There had seemed a frankness and openness about him that appealed to her, and of all the men she knew, only excepting her father, he alone possessed anything approximating poise and self-confidence in his intercourse with women. The others were either shy and blundering, or loud and coarse, or taciturn sticks like Bull, who seemed to be the only man on the ranch who was not desperately in love with her.

"We'll talk about something else," she announced.

"Isn't there any hope for me?" he asked.

"Why yes," she assured him. "I hope you will keep on loving me. I love to have people love me."

"But I don't want to do *all* the loving," he insisted.

"Don't worry—you're not. Even the cook is writing poems about me. Of all the foolish men I ever heard of Dad has certainly succeeded in corraling the prize bunch."

"I don't care a hang about that red-headed old

fool of a cook," he snapped. "What I want is for *you* to love *me*."

"Oh, well, that's a horse of another color. Now we *will* have to change the subject."

"Please, Di, I'm in earnest," he pleaded; "won't you give me a little to hope for?"

"You never can tell about a girl, Hal," she said.

Her voice was tender and her eyes suddenly soft, and that was as near a promise as he could get.

As Bull urged Blazes up the rough trail of Cottonwood Canyon the continued crack of rifles kept the man apprised of the direction of the origin of the sounds and approximately of their ever lessening distance ahead. Presently he drew rein and, pulling his rifle from its boot, dismounted, dropping the reins upon the ground.

"Stand!" he whispered to Blazes and crept forward stealthily.

The shooting was close ahead now — just around the brush covered shoulder of a rocky hill. The detonations were less frequent. Bull guessed that by now both hunters and hunted were under cover and thus able to take only occasional pot shots at one another's refuge.

To come upon them directly up the trail in the bottom of the canyon would have been to expose himself to the fire of one side, and possibly of both, for in this untamed country it was easily conceivable that both sides of the controversy might represent interests inimical to those of his employer. With this idea in mind the ex-foreman of the Bar Y Ranch clambered cautiously up the steep side of the hill that hid from his view that part of the canyon lying just beyond.

From the varying qualities of the detonations the man had deduced that five and possibly six rifles were participating in the affair. How they were divided he could not even guess. He would have a look over the crest of the hog-back and if the affair was none of his business he would let the participants fight it out by themselves. Bull, sober, was not a man to seek trouble.

Climbing as noiselessly as possible and keeping the muzzle of his rifle ahead of him he came presently to the crest of the narrow ridge where he pushed his way cautiously through the brush toward the opposite side, passing around an occasional huge outcropping of rock that barred his progress. Presently the brush grew thinner. He could see the opposite wall of the canyon.

A sharp report sounded close below him, just over the brow of the ridge. In front of him a huge outcropping reared its weather-worn surface twenty feet above the brush.

Toward this he crept until he lay concealed behind it. Then, warily, he peered around the up-canyon edge discovering that his hiding place rested upon the very edge of a steep declivity that dropped perpendicularly into the bottom of the canyon.

Almost below him five Apaches were hiding among the rocks and boulders that filled the bottom of the canyon. Upon the opposite side a single man lay sprawled upon his belly behind another.

Bull could not see his face, hidden as it was beneath a huge sombrero, but he saw that he was garbed after the fashion of a vaquero—he might be either an American or a Mexican. That made no difference now, however, for there were five against him, and the five were Indians. Bull watched for a moment. He saw that the Indians were doing all the firing, and he wondered if the man lying across the canyon was already dead. He did not move.

Cautiously one of the Indians crept from cover as the other four fired rapidly at their victim's position, then another followed him and the three remaining continued firing, covering the advance of their fellows.

Bull smiled, that grim, saturnine smile of his. There were some red-skins in the vicinity that were due for the surprise of their lives.

The two were working their way across the canyon, taking advantage of every particle of cover. They were quite close to the hiding place of the prone man now—in another moment the three upon Bull's side of the canyon would cease firing and the two would rush their unconscious quarry and finish him.

Bull raised his rifle to his shoulder. There followed two reports, so close together that it was almost inconceivable that they had come from the same weapon, and the two, who had already risen for the final attack, crumpled among the rocks beneath the blazing sun.

Instantly apprehending their danger, the other three Apaches leaped to their feet and scurried up the canyon, searching new cover as they ran; but it was difficult to find cover from a rifle holding the commanding position that Bull's held.

It spoke again, and the foremost Indian threw his hands above his head, spun completely around and lunged forward upon his face. The other two dropped behind large boulders.

Bull glanced across the canyon. He saw that the man had raised his head and was attempting to look around the edge of his cover, having evidently become aware that a new voice had entered the grim chorus of the rifles.

"Hit?" shouted Bull.

The man looked in the direction of the voice. "No," he replied.

"Then why in hell don't you shoot? There's only two of them left—they're up canyon on this side."

"Out of ammunition," replied the other.

"Well, you were in a hell of a fix," mused Bill as he watched the concealment of the two Indians.

"Any more of 'em than this bunch?" he called across to the man.

"No."

For a long time there was silence—the quiet and peace that had lain upon this age-old canyon since the Creation—and that would lie upon it forever except as man, the disturber, came occasionally to shatter it.

"I can't lie here all day," mused Bull. He crawled forward and looked over the edge of the cliff. There was a sheer drop of forty feet. He shook his head. There was a sharp report and a bullet tore up the dirt beneath him. It was followed instantly by another report from across the canyon.

Bull kept his eyes on the cover of the Indians. Not a sign of them showed. One of them had caught him napping—that was all—and ducked back out of sight after firing, but how was the man across the canyon firing without ammunition?

"I got one then," came the man's voice, as though in answer, "but you better lie low—he come near getting you."

"Thought you didn't have no ammunition," Bull called across.

"I crawled out and got the rifle of one of these you potted."

Bull had worked his way back to his cover and to the brush behind it and now he started up along the ridge in an attempt to get behind the remaining Indian.

A minute or two later he crawled again to the edge of the ridge and there below him and in plain sight the last of the red-skins crouched behind a great boulder. Bull fired and missed, and then the Apache was up and gone, racing for his pony tethered further up the canyon. The white man shrugged, rose to his feet and sought an easy way down into the bed of the canyon.

The other man had seen his action, which betokened that the fight was over, and as Bull reached the bottom of the cliff he was walking forward to meet him. A peculiar light entered the eyes of each as they came face to face.

"Ah!" exclaimed the one, "it is *Señor* Bull." He spoke now in Spanish.

"Gregorio!" said Bull. "How'd they git you in this fix?"

"I camped just above here last night," replied the other, "and this morning I walked down with my rifle on the chance of getting an antelope for breakfast. They come on me from above and there you are. They been shootin' at me since early this morning." He spoke English with scarce the slightest accent. "You have saved my life, *Señor* Bull, and Gregorio will not forget that."

"You haven't happened to see a bunch of Crazy J cows hereabouts, have you?" inquired Bull, ignoring the other's expression of gratitude.

"No, *Señor,* I have not," replied Gregorio.

"Well, I'll go get my horse and have a look up toward the head of the canyon, anyway," and Bull turned and walked down to get Blazes.

Fifteen minutes later, riding up again, he passed Gregorio coming down, the latter having found his pony and his belongings intact at his camp.

"*A Dios, Señor,*" called Gregorio in passing.

"So long," returned the American.

At the head of the canyon, where it narrowed to the proportions of a gorge, Bull examined the ground carefully and saw that no cattle had passed that way in many days; then he turned back and rode down the canyon.

Meanwhile, entering Cottonwood from below, Jim Weller, looking for lost horses, passed Gregorio coming out and, recognizing him, loosened his gun in its holster and kept one eye on the Mexican until he had passed out of sight around the shoulder of the hill that flanked the east side of the entrance to the canyon, for Gregorio bore an unsavory reputation in that part of the country. He was an outlaw with a price upon his head.

"Howsumever," mused Weller, "I ain't lost no outlaws—it's hosses I'm lookin' for," and he rode on with a sigh of relief that there was a solid hill between him and Gregorio's deadly aim. Ten minutes later he met Bull coming down from the head of Cottonwood. The two men drew rein with a nod.

Weller asked about horses, learning from Bull that there was no stock above them in Cottonwood, but he did not mention having met Gregorio. It was obvious to him that the two men could not have been in Cottonwood together without having met and if Bull did not want to mention it it was evident that he had some good reason for not doing so. It was not the custom of the country to pry into the affairs of others. Bull did not mention Gregorio nor did he speak of their brush with the Apaches; but that was because he was an uncommunicative man.

"I think I'll have a look up Sinkhole Canyon for them hosses," remarked Weller. Sinkhole was the next canyon west.

"Keep your eyes peeled for them Crazy J cows," said Bull, "and I'll ride up Belter's and if I see your horses I'll run 'em down onto the flat."

They separated at the mouth of Cottonwood, Weller riding toward the west, while Bull made his way eastwardly toward Belter's Canyon which lay in the direction of the home ranch.

Three hours later the semiweekly stage, careening down the North Pass trail, drew up in a cloud of dust at the junction of the Henders' Mine road at a signal from one of two men sitting in a buckboard. As the stage slowed down one of the men leaped to the ground, and as it came to a stop clambered to the top and took a seat beside the driver who had greeted him with a gruff jest.

The new passenger carried a heavy sack which he deposited between his feet. He also carried a sawed-off shot gun across his knees.

"The Saints be praised!" exclaimed a fat lady

with a rich brogue, who occupied a seat inside the coach. "Sure an' I thought we were after bein' held up."

An old gentleman with white whiskers down which a trickle of tobacco juice had cascaded its sienna-hued way reassured her.

"No mum," he said, "thet's the messinger from the mine with a bag o' bullion. This here stage ain't been held up fer three weeks. No mum, times ain't what they uset to be with all these here new-fangled ideas about reform what are spilin' the country."

The fat lady looked at him sideways, disdainfully, and gathered her skirts closer about her. The stage lurched on, the horses at a brisk gallop, and as it swung around the next curve the fat lady skidded into the old gentleman's lap, her bonnet tilting over one eye, rakishly.

"Be off wid ye!" she exclaimed, glaring at the little old gentleman, as though the fault were all his. She had scarcely regained her own side of the seat when another, and opposite, turn in the road precipitated the old gentleman into her lap.

"Ye spalpeen!" she shrilled, as, placing two fat hands against him, she thrust him violently from her. "Sure, an' it's a disgrace, it is, that a poor widdy-lady can't travel in pace without the loikes o' ye takin' advantage o' her weak an' unprotected state."

The little old gentleman, though he had two huge

guns strapped at his hips, appeared thoroughly cowed and terrified—so much so, in fact, that he dared not venture even a word of protest at the injustice of her insinuations. From the corners of his weak and watery blue eyes he surveyed her surreptitiously, wiped the back of his perspiring neck with a flamboyant bandana, and shrank farther into the corner of his seat.

A half hour later the stage swung through the gap at the foot of the pass. Before it lay the rolling uplands through which the road wound down past the Bar Y ranch house and the town of Hendersville on the flat below. The gap was narrow and winding and the road excruciatingly vile, necessitating a much slower pace than the driver had been maintaining since passing the summit.

The horses were walking, the coach lurching from one chuck-hole to another, while clouds of acrid dust arose in almost vapor lightness, enveloping beasts, vehicle and passengers. Through the nebulous curtain rising above the leaders the driver saw suddenly materialize the figures of two men.

"Halt! Stick 'em up!"

The words snapped grimly from the taller of the two. The messenger on the seat beside the driver made a single move to raise his sawed-off shot gun. A six-gun barked and the messenger toppled forward, falling upon the rump of the near wheel-horse. The horse, startled, leaped forward into his collar. The driver attempted to quiet him. The two men moved up beside the stage, one covering the driver and a passenger on top, the other threatening the two inside. The fat lady sat with her arms folded glaring at the bandit. The little old gentleman's hands touched the top of the stage.

"Stick 'em up!" said the bandit to the fat lady.

She did not move.

"Sure an' I'll not stick 'em up an inch fer the loikes o' yese," she shrilled; "an' lucky it is for ye, ye dhirty spalpeen, that Mary Donovan hasn't the bit ov a gun with her—or that there ain't a *man* along to protect a poor, helpless widdy lady," and she cast a withering glance of scorn in the direction of the little old gentleman, who grew visibly red through the tan of his weather-worn countenance.

The other bandit stepped to the hub of the front wheel, seized the messenger's bag and stepped down again.

"Don't move, or look back, for five minutes," he admonished them, "then pull yer freight."

The two then backed away up the road behind the stage, keeping it covered with their guns. The messenger lay in the road moaning.

The fat lady unfolded her arms, opened the door and stepped out. "Get back there, you!" called one of the bandits.

"Go to the divil!" retorted Mary Donovan, as she stooped beside the wounded messenger.

The man opened his eyes and looked about, then

he essayed to rise and with Mary Donovan's help came to his feet. "Jest a scratch, me b'y," she said in a motherly tone as she helped him to the stage. "Ye'll be all right the mornin'. Git a move on ye inside there, ye ould woman with the artilery," she yelled at the little old gentleman, "an' give this b'y a hand in."

Together they helped the wounded man to a seat. The bandits were still in sight, but they had not molested her—doubtless because she was a woman and unarmed; but no more had she deposited the messenger upon the seat than she turned upon the old man and wrenched one of his guns from its holster.

"Drive like the divil, Bill," she cried to the driver, sticking her head out of the window, and as he whipped up his team she turned back toward the two bandits and opened fire on them. They returned the fire, and the fusillade continued until the stage disappeared in a cloud of dust around a curve below the gap, the old gentleman and the passenger on top now taking part in the shooting.

CHAPTER III

SUSPICIONS

AS THE stage swirled through the dusty street of Hendersville an hour later and drew up before The Donovan House the loiterers about the hotel and the saloons gathered about it for the news and the gossip from the outer world. Gum Smith, sheriff, was among them.

"Stuck up again, Gum, at the gap," the driver called to him. "They bored Mack."

Mary Donovan and the little old gentleman were assisting the messenger from the stage, though he protested that he was all right and required no assistance. As the woman's eyes alighted upon the sheriff, she turned upon him, her arms akimbo.

"Sure, yese a fine spicimin uv a sheriff, Gum Smith, that ye are—not!" she yelled in a voice that could be heard the length of the single street. "Three holdups in the two months right under yer nose, and all ye do is 'depatize' an' 'depatize' an' 'depatize.' Why don't ye git out an' git 'em—ye ould woman," she concluded scornfully, and then turning to the wounded man, her voice instantly as soft as a lullaby.

"Get inside wid ye, ye poor b'y, an' Mary Donovan'll be after makin' ye comfortable 'til we get hould uv the ould saw-bones, if he's sober, which he ain't, or I'm no lady, which I am. Come on now, aisy like, there's a good b'y," and she put a motherly arm about the lad and helped him to the porch of the hotel, just as Diana Henders appeared from the interior, attracted by the sounds from without.

"Oh, Mrs. Donovan!" she exclaimed. "What has happened? Why, it's Mack! The Black Coyote again?" she guessed quickly.

"Shure an' it was none other. I seen him wid me own eyes—the black silk handkerchief about the neck uv him an' another over his ugly face. An' his pardner—sure now I couldn't be mishtaken wid the rollin' walk uv him—if it wasn't that dhirty greaser, Gregorio, me name's not Mary Donovan, which it is."

Together the two women helped the messenger into a bedroom where Mary Donovan, despite the embarrassed protests of her patient, undressed him and put him to bed while Diana Henders went to the kitchen for hot water and cloths.

Mack had an ugly flesh wound in his side, and this they had cleansed as best they could by the time the doctor arrived—a drink-broken old man who had drifted in from the East. His knowledge and skill were of the first rank and Hendersville boasted that it owned the best doctor in the Territory—when he was sober.

In *Gum's Place—Liquors and Cigars*—the male population was listening to the account of the holdup as expounded by the little old gentleman and the other passenger, the latter being a stranger in the community.

It was he who had the floor at the moment.

"I never laughed so much in my life," he averred, "as when the old woman calls the old man here the 'ould woman with the artillery.'"

The little old gentleman was standing at the bar with a glass of whiskey in his hand. Apparently with a single movement, so swift was he, he dashed the glass and its contents in the face of the stranger, whipped out both guns and commenced shooting.

A stream of lurid profanity accompanied his act, yet through the flood of incoherent obscenity the nub of an idea occasionally appeared, which was to the effect that "no blankety, blank tin-horn could git gay with Wildcat Bob." Almost instantly, as if a magician had waved his wand, the room, that had been comfortably filled with men, became deserted, as far as human eye could discern, except for the little old gentleman with the tobacco-dewed whiskers.

The front door had accommodated some, while heavy pieces of furniture and the bar accounted for the rest—all but the stranger with the ill-directed sense of humor. He had gone through the back window and taken the sash with him.

The shooting over, the company reappeared, grinning. Most of them knew Wildcat Bob. It had been the stranger's misfortune that he had not.

"I'd orter 'a' bored him, the dinged pole-cat," growled the little old gentleman, filling a fresh glass; "but I guess I larnt him his lesson. The idear of him a-speakin' of Mrs. Donovan disrespectful-like like that—callin' her the 'old woman'! Why, she's the finest lady ever drew breath.

"An' says she to me, says she, Mister Bob, says she, 'It's such a relief to have a man like you along when there's danger,' says she, but she can't stand bloodshed, bein' that timid and shrinkin' and she begged me not to start shootin' at the varmints, otherwise than which I shore would of messed them up somethin' awful," interspersed with which were quite two oaths or obscenities to each word.

The shooting over and quiet restored, Gum Smith made his belated appearance. At sight of the little old gentleman he smiled affably.

"Dog-gone my hide if it ain't Bob," he exclaimed, crossing the room with extended hand. "Have a drink on the house, Bob."

Wildcat Bob ignored the proffered hand. "I got the dust to cover my own drinks, *Mister* Sheriff," he replied, "an' instid of loafin' around here buyin' drinks why ain't you-all out scoutin' after that there Black Coyote hombre? You're shore a hell of a sheriff, you are, Gum Smith."

"Don't git excited, Bob," urged the sheriff, flushing. "Give a man time. Ah got to git me a posse, ain't Ah? Thet's jest what Ah was allowin' to do right now, an' Ah'll start by depatizin' yo."

"You'll deputize me—hell, you will, Gum Smith," returned the old man with a snort of disgust. "I ben out with you-all before. When you thinks danger's north you heads south. I had all the travelin' I wants today."

The sheriff mumbled something beneath his breath and turned away. Some half-hour later he rode out of town with a posse consisting of half a dozen of his cronies and leisurely took his way toward the gap.

In Mrs. Donovan's sitting room Mary Donovan sat rocking comfortably and chatting with Diana Henders. Mack had been made as comfortable as circumstances permitted. The doctor had assured them that he was in no danger and had gone his way—back to *Gum's Place—Liquors and Cigars.*

"And what are you doin' in town this day, Diana?" inquired Mrs. Donovan.

"I rode in with Hal Colby, he's foreman now," replied the girl. "I wanted to buy a few things while Hal rode on over to the West Ranch. We have some horses over there. He ought to be back any minute now."

"So Colby's foreman. What's become of Bull—quit?"

"He got drunk again and Dad broke him. I'm so sorry for him."

"Don't be after wastin' your pity on the loikes ov him," advised Mary Donovan. "There's not the wan ov thim's fit to black your boots, darlin'."

"I don't understand Bull," continued the girl, ignoring the interruption. "Sometimes I think he's all right and then again I'm afraid of him. He's so quiet and reserved that I feel as though no one could ever know him, and when a man's like that, as Hal says, you can't help but think that maybe he's done something that makes him afraid to talk, for fear he'll give himself away."

"So Hal Colby was after sayin' that? Well, maybe he's right an' maybe he's wrong. It's not Mary Donovan that'll be sayin' as don't know. But this I do be after knowin'—they're both ov thim in love with ye, and——"

"Hush, Mrs. Donovan! The boys all think they're in love with me, but I hate to hear anyone else say it seriously. It's perfectly silly. They'd be just as much in love with any other girl, if she chanced to be the only girl on the ranch, as I am, and pretty nearly the only girl in the county, too. There's Hal now. I must be going. Good-bye, Mrs. Donovan."

"Good-bye, darlin', an' be after comin' over again soon. It's that lonesome here, you never could imagine! An' what wid that ould scoundrel back in town again, to say nothin' ov Gum Smith!"

"What old scoundrel?" inquired the girl.

"Sure, no one else but Wildcat Bob, the spalpeen!"

Diana Henders laughed. "He's a very persistent suitor, isn't he, Mrs. Donovan?"

"Sure he's a very pestiferous shooter, that's what he is—the ould fool. Actin' like a wild broth ov a b'y, an' him sivinty if he's a day. He ought to be ashamed of himself, I'm sayin'; but at that he's better than Gum Smith—say, that man's so crooked ye could pull corks wid him."

The girl was still laughing as she emerged from the hotel and mounted her pony. Hal Colby sat his horse a few yards away, talking with half a dozen men. At sight of Diana Henders he reined about and joined her.

"The boys were just telling me about the latest holdup in Hell's Bend," he said, as they cantered, stirrup to stirrup, out of town. "How's Mack?"

"The doctor says he'll be all right," replied Diana. "Just a bad flesh wound. I don't see why something isn't done to put a stop to these hold-ups. Gum Smith doesn't seem to care whether he gets The Black Coyote or not."

"Oh, Gum's doin' the best he can," Colby assured her good-naturedly.

"You're too easy, Hal. You never like to say anything against a man, and of course that is right, too; but the lives and property of all of us are under Gum Smith's protection, to a greater or less extent, and if he was the right sort he'd realize his responsibility and make a determined effort to run down this fellow."

"He went out after him with a posse—the boys just told me so. What more can he do?"

"It was half an hour or more after the stage pulled in before Gum started," she retorted. "Does he or anyone else imagine that those two scoundrels are going to wait around the gap until Gum gets there? And he'll be back with his posse right after dark. He'll say he lost the trail, and that'll be the end of it until next time."

The man made no reply and the two rode on in silence for a few minutes.

It was the girl who spoke again first.

"I wonder," she said, "who this Black Coyote really is."

"Everybody seems pretty sure it was The Black Coyote," remarked Colby. "How did they know?"

"The black silk handkerchief he uses for a mask, and the other one about his neck," she explained. "It must be the same man. Everyone has noticed these handkerchiefs on one of the men in every holdup in Hell's Bend Pass during the last six months. There is scarce any one that isn't positive that the second man is the Mexican, Gregorio; but no one seems to have recognized the principal."

"I got my own opinion," said Colby.

"What do you mean? Do you know who The Black Coyote really is?"

"I wouldn't want to say that I know, exactly; but I got my own opinion."

"Well!" she urged.

"I wouldn't want to mention no names—until I was shore. But," after a pause, "I'd like to see his cayuse. No one ever sees either his or his pardner's. They keep 'em hid out in the brush alongside the trail; but I got a guess that if anyone ever seed The Black Coyote's pony we'd all know for shore who The Black Coyote is."

She did not insist further when she saw that he was apparently shielding the name of some man whom they both knew, and whom he suspicioned. It was only right that he should do this, she thought, and she admired him the more for it. So they talked of other things as they jogged along the dusty road toward home, the man riding a stirrup's width behind that he might feast his eyes upon the profile of his companion. As they neared the ranch they saw the figure of a solitary horseman approaching from the north.

"Looks like Blazes," remarked the girl.

"It is," said the man. "I sent Bull up to Cottonwood this morning. I don't see what he's doin' comin' in from the north. The Cottonwood trail's almost due west."

"He might have come back along the foot hill trail," suggested Diana.

"He might, but it's farther, an' I never seed a puncher yet that'd ride any farther than you told him to."

"Bull's different," she replied, simply. "If you sent him out for any purpose he'd accomplish it no matter how far he had to ride. He's always been a good hand."

A moment later the ex-foreman joined them where the two trails met. He accorded the girl the customary, "Howdy, Miss," of the times, and nodded to Colby. His mount was streaked with sweat and dust. It was evident that he had been ridden hard.

"Did you find them cows?" asked the foreman.

Bull nodded.

"In Cottonwood?"

"No, Belter's."

Diana Henders glanced at the foreman as much as to say, "I told you so!" Then, glancing back at Bull, she noticed a reddish brown stain on the side of his shirt, and gave a little exclamation of concern.

"Oh, Bull!" she cried, "you've been hurt—that's blood, isn't it? How did it happen?"

"Oh, that ain't nothin', Miss, just a little scratch," and he closed up, like a clam, spurring ahead of them.

Neither Colby nor the girl spoke, but both were thinking of the same things—that Bull wore a black silk handkerchief about his neck and that Mary Donovan had fired back upon The Black Coyote and his confederate following the holdup in Hell's Bend earlier in the afternoon.

Mrs. Donovan, her hands on her hips, stood just inside the dining room door as her guests filed in for supper that evening and seated themselves at the long deal table covered with its clean red and white cloth. She had a good-natured word for each of them, until her eyes alighted upon Wildcat Bob, attempting to sneak in unnoticed behind the broad figure of Jim Weller.

"So-o!" she exclaimed scornfully. "Ye ould fool—yer drunk again. Ta-ake off thim guns an' give thim to me."

"I haven't had a drink, Mary," expostulated the old man.

"Don't 'Mary' me, ye ould reprobate, an' be after givin' me thim guns, quick!"

Meekly he unbuckled his belt and passed it over to her. "I was just bringin' 'em in to you, Ma—Mrs. Donovan," he assured her.

"Yed better be. Now go an' sit down. I'll feed you this night, but don't you iver step foot into Mary Donovan's dining room again in liquor."

"I tell you I ain't had a drink," he insisted.

"Pha-at?" The word reeked with disbelief.

"Only just a drop to settle the dust after we pulled in," he qualified his original statement.

"Ye must uv been that dusty then!" she exclaimed scornfully.

"I was."

"Don't talk back. And did ye find yer horses, Jim Weller?" she inquired of the big man behind whom Wildcat Bob had made his unimpressive entrance.

Weller shook his head, negatively, his mouth being full of baked beans.

"Patches probably run 'em off," suggested Bill Gatlin, the stage driver.

"What with renegades and holdups this country ain't safe to live in no more," remarked Mrs. Donovan. "If some of these here would-be bad-men would git out an' shoot up the bandits and the Injuns instid of shootin' up saloons," she stated meaningly, casting a baneful look at Wildcat Bob.

"Hadn't orter be hard to find 'em, least wise one of 'em," stated Weller, "when every son-of-a-gun in the county knows who he is."

"Meanin'?" inquired the stage driver.

"Gregorio, in course," said Weller. "I seen him comin' out o' Cottonwood not three hours before the stage was stuck up, an' he was headin' towards Hell's Bend—him an' that Bar Y Bull feller."

"You mean them two was together?" asked Gatlin.

"Well, they warn't exactly together. Gregorio comes out fust an' about five minutes later I meets Bull acomin' down the canyon; but they couldn't have both been up there without t'other knowin' it."

"I don't believe Bull would be doin' it," said Mary Donovan.

"You can't never tell nothin' about them quiet fellers," remarked Gatlin, sententiously.

There was a pounding of hoofs without, the creaking of leather as men dismounted and a moment later the sheriff and some of his posse entered the dining room.

"I suppose ye got 'em, Gum Smith," said Mrs. Donovan, with sarcasm, "or ye wouldn't be back this soon."

"Ah ain't no cat, Mrs. Donovan," said the sheriff, on the defensive, "to see in the dark."

"Yese ain't no sheriff nayther," she shot back.

Wildcat Bob succeeded in calling attention to derisive laughter by pretending to hide it. Gum Smith looked at his rival angrily, immediately discovering that he was unarmed.

"What's the matter with the old woman with the artillery—is she chokin'?" he inquired sweetly.

Wildcat Bob went red to the verge of apoplexy, seized a heavy cup half-filled with coffee and started to rise.

"Sit down wid ye!" roared the stentorian voice of Mary Donovan.

"I—" started Wildcat Bob.

"Shut up an' sit down!"

The Wildcat did both, simultaneously.

"It's a sha-ame, that it is, that a respictable widdy lady should be redjuced to fadin' the likes o' yese fer a livin'," wailed Mrs. Donovan, sniffing, as she dabbed at her eyes with the corner of her apron, "all alone and unproticted as I am. Sure an' if poor Tim was here he'd wipe the ground wid the both ov yese."

Wildcat Bob, very red and uncomfortable, ate diligently, his eyes glued to his plate. Well did Mary Donovan know how to handle this terror of an earlier day, whose short temper and quick guns still held the respect and admiration of the roughest characters of the great empire of the southwest, but whose heart could be dissolved by a single tear.

As for Gum Smith, he was only too glad to be relieved of the embarrassment of the Wildcat's further attentions and he too gave himself willingly over to peace and supper. For the balance of the meal, however, conversation languished.

At the Bar Y Ranch the men sat smoking after the evening meal. Bull was silently puffing upon a cigarette. Hal Colby, always good-natured and laughing, told stories. During the silences Texas Pete strove diligently to recall the half-forgotten verses of *The Bad Hombre.*

But over all there hovered an atmosphere of restraint. No one could have put his finger upon the cause, yet all sensed it. Things were not as they had been yesterday, or for many days before. Perhaps there was a feeling that an older man should have been chosen to replace Bull, for Colby was one of the newer hands. Without volition and unconsciously the men were taking sides. Some, mostly the men who had worked longest for Henders, drew imperceptibly nearer Bull. Texas Pete was one of them. The others laughed a little louder, now, at Colby's stories.

"By gollies!" exclaimed Pete, "I remember some more of it:

"'I am the original bad un, I am;
I eats 'em alive an' I don't give a damn
Fer how fast they come er how many they be—
Of all the bad hombres the wust one is me.'"

sang Texas Pete. "Good night, fellers, I'm goin' to turn in."

CHAPTER IV

"I LOVE YOU"

DIANA HENDERS was troubled. Ever since the holdup several days before she had not been able to expunge from her thoughts a recollection of the sinister circumstances that pointed an accusing finger at Bull. There had always been a deep seated loyalty existing between the Henders and their employees and this alone would have been sufficient to have brought the girl to arms in the defense of the reputation of any of her father's "boys." In the case of Bull there were added reasons why she could not bear to foster a suspicion of his guilt.

Not only had he been a trusted foreman, but there was something in the man himself, or rather in his influence upon the imagination of the girl, that made it almost impossible for her to believe that he had shot Mack Harber, another employee, and stolen the bullion from her father's mine. He had always been reticent and almost shy in her presence. He had never presumed to even the slight familiarity of addressing her by her given name —a customary procedure among the other men, many of whom had seen her grow so gradually from a little girl to a young lady that they scarce yet discerned the change.

Yet she knew that he liked to be with her, though she was far from being sure that she cared for his company. He was quiet to taciturnity and far from being the pleasant companion that she found in Hal Colby. There was something, however, that she felt when in his company to a much greater degree than when she was with other men — absolute confidence in his integrity and his ability to protect her.

Now she was sorry for him since his reduction from a post of responsibility and her loyalty aroused by the inward suspicions she had permitted herself to entertain, to the end that she was moved by something akin to remorse to make some sort of overtures of friendship that he might know that the daughter of his employer still had confidence in him.

It was a quiet Sunday morning. The men were lazily occupying themselves with the overhauling of their outfits, replacing worn latigo and stirrup leather lacings, repairing hackamores and bridles, polishing silver and guns, cleaning boots with bacon grease and lamp black, shaving, or hair-cutting.

Down past the bunk-house, toward the corrals, came Diana Henders. Presently she would pause near the men and ask one of them to catch up a horse for her. The lucky fellow whom she asked would ride with her.

It was a custom of long standing; but she was earlier than usual this Sunday morning and several of the men worked frantically to complete the jobs they were engaged upon before she should arrive within speaking distance. Two or three affected attitudes of careless idleness indicative of perfect readiness to meet any call upon their time or services.

Texas Pete was cutting the hair of another puncher. He had reached a point where his victim was entirely shorn upon one side, the other displaying a crop of thick, brown hair four or five inches long, when he looked up and saw Diana approaching. Pete tossed the shears and comb into the lap of the victim.

"You-all don't need a hair-cut nohow," he announced, strolling away with what he believed to be a remarkable display of nonchalance, along a line that would, quite by accident of course, intercept Diana's course to the corrals.

The deserted and disfigured puncher wheeled upon him with a loud yell.

"Come back here, you knock-kneed, bowlegged, son-of-a—," then his eyes, too, alighted upon Diana. His fountain of speech dried at the source, his tanned face assumed a purple cast, and in two jumps he had reached the seclusion of the bunk-house.

Hal Colby walked deliberately forward to meet the girl, a pleasant smile of greeting upon his handsome face as he raised his wide sombrero in salutation. Had he been on trial for his life at that moment the entire outfit would have voted unanimously to hang him on the spot; but, gosh, how they envied him!

Bull sat, apparently unmoved, with his back against a cottonwood tree, running a wiping rag through the barrel of a revolver. He did not even look up, though he had seen Diana Henders from the moment that she left the house. Bull realized that after the affair in town that had caused his downfall there was no chance for him to ride with her again for many long days—possibly forever.

"Going for a ride, Di?" asked Colby, confidently, as the girl came abreast of the men.

"Why, yes, I was thinking of it," she replied sweetly. "I was just going to ask Bull if he wouldn't catch up Captain for me—the rest of you all seem so busy."

Colby appeared abashed but not defeated. "I haven't a thing to do," he assured her.

"But I've made you ride with me so much lately, Hal," she insisted.

"I'd rather ride with you than eat," he whispered.

Texas Pete had made a feeble pretense of searching for something on the ground, apparently given it up in despair, and was passing them on his way back to the bunk-house.

"I don't think you oughter ride with—with him, nohow," continued Colby.

The girl drew herself up, slightly. "Don't be nasty, Hal," she said.

"You know I hate to say that," he assured her. "I set a heap of store by Bull. He's one of my best friends, but after what's happened—you can't blame me, Di. I think your dad would say the same thing if he knew."

Bull was halfway to the corrals.

"I'll have the hosses up in a jiffy, Miss," he called back over his shoulder.

"Good-bye, Hal," laughed the girl, teasingly. "You'll have plenty of time to lay out the work for tomorrow—a foreman's *always* busy, you know," and she walked away briskly after Bull.

As Colby turned back toward the men he saw broad grins adorning the faces of most of them. Texas Pete, just approaching the bunk-house door, halted, removed his hat with a flourish, bowing low.

"Goin' to git your hair cut, Jim?" he inquired sweetly. "You know I'd rather cut your hair than eat."

A loud roar of laughter acknowledged this sally.

Colby, flushing crimson, beat a hasty retreat toward the office.

"Which way?" asked Bull, when the two had mounted.

"I'm going to town to see how Mack is getting along," replied the girl, watching his face.

"I seen Wildcat Bob yesterday. He said he was getting along fine. Nothing but a flesh wound."

Neither his voice nor his expression betrayed more than ordinary concern.

"Have you seen Mack since he was shot?" she inquired.

"Ain't had time. Colby keeps me pretty busy. Mack was a dinged fool fer gettin' creased anyhow," he observed. "When a feller's got the drop on you, stick 'em up. They ain't nothin' else to do. Mack orter known better than to make any funny gun-play with them two hombres coverin' him."

"It was mighty brave of him," said Diana. "He's no coward—and he was loyal to Dad."

"I don't see nothin' brave about it," he replied. "It was just plumb foolishness. Why he didn't have a chanct on earth."

"That's what made his act so courageous," she insisted.

"Then the feller what commits suicide must be a regular hero," he rejoined, smiling. "I never looked at it that way. I reckon Mack must have been aimin' to commit suicide."

"You're horrid, Bull. I believe you haven't any heart at all."

"I shore have. Leastways I did have one until —" He hesitated, looked at her in a peculiar way, then let his eyes drop to his saddle horn. "Oh, shucks! what's the use?" he exclaimed.

There was silence for a brief interval. The spirit of coquetry, that is strong in every normal girl, prompted her to urge him on; but a natural kindliness coupled with the knowledge that it would be unfair to him kept her silent. It was the man who spoke again first.

"I was sorry Mack got hurt," he said, defensively; "but he was lucky he wasn't killed. That Black Coyote feller must have been a friend of his'n."

"The brute!" she exclaimed. "He ought to be strung up to the highest tree in the county."

"Yes," he agreed, and then, with another of his rare smiles, "let's speak to Gum Smith about it when we get to town."

"Gum Smith!" Were it possible to snort Gum Smith she had accomplished it. "If an honest vote had been taken for the *worst* man for sheriff Gum Smith would have been elected unanimously."

"Why Gum's a good sheriff," he teased, "—fer tin horns and bandits."

She did not reply. Her thoughts were upon the man at her side. Nothing that he had said had exactly tended to weaken her faith in him, yet it had not materially strengthened it, either.

His apparent callous indifference to Mack's suffering might have been attributed with equal fairness to the bravado of the guilty desperado, or to the conditions and the times in which they lived which placed shootings and sudden death in the category of the commonplace. His suggestion that The Black Coyote must have been a friend of Mack, as an explanation of a flesh wound rather than a mortal one, appeared a trifle sinister, though it was amenable to other interpretations. On the whole, however, Diana Henders was not wholly pleased with the result of her probing.

At The Donovan House they found Mack sufficiently recovered to be able to sit upon the veranda, where there were gathered a number of Mrs. Donovan's other guests, including Wildcat Bob and the sheriff. Mary Donovan stood in the doorway, one hand on a hip and the other, the fist doubled, emphasizing some forceful statement she was delivering.

As Diana Henders and Bull appeared suddenly before them, the argument, which had been progressing merrily, lapsed into an embarrassed silence. It would have been evident to the most obtuse that one or the other of the newcomers had been the subject of the conversation, and neither Bull nor Diana was obtuse, the result being that they shared the embarrassment of the others.

The silence, which really lasted but a brief moment, was broken by Mary Donovan's hearty greeting to Diana, followed by a cordial word to Bull, which was seconded by Wildcat Bob. The others, however, spoke only to Diana Henders, appearing not to be aware of the presence of her escort.

"Come now," cried Mary Donovan, "into the house wid ye an' have a bit o' cake an' a cup o' tay." But Diana Henders did not dismount.

"No, thank you, Mrs. Donovan," she replied.

"We just rode down to see how Mack was getting along and to ask if there was anything we could do for him." She turned her glance toward the wounded man.

"I'm all right, Miss," he replied. "'T wasn't nothin' but a scratch. I'll be back at the mine in a couple o' days—an' guardin' the bullion shipments, too, same as usual." He looked straight at Bull as he made this final statement.

"Well," exclaimed Diana, hastily, "I'm glad you're so much better, Mack, and if there isn't anything we can do for you we'll start back for the ranch." She sensed the sullen attitude of most of the men there, the scowls they cast at Bull, and she knew that it would require little to precipitate a direct accusation, which would have been almost certain to have been followed by gunplay. "Come, Bull," she said, and reined her pony about.

They had ridden well out of town when she looked casually into the man's face. It bore a troubled expression and he must have guessed that she noted it.

"I wonder what was eatin' them fellers," he remarked. "No one only Wildcat Bob even spoke to me, an' Mack seemed gosh-almighty sore about somethin'. Well, they ain't none of 'em got their brand on me. If I did shoot up Gum Smith's joint it ain't no hair offen none of them."

The girl wondered if he really was ignorant of the suspicions directed against him, or if he took this means to make her believe that the cause of the altered attitude toward him was his drunken gunplay in the sheriff's saloon.

"I was right sorry about that, Miss," he blurted suddenly. "I never aimed for to do it. I wasn't goin' to drink too much no more after what I'd promised you. I'm right sorry. Do you think that, maybe, you—you might forgive me—and give me another chance?"

His voice was pleading and he was very much in earnest. The girl knew how difficult it was for a rough man like Bull to say what he had just said and she felt a sudden compassion for him.

"It made me sorry, too, Bull," she said. "I trusted you and I hated to be so disappointed in you."

"Please don't say you don't trust me, Miss," he begged. "I want you to trust me, more'n anything else."

"I want to trust you, Bull," and then, impulsively: "I do trust you!"

He reached across the interval between them and laid his rough hand upon her soft one.

"I love you, Diana," he said, very simply and with a quiet dignity that was unmarred by any hesitancy or embarrassment.

She started to speak, but he silenced her with a gesture.

"Don't say anything about it, please," he urged. "I don't expect you to love me; but there's nothing wrong about my loving you. I just wanted you to know it so that you'd always know where I stood and that you could always call on me for anything. With yer dad an' all the other men around that loves you there isn't much likelihood that you'll ever need me more'n another, but it makes me feel better to know that you know now. We won't talk about it no more, Miss. We both understand. It's the reason I didn't quit when yer dad busted me."

"I'm glad you told me, Bull," she said. "It's the greatest honor that any man can bestow upon a girl. I don't love any man, Bull, that way; but if ever I do he'll know it without my telling him. I'll do something that will prove it — a girl always does. Sometimes, though, the men are awfully blind, they say."

"I wouldn't be blind," said Bull. "I'd know it, I think, if a girl loved me."

"The right one will, some day," she assured him.

He shook his head. "I hope so, Miss."

She flushed, sensing the unintentional *double entendre* he had caught in her words. She wondered why she flushed.

They rode on in silence. She was sorry that Bull loved her, but she was glad that, loving her, he had told her of his love. He was just a common cowhand, unlettered, rough, and occasionally uncouth, but of these things she did not think, for she had known no other sort, except her father and an occasional visitor from the East, since childhood. Had she cared for him she would not have been ashamed She looked up at him with a smile.

"Don't call me 'Miss,' Bull, please—I hate it."

"You want me to call you by your first name?" he inquired.

"The other men do," she said, "and you did—a moment ago."

"It slipped out that time." He grinned sheepishly.

"I like it."

"All right, Miss," he said.

The girl laughed aloud, joyously.

"All right, Diana, I mean," he corrected himself.

"That's better."

So Diana Henders, who was really a very sensible girl, instead of merely playing with fire, made a big one of a little one, all very unintentionally, for how was she to know that to Bull the calling of her Diana instead of Miss was almost as provocative to his love as would have been the personal contact of a kiss to an ordinary man?

As they approached the ranch house at the end of their ride they saw a buckboard to which two bronchos were harnessed hitched to the tie rail beneath the cottonwoods outside the office door.

"Whose outfit is that?" asked Diana. "I never saw it before."

"The Wainrights from the north side o' the hills. I seen 'em in town about a week ago."

"Oh, yes, I've heard of them. They're from the

East. Mr. Wainright don't like the country north of the mountains."

"He's lookin' fer range on this side," said Bull. "Like as not that's what he's here fer now. They ain't enough water fer no more outfits though, nor enough feed neither."

They drew rein at the corral and dismounted. "Thanks, Bull," said the girl, as she passed him her bridle reins. "We've had a lovely ride."

"Thanks—Diana."

That was all he said, but the way he spoke her name was different from the way any other man had ever spoken it. She was sorry now that she had asked him to call her Diana.

As she was passing the office to go to her room her father called to her.

"Come in, Di; I want you to meet some new neighbors," and when she had entered, "My daughter, Mr. Wainright."

Diana extended her hand to a fat man with close-set eyes, and then her father presented the younger Wainright.

"Mr. Jefferson Wainright, Jr., Diana," he said.

The son was a well-groomed appearing, nice-looking young fellow of twenty-one or twenty-two. Perhaps his costume was a trifle too exaggerated to be in good taste, but he had only fallen into the same mistake that many another wealthy young Easterner has done before and since upon his advent to the cow-country. From silver banded sombrero to silver encrusted spurs there was no detail lacking.

"By gollies, he looks like a Christmas tree," had been Texas Pete's observation the first time that he had seen him. "All they forgot was the candles."

"You live north of the mountains?" inquired Diana, politely.

"Yep," replied the elder Wainright; "but we don't calc'late to stay there. We're from Mass-'chusetts—Worcester—blankets—made a fortune in 'em—made 'em for the gover'ment mostly. Jeff got it in his head he wanted to go into the cattle business—come by it natch'ral I allow. I used to be in the livery stable business before I bought the mills—so when he graduates from Harvard a year ago we come out here—don't like it tother side the mountains—so I calc'lates to come over here."

"I was just explaining to Mr. Wainright that there is scarcely enough feed or water for another big outfit on this side," interjected Mr. Henders.

"Don't make any difference—set your price—but set it right. I'll buy you out. I c'd buy half this territory I calc'late—if I had a mind to—but the price's got to be right. Ol' Jeff Wainright's got a name for bein' a pretty shrewd trader—fair'n honest, though—fair'n honest. Just name your price—how much for the whole shebang—buildin's, land, cattle—everything?"

Elias Henders laughed good naturedly. "I'm afraid they're not for sale, Mr. Wainright."

"Tut, tut! I'll get 'em—you'll sell—ol' Jeff

Wainright's always got everything he went after. Well, son, I calc'late we'd better be goin'."

"You'll have dinner with us first, of course," insisted Diana; "it must be almost ready now."

"Well, I don't mind if we do," returned the elder Wainright, and so they stayed for the noon day meal.

Diana found the younger Wainright a pleasant, affable companion. He was the first educated man near her own age that she had ever met and his conversation and his ways, so different from those of the rough vaqueros of her little world, made a profound impression upon her. He could talk interestingly from the standpoint of personal experience of countless things of which she had only secondhand knowledge acquired from books and newspapers. Those first two hours with him thrilled her with excitement—they opened a new world of wondrous realities that she had hitherto thought of more as unattainable dreams than things which she herself might some day experience.

If he had inherited something of his father's egotism she forgot it in the contemplation of his finer qualities and in the pleasure she derived from association with one somewhere near her own social status in life. That the elder Wainright was impossible she had sensed from the first, but the son seemed of different fiber and no matter what his antecedents, he must have acquired something of permanent polish through his college associations.

The disquieting effect of the Wainrights' visit was apparent elsewhere than at the ranch house. There was gloom at the bunk-house.

"Dog-gone his hide!" exclaimed Texas Pete.

"Whose?" inquired Shorty.

"My ol' man's. If he hadn't gone an' got hung he might 'a' sent me to Havaad. What chanct has a feller got agin one o' them paper-collared, cracker-fed dudes anyway!"

CHAPTER V

THE ROUND-UP

"I HAD a letter from Wainright in the mail today, Di," said Elias Henders to his daughter about a week later. "He is after me again to put a price on the whole 'shebang.'"

"We could go East and live then, couldn't we?" asked the girl.

Henders looked at her keenly. There had been just the tiniest trace of wistfulness in her tone. He crossed the room and put an arm about her.

"You'd like to go East and live?" he asked.

"I love it here, Dad; but there is so much there that we can never have here. I should like to see how other people live. I should like to go to a big hotel, and to the theaters and opera, and meet educated people of my own age. I should like to go to parties where no one got drunk and shot the lights out," she concluded with a laugh.

"We don't have to sell out to go back," he told her. "I am afraid I have been selfish. Because I never wanted to go back after your mamma left us, I forgot that you had a right to the same advantages that she and I enjoyed. The ranch seemed enough — the ranch and you."

"But there'd be no one to manage things if you went away," she insisted.

"Oh, that could be arranged. I thought you felt that we couldn't afford to go unless we sold."

"It would be nice if you were relieved of all responsibility," she said. "If you sold the ranch and the brand you wouldn't have to worry about how things were going here."

"Old Wainright wouldn't pay what they are worth, even if I was ready to sell," he explained. "I'll tell you what I'll do—I'll make him a price. If he takes it I'll sell out, and anyway, whether he does or not, we'll go East to stay, if you like it."

"What price are you going to ask?"

"Seven hundred and fifty thousand dollars for the ranch and the brand. They might bring more if I wanted to make an effort to get more, but that will show a fair profit for us and I know will be satisfactory to John. He has asked me a dozen times in his letters why I didn't sell the cattle end of the business and come East."

"Yes, I know Uncle John has always wanted us to come back," she said.

"But old Wainright really doesn't want the ranch and cattle at all," said her father. "What he wants is the mine. He has offered me a million dollars for all our holdings in the county, including the mine. He mentions the fact that the workings have pretty nearly petered out, and he's right, and he thinks I'll grab at it to unload.

"I suspect he's had a man up there for the past six months—the new bookkeeper that Corson sent out while your Uncle John Manill was in Europe—and he thinks he's discovered something that I don't know—but I do. For years, Di, we've been paralleling a much richer vein than the one we've been working. I've known it for the past two years, but John and I figured we'd work out the old one first—we've all the money we need anyway. The mine alone is worth ten or twenty millions."

"Uncle John knows it? There wouldn't be any danger that someone might trick him into a deal?"

"Not a chance, and of course, as you know, he wouldn't do anything without consulting me. Ours is rather a peculiar partnership, Di, but it's a very safe one for both of us. There isn't the scratch of a pen between us as far as any written agreement is concerned, but he trusts me and I trust him. Why before either of us married the only precautions we took to safeguard our interests was to make our wills—I left everything to him and he left everything to me. After we married we made new wills, that was all.

"If I die first everything goes to him, and when he dies it is all divided equally between our surviving heirs; or just the other way around if he dies first. Each of us felt that we could thus best safeguard the interests of our respective families, since we both had implicit confidence in the other's honesty and integrity."

"Oh, let's not talk about it," exclaimed the girl. "Neither one of you is ever going to die."

"All right, Di," laughed her father; "just as you say—you've always had your own way. Now we'll plan that Eastern trip. Can't very well go until after the spring round-up, and in the meantime we can be sizing up Colby. If he takes hold all right we couldn't do better than to leave him in charge. I never did like the idea of importing a new man as superintendent if you could possibly use one of your own men. What do you think of him, Di?"

"I don't know yet Dad," she replied. "I like him immensely, and I think he's honest and loyal, but he don't know stock, nor the range, as well as Bull."

"Bull is out of the question," replied her father. "I could never trust him again."

"I know how you feel. I feel the same way, and yet there is something about him, Dad—I can't explain it; but when I am with him I cannot doubt him."

"He's got you hypnotized. I hope he hasn't been making love to you," he concluded, seriously.

"Oh, they all do," she cried, laughing; "but Bull least of all."

"I suppose you'll have to be marrying one of these days, and if you were going to live here I'd rather you married a Western boy; but if you are going East you mustn't fall in love yet, for you are sure to find a great difference between the boys you have known and the boys back there."

"Don't worry, Dad, I haven't fallen in love yet; but if I do soon I'm afraid it's going to be either Hal Colby or Jefferson Wainright."

"Senior?" he asked.

"Oh, isn't he funny—and impossible!" she cried.

"He's all of that and more too," replied her father.

"What do you mean?"

"I mean that I wouldn't trust him as far as I could throw a bull by the tail. He's one of those blue-bellied Yankees who considers any means as honest that keep him on the right side of a jail door; but the boy appears to be a much more decent sort."

"He is delightful and wonderful," said Diana.

The days passed, lovely, sunshiny days during which Diana spent long hours dreaming of the coming Eastern trip. She rode much, as usual, sometimes with one man, again with another, but more often with her father or Hal Colby.

Bull's assignments usually took him too far afield for her to accompany him. If he thought that Colby had some such purpose in mind when he laid out the work from day to day he said nothing of it; but he could not have failed to notice that following each of the few occasions upon which Diana accompanied him, usually a Sunday, he was given work the next day that kept him in the saddle until late at night, and upon several occasions away from the ranch for two days or more.

At last the time of the spring rodeo arrived. Riders from other outfits commenced straggling in, some from a hundred miles away, until the Bar Y Ranch commenced to take on the appearance of an army camp. The chuck wagon was overhauled and outfitted. The *cavvy* was brought over from West Ranch—wild, half-broken horses, with a sprinkling of colts that had never felt leather—and assigned to the riders. There were enough to give each man a string of eight horses.

With the others came Jefferson Wainright, Jr., arrayed like Solomon. At first the men had a lot of fun with him, but when he took it good-naturedly they let up a bit, and after a few evenings, during which he sang and told stories, they accepted him almost as one of them. He was much with Diana Henders, with the result that he found himself with four unbroken bronchs in his string. The Bar Y hands grinned when Colby picked them for him, and everyone was present when he first essayed to ride one of them.

Diana was there too. She chanced to be standing near Bull when the first of the four, having been roped, thrown and hogtied, was finally saddled, bridled and let up. It was a ewe-necked, wall-eyed, Roman-nosed pinto and its back was humped like a camel's.

"He shore looks mean," remarked Bull to the girl.

"They ought not to let Mr. Wainright ride him," she replied. "He's not used to bad horses and he may be killed."

"I reckon that's just about how Hal figgered it," said Bull.

"I didn't think it of him. It's a shame!" she exclaimed. "Some one ought to top that horse for Mr. Wainright—some one who can ride—like you, Bull," she added flatteringly.

"You want me to?" he asked.

"I don't want to see the poor man killed."

Bull stepped forward and climbed into the corral. Wainright was standing several feet from the pinto watching several men who were trying to readjust the blind over the brute's eyes. Bull saw that the man was afraid.

"Want me to top him for you, young feller?" he asked.

"Don't you think he's safe?" asked Wainright.

"Oh, yes, he's safe—like a Kansas cyclone."

Wainright grinned a sickly grin. "I'd appreciate it," he said, "if you'd try him first. I'd be glad to pay you for your trouble."

Bull approached the men with the horse. "Lead him out," he said. "When I rides one like that I wants elbow room."

They ran the pony, bucking, out of the corral. Bull stepped to the animal's side.

"What you doin'?" demanded Colby, who had been standing too far away to overhear the conversation.

"Toppin' this one for the dude," replied Bull.

"No you're not," snapped Colby. His voice was angry. "You'll ride the hosses I tells you to and so will he."

"I'm ridin' this one," replied Bull. He had grasped the cheek strap with his left hand, his right was on the horn of the saddle. Carefully he placed his left foot in the stirrup. Then he nodded to a man standing at the horse's head.

The blind was snatched away and the man leaped aside. The horse reared, wheeled and struck at Bull, but Bull was not there—he was in the saddle. The animal lunged forward awkwardly once, then he gathered himself, stuck his nose between his front feet and went to pitching, scientifically and in earnest, and as he pitched he lunged first to the right and then to the left, twisting his body, squealing and kicking. Bull waved his sombrero and slapped the beast on neck and rump with it and the pinto bucked the harder.

Finding that these tactics failed to unseat the rider he commenced suddenly to turn end for end in air at each jump, yet still the man stuck, until the beast, frantic with combined terror and rage, stopped in his tracks and turned savagely to bite at Bull's legs. Just a moment of this until he felt the sting of the quirt and then he reared quickly and threw himself over backward in an effort to crush his rider, nor did he miss him by a matter of more than inches.

There are those who will tell you just how you should throw yourself safely to one side when a horse falls, but any man who has had a horse fall with him, or deliberately throw himself backward, knows that it is five parts chance and the rest luck if he isn't caught, and so it was just luck that Bull fell clear.

Diana Henders felt a sudden lump in her throat and then she saw the horse scramble to his feet and the rider too, just in time to throw a leg across the saddle, and come up with a firm seat and both feet in the stirrups. The quirt fell sharply first on one flank and then on the other, the pinto took a dozen running jumps and then settled down to a smooth run across the open.

Five minutes later he came loping back, blowing and sweaty, still trembling and frightened, but with the hump out of his back.

"You kin ride him now," said Bull to young Wainright, as he dismounted carefully and stood stroking the animal's neck.

Hal Colby came forward angrily, but Bull had dismounted close to where Diana Henders stood, and it was she who spoke to him first, and Colby, approaching, heard her words.

"Thank you, ever so much, Bull," she said. "I was sorry afterwards that I asked you to ride him, for I thought you were going to be hurt when he threw himself — I should never have forgiven myself."

"Shucks!" said Bull. "It wasn't nothin'."

Colby walked off in another direction. If there had been bad blood between the two men in the past it had never been given outward expression, but from that moment Colby made little or no effort to hide the fact that he had no use for Bull, while the latter in many little ways showed his contempt for the foreman.

Better friendships than had ever existed between these two have been shattered because of a woman, but there were other exciting causes here. That Colby had gotten Bull's job might have been enough to cause a break, while the foreman's evident suspicion that Bull knew a great deal too much about the holdups in Hell's Bend and the shooting of Mack Harber would have turned even more generous natures than Hal Colby's against the ex-foreman.

In spite of herself Diana Henders could not deny a feeling of chagrin that Jefferson Wainright had permitted another man to top a bad horse for him, although it had been she who had arranged it. Perhaps she was a trifle cool to the young Easterner that evening, but she thawed gradually beneath the geniality of his affable ways and entertaining conversation, and in the weeks that followed, during which she accompanied the outfit throughout the round-up, she was with him much of the time, to the great discomfiture of Hal Colby and others.

The Bar Y foreman had, however, after the day that Bull rode the pinto for Wainright, left the latter severely alone, for the following morning Elias Henders had come to the corral and selected a new string of horses for the "dude" and spoken a few words into the ear of his foreman.

The long, hard days in the saddle left them all ready to turn in to their blankets soon after supper. A smoke, a little gossip and rough banter and the men jingled away through the darkness in search of their bed-rolls to the accompaniment of their tinkling spurs.

"I seen Injun signs today," remarked a tall, thin Texan one evening. "'Bout a dozen of 'em been campin' over yender a piece in them hills. Signs warn't over four hour old."

"They mought be peaceable Injuns on pass from the reservation," suggested another.

"More likely they're renegades," said Shorty. "Anyhow I ain't a-takin' no chances on no Injuns —I shoots fust an' axes for their pass later."

"You ain't never seed a hos-tyle Injun, Shorty," said Texas Pete.

"A lot you know about it, you sawed-off, hammered-down, squint-eyed horse thief," retorted Shorty courteously; "I'm a bad man with Injuns."

"By gollies!" exclaimed Pete, "thet reminds me of another verse:

"'So bring on yore bad men, yore killers an' sich
An' send out some Greasers to dig me a ditch,
Fer when I gits through, ef I takes any pains,
You'll need a big hole fer to plant the remains.'"

On the opposite side of the chuck wagon, where a tent had been pitched for Diana Henders, a little group surrounded her fire. Beside the girl there were her father, Hal Colby and Jefferson Wainright, Jr. The two young men always gravitated in Diana's direction when off duty. Colby had been quick to realize the advantage that the other's education gave him and bright enough to remain a silent observer of his manners and conversation. Inwardly he held the Easterner in vast contempt, yet he cultivated him and often rode with him that he might learn from him something of those refinements which he guessed constituted the basis of Diana's evident liking for Wainright. He asked him many questions, got him to talk about books, and made mental note of various titles with the determination to procure and read the books that he had heard the man discuss with Diana.

Bull, on his part, kept away from the Henders' fire in the evening and in the day time Colby saw to it that his assignments sent him far afield from where there was much likelihood of Diana being, with the result that he saw less of her than was usual at home.

The ex-foreman's natural reserve had degenerated almost to sullenness. He spoke seldom and never smiled, but he rode hard and did his work well, until he came to be acknowledged as the best all-round man in the outfit. There was no horse that he wouldn't ride, no risk that he wouldn't take, no work that he would ever refuse, no matter how unfair the assignment, with the result that the men respected him though there was none who seemed to like his company, with the exception of Texas Pete.

"Well, boys," said Elias Henders, rising, "I guess we'd better be turning in. Tomorrow's going to be a hard day."

The two younger men rose, Colby stretching and yawning. "I reckon you're right, Mr. Henders," he agreed, but waiting for Wainright to make the first move to leave. The latter paused to roll a cigarette—an accomplishment that he had only recently brought to a state even approximating perfection. He used both hands and was rather slow. Colby eyed him, guessing that he was merely fighting for time in order to force the foreman to go first. Slowly the latter withdrew his own pouch of tobacco from his shirt pocket.

"Reckon I'll roll a smoke by the light of your fire, Di, before I go," he remarked.

He creased the paper, poured in a little tobacco, and, as he drew the pouch closed with his teeth and left hand, deftly rolled the cigarette with his right, bending it slightly in the center to keep it from opening up. Wainright realized that if he had a conversational advantage over Colby there were other activities in which the foreman greatly outshone him. Rolling a smoke was one of them and that was doubtless why Colby had chosen to roll one at a moment that odious comparison might be made.

Wainright lighted his and shifted to the other foot. Would Colby never leave! Colby permitted three matches to burn out before he finally succeeded in getting a light, thus gaining a considerable advantage in time over Wainright. Elias Henders had repaired to his blankets, just beyond Diana's tent and out of sight.

The girl realized the game that the two men were playing and could scarce repress an inclination to laughter. She wondered which would win, or if she would have to call it a draw and send them both about their business. Wainright decided the matter.

"Come on, Colby," he said, throwing an arm about the other's shoulders, "we're keeping Miss Henders up. Good night, Miss Henders," and raising his hat he moved off, taking Colby with him. They had taken about twenty steps when Wainright halted and wheeled about.

"Oh, I say, Miss Henders," he called, "there's something I wanted to ask you," and he started back. "Don't wait for me, Colby," he threw over his shoulder; "I'll be along in a moment."

Colby glared at the other's retreating back

through the darkness, hurled his cigarette to the ground and stamped away, out generaled. "I'll get him yet," he mumbled. "He may be pretty slick at them parlor tricks, but they ain't many parlors in Arizona. The damn dude!"

Wainright rejoined Diana by the fire. "It's too beautiful an evening to go to bed," he said, "and I haven't had half a chance to talk with you. Colby hangs around as though he had a mortgage on your time and was going to foreclose. He sort of puts a damper on conversation unless it revolves about cows—that's all he can talk about."

"It's a subject that is always of interest to us out here," replied the girl loyally. "Cows are really our lives, you know."

"Oh, that's all right for men; but there are other things in life for a girl like you, Miss Henders. You deserve something better than cows—and cowboys. You love music and books, and you can't deny that you like to talk about them. You belong East—you belong back in Boston."

"We're going back, not to Boston, but to New York, after the round-up—Dad and I," she told him.

"No! really? How funny! I've got to go back too. Maybe we could all go together."

"That would be fine," she agreed.

"Wouldn't you like to stay back there?" he asked, almost excitedly, and then quite unexpectedly he took her hand. "Miss Henders!" he exclaimed.

"Diana! Wouldn't you like to stay there always? I'd make a home for you there—I'd make you happy—I love you, Diana. We could be married before we left. Wouldn't it be wonderful, going back there together on our honeymoon! And then to Europe! We could travel everywhere. Money would mean nothing. I don't have to tell you how rich we are."

"No," she replied, "I have heard your father mention it," and withdrew her hand from his.

He did not seem to notice the allusion to his father's boastfulness.

"Tell me that you love me," he insisted. "Tell me that you will marry me."

"But I don't know that I do love you," she replied. "Why, I scarcely know you, and you certainly don't know me well enough to know that you would want to live with me all the rest of your life."

"Oh, yes, I do!" he exclaimed. "If there was only some way to prove it. Words are so futile—they cannot express my love, Diana. Why, I worship you. There is no sacrifice that I would not willingly and gladly make for you or yours. I would die for you, dear girl, and thank God for the chance!"

"But I don't want you to die for me. I want you to go to bed and give me a chance to think. I have never been in love. Possibly I love you and do not know it. There is no need for haste anyway.

I will give you my answer before I go East. Now run along, like a good boy."

"But tell me, darling, that I may hope," he begged.

"You will do that anyway, if you love me," she told him, laughingly, as she turned and entered her tent. "Good night!"

CHAPTER VI

THE RENEGADES

THE next morning Colby took Wainright with him. Deep in the foreman's heart was a determination to ride hard over the roughest country he could find and if the "dude" got killed it wouldn't be Colby's fault—nor would it be Colby's fault if he didn't. But the foreman's plans were upset at the last moment by Elias Henders and Diana, who elected to accompany him.

"You and Wainright ride ahead, Hal," directed Henders, "and Di and I will trail along behind."

The foreman nodded silently and put spurs to his pony, and in silence Wainright loped at his side. The arrangement suited neither and each was busy concocting schemes whereby the other might be paired off with Elias Henders, though under ordinary circumstances either would have been highly elated at the prospect of spending a whole day in company with "the old man."

"Glorious morning!" ejaculated Henders to his daughter. "God may have forgotten Arizona in some respects, but he certainly remembered to give her the most wonderful mornings in the world."

"Don't they fill one with the most exquisite sensations!" she exclaimed.

"Almost as intoxicating as wine," he agreed, and then: "By the way, Bull's been doing fine, hasn't he? I don't believe he's touched a drop since that night at Gum's."

"He's working hard, too," said the girl.

"He always did that—he's the best cow-hand I ever saw and a hog for work. There isn't a man in seven counties that can commence to touch him when it comes to riding, roping, parting, calling brands, judging ages or weights, or handling cattle with judgment under any conditions, nor one that knows the range within a hundred miles like he does. Why, day before yesterday he had to give a fellow from the Red Butte country some pointers about the fellow's own range—Bull knew it better than he did."

"He's wonderful," said Diana. "I love to see him in the saddle, and anywhere in the cow-country he fits into the picture. I'm always proud that Bull is one of our men. Oh, I hope he don't ever drink again."

Elias Henders shook his head. "I'm afraid he'll never quit," he said. "A man's got to have something to quit for, and Bull has no incentive to stop—only just his job, and when did a little thing like a job keep a man from drinking, especially the best cow-hand in the territory? There isn't an outfit anywhere that wouldn't hire him, drunk or sober. He don't seem to be hanging around you much lately, Di, and I'm glad of that. I'd hate to see you interested in a man like Bull. I don't take much to garrulous people, but neither do I want 'em as tightmouthed as Bull. I'm afraid he's got something to hide that makes him afraid to talk for fear he'll let it out."

"What do you suppose happened last night, Dad?" asked Diana, suddenly.

"I don't know, I'm sure—what?" he asked.

"Jefferson Wainright proposed to me."

"No! What did you tell him?"

"What should I have told him?"

"That depends upon how much or little you think of him," replied her father.

"Would you like him for a son-in-law?"

"If you choose him, I shall like him—I should like the Devil if you chose to marry him."

"Well, he isn't quite as bad as all that, is he?" she cried, laughing.

"I didn't mean it that way. He seems to be a nice boy. He could give you everything and he could take you among the sort of people that you belong among, and you wouldn't have to be ashamed of him; but I don't like his father."

"His father is something of an embarrassment," she assented.

"Do you love the boy, Di?" he asked.

"I don't know, and I told him so. He wants me to marry him before we go East, and all go together."

"What a lovely idea—taking your fathers on

a honeymoon! You can count me out, and anyway if some other man is going to take you East I won't have to go at all."

"Well, I haven't gone with him, yet. I told him I'd give him his answer before we left."

"That would be a good idea—if he is going—he might want a few minutes' notice," he bantered, "but how about Hal? I thought you leaned a little in that direction."

"I do," laughed the girl. "When I m with one I like that one best, and when I'm with the other I like him."

"And when they are both with you at the same time—possibly you can find your answer there."

"I have thought of that, because then I always compare the two—and Hal always suffers by the comparison. That is when we are sitting talking—but when they are in the saddle it is the other way round."

"People can't spend their married lives in the saddle," he reminded her.

She sighed. "I am terribly perplexed. Of only one thing am I sure and that is that I shall marry either Hal Colby or Jefferson Wainright."

"Or some one else," he suggested.

"No! no one else," she stated emphatically.

It was past noon and they had turned back, gathering up the little bunches of cattle that they had driven down out of canyon and coulee onto the flat below. Elias Henders and Diana were riding quite apart from the foreman and Wainright when Henders turned back to ride to the summit of a low elevation for a final survey of the country for any straggling bunch that might have escaped their notice. Diana was a few yards in rear of him as he drew rein on top of the hillock. It was very quiet. The cattle were at a distance from them, moving slowly off down the valley. There was only the sound of her horse's unshod hoofs in the soft dirt and the subdued noise of a well-worn saddle as she urged her mount toward the side of her father.

Suddenly there was the crack of a rifle and Elias Henders' horse dropped in its tracks. Henders fell clear and whipped out his revolver.

"Get out of here, Di!" he called to the girl. "It's Indians. You've got time if you keep behind this butte and ride like Hell."

She turned and looked toward the two men a quarter of a mile away—Colby and Wainright. She saw them wheel their horses and look toward the point from which the shot had come and from their position she guessed that they could see the Indians, though she could not.

Then she saw Hal Colby put spurs and quirt to his mount until the wiry beast fairly flew over the ground toward her. Wainright hesitated, looked toward the Indians and then back down the valley in the direction of the camp fifteen miles away. Suddenly he wheeled his horse and dashed off.

To her mind flashed the impassioned words that he had poured into her ears only the night before: "I worship you. There is no sacrifice that I would not willingly and gladly make for you or yours. I would die for you, dear girl, and thank God for the chance!"

Her lip curled and her eyes shot a single scornful glance in the direction of the retreating figure of Jefferson Wainright before she turned them back toward Colby. How magnificent he was! He had drawn one of his six-guns and was riding, not for the hill, but straight for the Indians, and just as he passed out of her sight behind the hillock he opened fire. She could hear the crack of his gun mingling with those of the Indians, and then her father, pausing in his fire, turned to her again.

"My God, Di, haven't you gone?" he cried. "Hurry! There is time yet. Hal has got 'em on the run now, but they'll be back again. There must be a dozen of them. Ride back to camp for help."

"Mr. Wainright has already gone, Dad," she told him. "We have always been together, all my life, Dad, and it don't take two to get help. We need all the guns here we can get until the boys come," and she dismounted and crawled to his side, despite his protests.

Over the crest of the hill she could see Colby galloping toward them, while the Indians, a quarter of a mile beyond him, were just circling back in pursuit. In the foreground a dead Indian lay sprawled in the open. To the right a riderless pony was loping away to join its fellows.

Diana lay a few feet from her father, both in readiness to cover Colby's retreat when the Indians came within revolver range.

"Wish we had a couple of rifles," remarked Elias Henders. "If I had a thirty-thirty I could hold 'em off alone until the boys get here."

"We ought to be able to hold out for an hour, Dad. The boys should be here in that time."

"We'll do the best we can, but, Di—" he paused, a little catch in his voice—"don't let them get you, dear. The boys might not get here in time.

"Wainright is not much of a rider—he won't make the time that one of our boys would. They'd kill the horse, but they'd get there. And then there may not be anyone in camp but the cook that time of day—that's what I'm really most afraid of.

"We'll do the best we can. Likely as not we'll pull through; but if we don't, why, remember what I said, don't let 'em get you—save one shot. You understand?"

"I understand, Dad."

Colby, his horse stretched to quirt and spur, swung around to their side of the hill, threw his horse to its haunches as he reined in close to them and leaped from the saddle. Without a word he dragged the blowing, half-winded animal directly in front of them, raised his six-shooter to its forehead and shot it between the eyes.

Diana Henders voiced a little gasp of dismay, and then she saw the man turn toward her own pony; but she only covered her eyes with her palms and bit her lip to stifle a sob. A moment later there was a shot and the sound of a falling body.

"Crawl behind that cayuse of mine, Di," said Colby. He was tugging at the body of the girl's pony to drag it closer to the others, in order to form a rude triangle with the two other dead horses. Henders rose to his knees and gave Colby a hand, while Di opened fire upon the approaching braves.

"Reckon we orter hold out here till the boys come," remarked the foreman.

He was cool and self-possessed—just as cool and self-possessed as Jefferson Wainright would have been in a Boston drawing-room. Even as she took careful aim at a half-naked, yelling buck, and missed him, Diana Henders' mind was considering this fact. She fired again and this time the buck ceased to yell, grasped his stomach with both hands and toppled headlong to the ground. Hal Colby might learn to be cool and self-possessed in a Boston drawing-room, but could Jefferson Wainright ever learn to be cool and self-possessed inside a yelling circle of painted savages thirsting for his life's blood?

The Indians were now riding a wide circle entirely about the hillock, firing as they rode. Naturally their aim was execrable, and the three were in danger only of a chance hit. After the warrior fell to Diana's bullet the circle widened to still greater proportions and a few minutes later the Indians withdrew out of effective revolver range and gathered in a compact group where the three on the hillock could see them gesticulating and talking excitedly.

"They're up to some new devilment," said Henders.

"I hope they don't charge from different directions before the boys git here," remarked Colby. "If they do we might as well kiss ourselves goodbye. I wish you wasn't here, Di.

"Damn that white-livered dude's hide. Ef he hadn't turned tail you could have gone. You could ride rings around that slab-sided maverick, an' besides you'd have been safe. Look! They're separatin' now."

"Yes, they're riding to surround us again," said Diana.

"If they charge, Hal," said Henders, "wait until they get close and then stand up and let them have it. Di, you lie as close to the ground as you can. Don't move. Just watch us, and when you see we're both down you'll know it's all up and—you must do what I told you to."

Hal Colby looked at the beautiful girl at his side, and scowled, for he guessed without being told, what her father meant. "Damn that dude!" he muttered.

"Mebby I hadn't orter shot all the hosses," he

said presently. "Mebby Di could have got away."

"No," Henders assured him. "You did just right, Hal. Di wouldn't go. I told her to, but she wouldn't. It was too late then anyway."

"I figgered it was too late," said Colby; "but mebby it wasn't. I wish I had thet damn dude here."

"They're coming!" cried Diana.

From four sides the Indians were racing toward them, their savage cries breaking hideously the silence of the sun-parched valley. The three crouched, waiting. No word was spoken until the nearest of the red-skins was no more than twenty-five yards away.

Then: "Now!" said Henders, leaping to his feet. Colby was up simultaneously, firing as he rose. Diana Henders, far from lying close to the ground as she had been directed, was on her feet almost as quickly as the men.

"Get down, Di!" commanded her father, but her only reply was a shot that brought down a warrior's pony twenty paces from them.

Colby and Henders had each shot an Indian and there was another pony down in front of Colby. The renegades were close now and presented splendid targets for the three whites, all of whom were excellent revolver shots. At each report of their weapons a hit was scored.

Now a pony screamed and wheeled away, bearing its rider in headlong flight down the gentle declivity of the hillside; another stumbled and crumpled to the ground, sprawling its painted master in the dust; a warrior, wounded, veered to one side and raced off to safety; or, again, one slumped silently to earth, never to charge again.

Two of the unhorsed warriors sprang into close quarters, clubbing their empty rifles. One was leaping toward Diana, the other for Colby. At the same instant Elias Henders lifted both hands above his head, his gun slipped from nerveless fingers, and he lunged forward across the body of his dead horse.

Colby put a shot through the stomach of the buck leaping upon him, then turned toward Diana. He saw the painted face of a tall chief just beyond Diana's; he saw the rifle swinging to brain her as she pulled the trigger of her Colt with the muzzle almost against the sweat streaked body; there was no answering report, and then Colby, leaping between them, seized the upraised rifle and tore it from the hand of the red man.

The two clinched, the Indian reaching for his knife, while the white, who had emptied both guns and had no time to reload, strove to brain his antagonist with one of them. Struggling, they fell.

Diana Henders, reloading her own weapon, looked hurriedly about. The other warriors, momentarily dispersed, had rallied and were returning with wild, triumphant yells, for they saw that the battle was already theirs.

Elias Henders raised himself weakly on one elbow and looked about. Instantly his gaze took in the situation.

"Di!" he cried, "my little girl. Quick! Don't wait! Shoot yourself before they get you."

"Not yet!" she cried, and turned toward the two men, the red and the white, battling at her feet. Stooping, she held the muzzle of her weapon close to the rolling, tossing men, waiting an opportunity to put a bullet in the chief when she could do so without endangering Colby.

From behind her the returning braves were approaching rapidly, the racing hoofs of their ponies pounding a dull tattoo on the powdery earth. They were almost upon her when Colby's fingers found the chief's throat and the latter's head was pushed momentarily away from that of the white man. It was the instant that Diana had awaited. She stepped in closer, there was the sound of a shot, and the renegade collapsed limply in Colby's grasp.

Simultaneously a wild yell arose from below them in the valley. The remaining Indians, almost upon them, were riding in a close mass from the opposite side. What could it be—more Indians?

Colby had hurled the dead chief aside and was on his feet beside the girl. They both looked in the direction of the new sound to see two horsemen racing madly toward them.

"It's Bull! It's Bull!" cried Diana Henders. "Bull and Texas Pete."

The ponies of the oncoming men were racing neck and neck. The riders were howling like demons. The Indians heard, paused in their charge and wheeled to one side—there were five of them left. The reinforcements were too much for them, and with a parting volley they galloped off.

But Bull and Texas Pete were of no mind to let them go so easily. For a mile or more they pursued them, until they realized that their already almost spent horses could not outdistance the mounts of the Indians. Then they turned and loped slowly back toward the three upon the hillock.

Instantly the immediate necessity of defense had passed Diana Henders kneeled beside her father and lifted his head in her arms. Colby stepped to the opposite side of the prostrate man to help her. Suddenly she looked up into his eyes, an expression of horror in her's.

"Oh, Hal! Hal! he's gone!" she cried, and burying her face in her arms, burst into tears.

The man, unaccustomed to a woman's tears, or a sorrow such as this, was at a loss for words, yet almost mechanically his arms went about her and drew her close to him, so that she stood with her face buried in the hollow of his shoulder as Bull and Texas Pete rode up the hill and dismounted beside them. They took in the pitiful scene at a glance, but they saw more in it than the death of "the old man," whom they both loved—at least Bull did.

In the attitude of Diana and Colby he read the death knell of whatever faint hope he might have entertained of ultimate happiness. It was a hurt and bitter man that lifted the dead body of his employer in strong arms and laid it across the saddle of his horse.

"You ride Pete's hoss, Miss," he said gently. "Colby, you walk ahead with her. Pete an' I'll come along with the old man."

They all did as he bid without question. There was something about the man that demanded obedience even if he was no longer foreman. It was always that way with Bull. Wherever he was he was the leader. Even though men mistrusted, or disliked him, and many did, they involuntarily obeyed him. Possibly because he was a strong man who thought quickly and accurately and was almost invariably right in his decision—it was certainly not because a large proportion of them loved him, for they did not. There was that something lacking in Bull—that quality which attracted the love of his fellows.

After Diana and Colby had gone ahead Bull and Pete roped the body of Elias Henders securely to the saddle and presently the sorrowful little cortege took its slow way back toward camp.

CHAPTER VII

EXIT WAINRIGHT

A WEEK or ten days after Elias Henders' funeral the Wainright buck-board drew into the Bar Y ranch yard and the Wainrights, senior and junior, alighted and approached the house. They found Diana in the office working on the books, which she had kept for her father when they were without a bookkeeper, which was the case at present.

She greeted them politely, but without marked cordiality. It was the first time that she had encountered either of them since her father's death, having refused to see the younger man on her return to the camp with Elias Henders' body.

"We been calc'latin' to drive over for several days past, Miss Henders," said the elder man. "Thought mebby you might want some advice or suthin'. Anything we can do, we're both at your service."

"That's very kind of you, indeed, I'm sure," replied the girl; "but really I have so many good friends here that I couldn't think of inconveniencing you. Everyone has been so kind and considerate."

"Well, they ain't no harm in offerin'," he continued. "Anything we can do, you know. If it's a little matter of money to tide you over till the estate's settled, why, just call on Jefferson Wainright—he's got a lot and he ain't stingy either."

"There is nothing, thank you," she said, with just the faintest tinge of asperity.

He rose slowly from his chair and shoved his fat hands into his pockets.

"I reckon I'll walk around a bit," he said. "I calc'late that you young folks got suthin' to say to one another," and he winked ponderously at them as he waddled through the doorway.

There was a strained silence for several minutes after he left. Jefferson Wainright, Jr., finally, after clearing his throat two or three times, broke it.

"The governor means all right," he said. "We'd really like to be of service to you, and after the—the talk we had that last night before—before your father was killed—you know—why, I hoped I might have the right to help you, Diana."

She drew herself up very straight and stiff. "I think we had better forget that, Mr. Wainright," she said.

"But you promised me an answer," he insisted.

"After what happened I should think you would know what the answer must be without being subjected to the humiliation of being told in words."

"Do you mean that you are blaming me, too, like the men did, for going for help. You would all have been killed if I hadn't. I think I did just the sensible thing," he concluded, half defiantly.

"Yes, I suppose so," she replied icily, "and Hal Colby did a very silly thing staying and risking his life for Dad and me."

"I think you're mighty unfair, Diana," he insisted, "and the way it turned out only goes to prove that I was right. I met Bull and that Texas person less than half way to camp and got them there in time."

"If they had been as sensible as you they would have gone on to camp for more reinforcements, as you did, but like most of our boys out here, Mr. Wainright, they haven't much sense and so they nearly rode their horses down to get to us—only two of them, remember, after you had told them that we were surrounded by a hundred Indians."

"Oh, pshaw, I think you might be reasonable and make some allowance for a fellow," he begged. "I'll admit I was a little excited and maybe I did do the wrong thing, but it's all new to me out here. I'd never seen a wild Indian before and I thought I was doing right to go for help.

"Can't you forgive me, Diana, and give me another chance? If you'll marry me I'll take you away from this God-forsaken country back where there are no Indians."

"Mr. Wainright, I have no wish to offend you, but you might as well know once for all that if you were the last man on earth I would never marry you—I could not marry a coward, and you are a coward. You would be just as much of a coward back East if danger threatened. Some of our boys are from the East—Hal Colby was born in Vermont—and the day that you ran away was his first experience, too, with hostile Indians, and if you want another reason why I couldn't marry you—the first and biggest reason—I'll give it to you."

Her voice was low and level, like her father's had been on the rare occasions that he had been moved by anger, but the tone was keen edged and cutting. "I feel now, and I shall always feel as long as I live, that had you remained instead of running away we might have held them off and Dad would not have been uselessly sacrificed."

She had risen while she spoke, and he rose too, standing silently for a moment after she had concluded. Then he turned and walked toward the door. At the threshold he paused and turned toward her.

"I hope you will never regret your decision," he said. The tone seemed to carry a threat.

"I assure you that I shall never. Good day, Mr. Wainright."

After he had gone the girl shuddered and sank down into a chair. She wished Hal Colby was there. She wanted someone to comfort her and to give her that sense of safety under masculine protection that her father's presence had always afforded.

Why couldn't all men be like Hal and Bull? When she thought of brave men she always thought of

Bull, too. How wonderful they had all been that day—Hal and Bull and Pete. Rough, uncouth they often were; worn and soiled and careless their apparel; afraid of nothing, man, beast or the devil; risking their lives joyously; joking with death; and yet they had been as gentle as women when they took her back to camp and all during the long, terrible journey home, when one of the three had always been within call every minute of the days and nights.

Of the three Bull had surprised her most, for previously he had always seemed the hardest and most calloused, and possessing fewer of the finer sensibilities of sympathy and tenderness; but of them all he had been the most thoughtful and considerate. It had been he who had sent her ahead with Colby that she might not see them lash her father's body to the horse; it had been he who had covered all that remained of Elias Henders with the slickers from his saddle and Pete's that she might not be shocked by the sight of her father's body rocking from side to side with the swaying motion of the horse; and it was Bull who had ridden all night to far-away ranches and brought back two buckboards early the next morning to carry her Dad and her more comfortably on the homeward journey. He had spoken kindly to her in an altered, softened voice, and he had insisted that she eat and keep her strength when she had wanted to forget food.

But the funeral over she had seen nothing more of him, for he had been sent back to the round-up to ride with it for the last few remaining days, while Hal Colby remained at the ranch to help her to plan for the future and gather together the stray ends that are left flying when even the most methodical of masters releases his grip for the last time.

She sat musing after Wainright left the room, the clock upon the wall above her father's desk ticking as it had for years—just as though this terrible thing had not happened—just as though her father were still sitting in his accustomed chair, instead of lying out there in the sandy, desolate little graveyard above Hendersville, where the rocks that protected the scattered sleepers from the coyotes offered sanctuary to the lizard and the rattle-snake.

Her revery was disturbed by the fall of heavy feet upon the veranda and she raised her eyes just as the elder Wainright entered the room. He was not smiling now, nor was his manner so suave as usual.

"We got to be goin' now, Miss Henders," he said brusquely; "but I wanted a mite of a word with you before we left. O' course, you don't know nothin' about it, but afore your father died we was negotiatin' a deal. He wanted to get out from under, now that the mine's runnin' out, an' I wanted to git a range on this side o' the mountains. We'd jest about got it all fixed up when this accident happened.

"Now here's what I wanted to say to you. Of course, the mine's no account, and the range's 'bout all fed off, and they ain't scarce enough water fer the number o' stock I was calc'latin' to put on, but Jefferson Wainright's a man o' his word an' when I says to your father that I'd give him two hundred and fifty thousand dollars fer his holdin's I won't back down now, even if I don't think they be worth so much as that.

"I'll get all the papers ready so's ye won't have to go to no expense fer a lawyer, and then ye can have the money an' go back East to live like ye always wanted to, an' like yer paw was fixin' fer ye."

The deeper he got into the subject the faster he talked and the more he relapsed into the vernacular of his earlier days. Finally he paused. "What do ye say?" he concluded.

"The ranch is not for sale, Mr. Wainright," she replied.

He opened his little eyes and his big mouth simultaneously in surprise.

"What's thet—not for sale? Why, you must be crazy, child. You don't know what you're talkin' about."

"I know exactly what I am talking about," she told him. "Father talked this all over with me and showed me your offer of a million dollars for our holdings. The ranch is not for sale, for a million dollars or any other price, to you, Mr. Wainright, and be careful that you do not stumble over that stool as you go out."

The man's fat face became suddenly empurpled with rage and for a moment he was inarticulate as, backing toward the doorway, he sought for words adequately to express his outraged feelings. He was not humiliated — there are certain types of men whose thick skin serves them as an invulnerable armor against humiliation.

He was just plain mad — mad all the way through to think that he had been caught at his trickery, exposed and thwarted by a chit of a girl, and, like the type he represented naturally would be, he was mad at her rather than at himself. As he reached the doorway he found his voice.

"You'll be sorry for this! You'll be sorry for this!" he cried, shaking a fist at her. "And, mark you, I'll get this property yet. Jefferson Wainright can buy and sell you twenty times over and he always gets what he goes after."

The figure of a tall man loomed suddenly behind him. Calloused and ungentle fingers seized him roughly by the collar of his coat. A low voice spoke softly in his ear.

"Don't you know better'n to shake your fist in a lady's face, you pot-bellied buzzard?" it inquired, and the elder Wainright was jerked unceremoniously through the doorway, whirled about and projected violently from the veranda, his speed simultaneously accelerated by the toe of a high-heeled cowboy boot. "I reckon you'd better make yourself damned scarce around here," continued the low tones of the speaker.

Wainright scrambled to his feet and turned upon the owner of the voice. He shook both fists now and fairly danced up and down in his fury. "I'll get you!" he screamed. "I'll get you! Don't you know who I am—why, I could buy and sell you a hundred thousand times over—I'm Jefferson Wainright, I am. I'll get you—layin' your hands on me—you low down, thirty-five dollar cow-puncher!"

"Vamoose!" said the man, "and do it pronto." He emphasized his injunction with a shot, the bullet kicking up a little spurt of dust between Wainright's feet.

The fat man started on a run for his buck-board which the younger Wainright had driven down to the corrals. The man on the veranda fired again, and again the dust rose about the fleeing feet of the terrified Easterner.

Diana Henders had come to the doorway where she stood leaning against the frame, smiling.

"Don't hurt him, Bull," she said.

The man cast a quick smile over his shoulder. "I ain't a-aimin' to hurt him," he said. "I'm just a-aimin' to eddicate him. Them corn-fed Easterners ain't got no eddication nohow. What they need is someone to larn 'em manners."

As he spoke he kept on firing at the fleeing Wainright and every shot kicked up a puff of dust close to the fat man's feet until he reached the corner of the bunk-house and disappeared behind it.

The shots had called out the cook and the few men who were about, with the result that a small yet highly appreciative audience witnessed Wainright's discomfiture. A part of it was Texas Pete, who rocked to and fro in unholy glee.

"By gollies! did you see him?" he yelled. "He never hit nothin' but the high spots. I'll bet he busted all the world's records between the office and the bunk-house. Why, he done it in nothin' flat, an' you could have played checkers on his coat-tails. He shore stepped high, wide an' handsome."

On the veranda of the ranch house Bull had shoved his gun back into its holster. The smile had left his face.

"I thought you were still out with the outfit, Bull," said the girl.

"We finished up last night," he told her, "and I come in ahead." He looked down at his feet in evident embarrassment. "I come in ahead for my time, Miss."

"Your time! Why, Bull, you're not goin' to quit?"

"I reckon I better," he replied. "I been aimin' to move on fer some spell."

The girl's eyes were wide, and almost noticeably moist, and there was a surprised, hurt look in them, that he caught as he chanced to glance up at her.

"You see, Miss," he hastened to explain, "things ain't very pleasant for me here. I ain't complainin', but there are those that don't like me, an' I figgered I'd quit before I was let out. As long as your paw was alive it was different, an' I don't need to tell you that I'd be powerful proud to work for you always, if there wasn't no one else; but there is. I reckon you got a good man an' it will be pleasanter all around if I ain't here no more."

At the mere thought of his going a lump rose in Diana Henders' throat, and she realized how much she had come to depend on him—just the mere fact that she had known Bull was around had given her a feeling of greater security—he had become in the nature of a habit and it was going to be hard to break the habit.

"Oh, Bull," she cried, "I can't let you go now—I can't spare both you and Dad at the same time. You're like a brother, Bull, and I need a brother mighty badly right now. You don't *have* to go, do you? You don't really *want* to?"

"No, Miss, I don't have to an' I don't want to—if you want me to stay."

"Then you *will* stay?"

He nodded. "But I reckon' you'd better tell Colby," he said, "for I expect he's aimin' to give me my time."

"Oh, no, I'm sure he's not," she cried. "Hal likes you, Bull. He told me you were one of his best friends, and he was so sorry about your losing the job as foreman. He said he hated to take it."

Bull made no comment and whatever his thoughts his face did not betray them. Presently he jerked his head in the general direction of the corrals where the Wainrights, having hastily clambered into their buck-board, were preparing to depart.

"Say the word," he told her, "and I'll run them short sports so far outta the country they won't never find their way back."

"No," she replied, smiling; "let them go. They'll never come back here, I'm sure."

"I reckon the old gent figgers he ain't very popular round these diggins," said Bull, with the faintest trace of a smile; "but I don't know so much about how thet young dude stands." He looked questioningly at Diana.

"About deuce high, Bull," she replied. "I saw enough of him to last me a couple of life times the day the renegades jumped us."

"I reckoned as much, Miss, knowin' you as I do. Scenery an' the gift o' gab ain't everything, but sometimes they fool wimmen folks—even the brightest of 'em."

"He was awfully good company," she admitted.

"When they warn't no Injuns around," Bull completed the sentence for her. "The old feller seemed all het up over somethin' about the time I happened along. I heered him say he was set on gettin' this property. Is that what they come over fer?"

"Yes. He offered me a quarter of what he'd offered Dad for it, and his offer to Dad was only about twenty per cent of what it's worth. You see, Bull, what they want is the mine. They are just using the range and the cattle as an excuse to get hold of the mine because they think we don't know the real value of the diggings; but Dad did know. There's another vein there that has never been tapped that is richer than the old one. Dad knew about it, and somehow Wainright learned of it too."

"The old skunk!" muttered Bull.

The Wainrights were driving out of the ranch yard and heading toward Hendersville. The older man was still breathing hard and swearing to himself. The younger was silent and glum. They were going to town for dinner before starting on the long drive back to their ranch. Approaching them along the trail at a little distance ahead was a horseman. Young Wainright recognized the rider first.

"That's Colby," he said. "He hasn't any use for that fellow Bull. They are both stuck on the girl. It might not be a bad plan to cultivate him —if you want to get even with Bull."

As they came nearer it appeared evident that Colby was going by them with nothing more than a nod. He did not like either of them— especially the younger; but when they drew rein and the older man called to him he turned about and rode up to the side of the vehicle.

"You're still foreman here, ain't ye?" asked Wainright senior.

Colby nodded. "Why?" he inquired.

"Well, I jest wanted to tell ye that some of your men ain't got a very pleasant way of treatin' neighbors."

"How's that?"

"Well, I was jest a-leavin' after a social call when one of yer men starts shootin' at me. Thet ain't no way to treat friends an' neighbors. Suppose we was to shoot up your men when they came over our way?"

"Who was it?" demanded Colby.

"Bull," said the younger Wainright. "I suppose he was drunk again, though. They say he always goes to shooting whenever he gets drunk. When we left he was up at the house making love to Miss Henders," he added. "I shouldn't think she'd feel safe with a fellow like that around."

Colby scowled. "Thanks fer tellin' me," he said. "I reckon I'll have to fix that feller. He's gettin' too damn fresh."

"Well, I thought ye'd orter know," said Wainright senior. "Well, so long, an' if ye ever git over our way drop in."

"Giddap!" said Jefferson Wainright, Jr., and the two rolled away through the deep dust of the parched road.

Colby rode on at a brisk gallop and as he swung from his saddle cast a glance in the direction of the house where he saw Bull just descending the steps from the veranda where Diana Henders stood. Colby bit his lip and the frown on his face became deeper.

Dragging saddle and bridle from his pony he turned the animal into the corral with a final slap on the rump—a none too gentle slap which reflected the state of his feelings—then he headed straight for the bunk-house which he reached just in time to intercept Bull at the entrance.

"Look here, Bull," said Colby without any preamble, "this business of drinkin' an' shootin' things up has gone about far enough. I ain't a-goin' to have it around here no more. I reckon you'd better ask fer your time."

"All right," said Bull, "you go an' git it fer me while I'm packin' my war-bag."

Colby, rather surprised and at the same time relieved that Bull took the matter so philosophically, started for the office, while the latter entered the bunk-house, where Shorty, Texas Pete and a couple of others who had overheard the conversation outside the door looked up questioningly.

"By gollies!" exclaimed Texas Pete, "I'm a-goin' to quit. I'm a-goin' after my time right now, pronto," and he arose and started for the doorway.

"Wait a minute, old hoss," advised Bull. "I ain't went yet."

"But didn't Colby jest let you out?" inquired Pete.

"He might change his mind," explained Bull.

Up at the house Colby was entering the office. "Hello, Di!" he cried. "Got your check-book handy?"

"Yes, why?"

"Bull's quittin'."

"Quitting? Why, he just promised me that he'd stay on. I don't understand."

"He just promised you that he'd stay on! You mean you asked him to?"

"Yes," replied Diana. "He came up here to quit. Said he thought he wasn't wanted any more, and I made him promise he wouldn't leave. I tell you, Hal, we could never replace him. Are you sure he was in earnest about quitting? Send him up here and I'll make him stay."

"Well, like as not I was mistaken," said Colby. "I reckon Bull was jest a-kiddin'. I'll ask him again and if he is plumb set on leavin' I'll send him up."

When he entered the bunk-house a few minutes later he nodded at Bull. "You kin stay on, if you want to," he said; "I've changed my mind."

Bull winked at Texas Pete who was vainly endeavoring to remember another verse of the seemingly endless self-glorification of the bad hombre.

"By gollies!" he exclaimed, "I believe I got another:

"He twirls two big guns an' he shoots out a light;
The fellows a-drinkin' there ducks out o' sight;

He shoots through a bottle thet stands on the bar;
An' shoots the ol' ashes plumb off my seegar."

"But it seems like I'd left out somethin' thet orter a-gone before."

"Nobody'd git sore if you left it all out," Shorty assured him.

"The trouble with you uneddicated cow-punchers," Texas Pete told him, "is thet you are too all-fired ignorant to appreciate my efforts to elivate you-all by means of good poetry. It shore is hell to be the only lit'ry gent in a bunch of rough-necks.

"'Come, set up the bottles, you gol darned galoot,'
Says he to the boss, ''Fore I opens yore snoot
With one o' these yere little babies o' mine,'
An' shoots out the *no* in the *no credit* sign."

CHAPTER VIII

"YOU DON'T DARE!"

THE stage lurched down the steep and tortuous gradiant of Hell's Bend Pass, bumped through the rutty gap at the bottom and swung onto the left fork just beyond. The right fork was the regular stage route to Hendersville. The left hand road led to town, too, but over Bar Y property and past the home ranch.

The driver never came this way unless he had passengers, express or important messages for the ranch, though the distance was no greater and the road usually in better repair. Today he had a telegram for Diana Henders.

There was a brief pause as he drew up his sweating team in the road before the ranch house, yelled to attract the attention of a ranch-hand working about the corrals, tossed the envelope into the road and then, with a crack of his long whip, was off again at a run, leaving billowing clouds of powdery dust in his wake.

The man working in the corrals walked leisurely into the road, picked up the envelope and, after scrutinizing the superscription and deciphering it laboriously, carried the message to the office, where Diana Henders was working over the books.

"Telegram fer ye, Miss," announced the man, crossing the room to hand it to her.

She thanked him and laid the envelope on the desk beside her as she completed an interrupted footing. The arrival of telegrams was no uncommon occurrence even on that far-away ranch, and as they always pertained to business they caused Diana no flurry of excitement. Buyers often wired, while Uncle John Manill used the comparatively new telegraph facilities upon the slightest pretext.

The footing finally checked to her satisfaction, Diana picked up the envelope, opened it and drew forth the message. At first she glanced at it casually, then she read it over again with knit brows as though unable fully to grasp the purport of its contents. Finally she sat staring at it with wide, strained eyes, until, apparently crushed, she lowered her head upon her arms and broke into sobs, for this is what she had read:

MISS DIANA HENDERS,
BAR Y RANCH, HENDERSVILLE,
VIA ALDEA, ARIZONA.
Mr. Manill died suddenly last night. Miss Manill and I leave for ranch soon as possible after funeral.
MAURICE B. CORSON.

For a long time Diana Henders sat with her face buried in her arms. Gradually her sobs subsided as she gained control of herself. Stunning though the effect of this new blow was, yet she grasped enough of what it meant to her to be almost crushed by it. Though she had not seen her Uncle John Manill since childhood, he had, nevertheless, constituted a very real and potent force in her existence. Her mother had adored him, her only brother, and Elias Henders had never ceased to proclaim him as the finest type of honorable gentleman that nature might produce. His Eastern connections, his reputation for integrity and his fine business acumen had all been potent factors in the success of the Henders and Manill partnership.

With the death of her father the girl had felt keenly only her personal loss — for Uncle John Manill loomed as a Rock of Gibraltar to protect her in all matters of business; but now she was absolutely alone.

There was no one to whom she might turn for counsel or advice now that these two were gone. Hal Colby, she realized keenly, was at best only a good cowman — in matters requiring executive ability or large financial experience he was untried.

Of Corson, Manill's attorney, she knew nothing, but she was reasonably sure that even though he proved honest and possessed of an excellent understanding of matters pertaining to the Eastern office, he would not be competent to direct the affairs of ranch and mine at the sources of production.

That she might have carried on herself under the guidance of John Manill she had never doubted, since she could always have turned to him for advice in matters of moment where she was doubtful of her own judgment; but without him she questioned her ability to direct the destinies of this great business with all its numerous ramifications.

Suddenly she arose and replaced the books in the office safe, dabbed at her tear-dimmed eyes with her handkerchief and, putting on her sombrero, walked from the office, adjusting her wavy hair beneath the stiff band of her heavy hat. Straight toward the corrals she made her way. She would saddle Captain and ride out into the sunshine and the fresh air where, of all other places, she knew she might find surcease of sorrow and an opportunity to think out her problems more clearly. As she entered the corral Hal Colby came running up from the bunk-house. He had seen her pass and followed her.

"Ridin', Di?" he asked.

She nodded affirmatively. She was not sure that she wanted company—not even that of Hal Colby—today when she desired to be alone with her grief.

"You weren't goin' alone, were you? You know it ain't safe, Di. Your dad wouldn't have let you an' I certainly won't."

She made no reply. She knew that he was right. It was not safe for her to ride alone, but today she felt that she did not care what happened to her. Fate had been cruel—there was little more that it could do to harm her.

In a way she half resented Hal's new air of

proprietorship, and yet there was something about it that carried a suggestion of relief from responsibility. Here there was at least someone who cared —someone upon whose broad shoulders she might shift a portion of her burden, and so she did not follow her first impulse to send him back.

Together they rode from the corral, turning down the road toward town and neither spoke for several minutes, after the manner of people accustomed to being much together in the saddle. The man, as was usual with him when they rode, watched her profile as a lover of art might gloat over a beautiful portrait, and as he looked at her he realized the change that had come over her face and noted the reddened lids.

"What's the matter, Di?" he asked presently. "You look like you'd been cryin'. What's happened?"

"I just got a telegram from New York, Hal," she replied. "Uncle John is dead—he died night before last. The stage just brought the message in from Aldea."

"Shucks," he said, at a loss for the proper words, and then, "that's shore too bad, Di."

"It leaves me all alone, now, Hal," she continued, "and I don't know what I'm going to do."

"You ain't all alone, Di. There ain't anything I wouldn't do for you. You know I love you, Di. Won't you marry me? It would make it easier all around for you if we was married. There's them that's always tryin' to take advantage of a girl or a woman what's left alone, but if you got a husband you got someone to look out for you an' your rights. I got a little money saved up."

"I have plenty of money, Hal."

"I know it. I wish you didn't have none. It makes me feel like you thought that was what I was after, but it ain't. Won't you, Di? Together we could run the ranch just like your dad was here."

"I don't know, Hal. I don't know what to do. I think I love you, but I don't know. I don't even know that I know what love is."

"You'd learn to love me," he told her, "and you wouldn't have to worry no more. I'd look after everything. Say yes, won't you?"

The temptation was great—greater even than the man himself realized—to have a place to lay her tired head, to have a strong man to carry the burden and the responsibilities for her, to have the arm of love about her as it had been all her life until her father had been taken away. She looked up at him with a faint smile.

"I won't say yes—yet," she said. "Wait a while, Hal—wait until after Mr. Corson and my cousin come and we see how things are going to turn out, and then—then I think that I shall say yes."

He leaned toward her impulsively and put an arm about her, drawing her toward him with the evident intention of kissing her, but she pushed him away.

"Not yet, Hal," she told him; "wait until I have said yes."

A week later a group of boarders were lounging on the veranda of The Donovan House in Hendersville. It was almost supper time of a stage day and the stage had not yet arrived. Mack Harber, whose wound had given more trouble than the doctor had expected, was still there convalescing, and Mary Donovan was, as usual, standing in the doorway joining in the gossip and the banter

"Bill ain't niver late 'less somethin's wrong," said Mrs. Donovan.

"Like as not he's been held up again," suggested Mack.

"I'd like to be sheriff o' this yere county fer 'bout a week," stated Wildcat Bob.

"Sure, an' phawt would ye be after doin'?" inquired Mary Donovan, acidly.

Wildcat Bob subsided, mumbling in his stained beard. For the moment he had forgotten that Mrs. Donovan was among those present.

"Here they come!" announced Mack.

With the clank of chain, the creaking of springs, and the rapid pounding of galloping hoofs the stage swung into the single street of Hendersville in a cloud of dust and with a final shrieking of protesting brakes pulled up before The Donovan House.

"Where's Gum Smith?" demanded Bill Gatlin from the driver's seat.

"Dunno. Held up agin?" asked one of the loungers.

"Yes," snapped Gatlin.

Mack Harber had risen from his chair and advanced to the edge of the veranda.

"The Black Coyote?" he asked.

Gatlin nodded. "Where's thet damn sheriff?" he demanded again.

"He ain't here an' he wouldn't be no good if he was," replied Wildcat Bob.

"We don't need no sheriff fer what we oughter do," announced Mack Harber, angrily.

"How's thet?" asked Wildcat.

"You don't need no sheriff fer a necktie party," said Mack, grimly.

"No, but you gotta get yer man fust."

"Thet's plumb easy."

"How come?" inquired Wildcat.

"We all know who The Black Coyote is," stated Mack. "All we gotta do is get a rope an' go get him."

"Meanin' get who?" insisted the little old man.

"Why, gosh all hemlock! you know as well as I do thet it's Bull," replied Mack.

"I dunno nothin' o' the kind, young feller," said Wildcat Bob, "ner neither do you. Ef ye got proof of what ye say I'm with ye. Ef ye ain't got proof I'm ag'in ye."

"Don't Bull always wear a black silk handkerchief?" demanded Mack. "Well, so does The

Black Coyote, an' they both got scars on their chins. There ain't no doubt of it."

"So ye want to string up Bull 'cause he wears a black bandanna and a scar, eh? Well, ye ain't goin' to do nothin' o' the kind while ol' Wildcat Bob can fan a gun. Git proof on him an' I'll be the fust to put a rope 'round his neck, but ye got to git more proof than a black handkerchief."

"Shure an' fer onct yer right, ye ould blatherskite," commended Mary Donovan. "Be after comin' to yer suppers now the all of yese an' fergit stringin' up dacent young min like Bull. Shure an' I don't belave he iver hild up nothin' at all, at all. He's that nice to me whinever he's here, wid his Mrs. Donovan, mum, this an' his Mrs. Donovan, mum, that, an' a-fetchin' wood fer me, which the loikes o' none o' yese iver did. The viry idea ov him bein' The Black Coyote—go on wid ye!"

"Well, we all know that Gregorio's one of them, anyway—we might string him up," insisted Mack.

"We don't know that neither," contradicted Wildcat; "but when it comes to stringin' up Gregorio or any other greaser I'm with ye. Go out an' git him, Mack, an' I'll help ye string him up."

A general grin ran around the table, for of all the known badmen in the country the Mexican, Gregorio, was by far the worst. To have gone out looking for him and to have found him would have been equivalent to suicide for most men, and though there were many men in the county who would not have hesitated had necessity demanded, the fact remained that his hiding place was unknown and that that fact alone would have rendered an attempt to get him a failure.

"Thar's only one way to git them, sonny," continued Wildcat Bob, "an' thet is to put a *man* on the stage with the bullion, 'stid o' a kid."

Mack flushed. "You was there when they got me," he fired back. "You was there with two big six-guns an' what did you do—eh? What did you do?"

"I wasn't hired to guard no bullion, an' I wasn't sittin' on the box with no sawed-off shotgun 'crost my knees, neither. I was a-ridin' inside with a lady. What *could* I a-done?" He looked around at the others at the table for vindication.

"Ye couldn't done nothin', ye," said Mary Donovan, "widout a quart o' barbed-wire inside ye an' some poor innocent tenderfoot to shoot the heels offen him."

Wildcat Bob fidgeted uneasily and applied himself to his supper, pouring his tea into his saucer, blowing noisily upon it to cool it, and then sucking it through his whiskers with an accompanying sound not unlike snoring; but later he was both mollified and surprised by a second, generous helping of dessert.

When word of the latest holdup reached the Bar Y ranch it caused the usual flurry of profanity and speculation. It was brought by a belated puncher who had ridden in from the West ranch by way of Hendersville. The men were gathered at the evening meal and of a sudden a silence fell upon them as they realized, apparently simultaneously and for the first time, that there was a single absentee. The meal progressed in almost utter silence then until they had reached the pudding, when Bull walked in, dark and taciturn, and with the brief nod that was his usual greeting to his fellows. The meal continued in silence for a few minutes until the men who had finished began pushing back their plates preparatory to rising.

"I reckon you know the stage was held up again, Bull, an' the bullion stolen," remarked Hal Colby, selecting a tooth-pick from the glassful on the table.

"How should I know it?" asked Bull. "Ain't I ben up Sink Hole Canyon all day? I ain't seen no one since I left the ranch this morning."

"Well, it was," said Colby. "The same two slick gents done it, too."

"Did they git much?" asked Bull.

"It was a big shipment," said Colby. "It always is. They don't never touch nothin' else an' they seem to know when we're shippin' more'n ordinary. Looks suspicious."

"Did you just discover that?" inquired Bull.

"No, I discovered it a long time ago, an' it may help me to find out whose doin' it."

"Well, I wish you luck," and Bull resumed his meal.

Colby, having finished, rose from the table and made his way to the house. In the cozy sitting-room he found Diana at the piano, her fingers moving dreamily over the ivory keys.

"Some more bad news, Di," he announced.

She turned wearily toward him. "What now?"

"The Black Coyote again—he got the bullion shipment."

"Was anyone hurt?"

"No," he assured her.

"I am glad of that. The gold is nothing—I would rather lose it all than have one of the boys killed. I have told them all, just as Dad did, to take no chances. If they could get him without danger to themselves I should be glad, but I could not bear to have one of our boys hurt for all the gold in the mine."

"I think The Black Coyote knows that," he said, "and that's what makes him so all-fired nervy. He's one of our own men, Di—can't you see it? He knows when the shipments are big an' don't never touch a little one, an' he knows your Dad's orders about not takin' no chances.

"I've hated to think it, but there ain't no other two ways about it—it's one o' our men—an' I wouldn't have to walk around the world to put my finger on him, neither."

"I don't believe it!" she cried. "I don't believe that one of my men would do it."

"You don't want to believe it, that's all. You

know just as well as I do whose doin' it, down in the bottom of your heart. I don't like to believe it no more'n you do, Di; but I ain't blind an' I hate to see you bein' made a fool of an' robbed into the bargain. I don't believe you'd believe it, though, if I caught him in the act."

"I think I know whom you suspect, Hal," she replied, "but I am sure you are wrong."

"Will you give me a chance to prove it?"

"How?"

"Send him up to the mine to guard the bullion until Mack gits well an' then keep Mack off the job fer a month," he explained. "I'll bet my shirt thet either there ain't no holdups fer a month or else they's only one man pulls 'em off instead o' two. Will you do it?"

"It isn't fair. I don't even suspect him."

"Everybody else does an' thet makes it fair fer it gives him a chance to prove it if he ain't guilty."

"It wouldn't *prove* anything, except that there were no holdups while he was on duty."

"It would prove something to my mind if they started up again pretty soon after he was taken off the job," he retorted.

"Well—it might, but I don't think I'd ever believe it of him unless I saw him with my own eyes."

"Pshaw! the trouble with you is you're soft on him—you don't care if your gold is stole if he gits it."

She drew herself to her full height. "I do not

care to discuss the matter further," she said. "Good night!"

He grabbed his hat viciously from the piano and stamped toward the doorway. There he turned about and confronted her again for a parting shot before he strode out into the night.

"You don't dare try it!" he flung at her. "You don't dare!"

After he had gone she sat biting her lip half in anger and half in mortification, but after the brief tempest of emotion had subsided she commenced to question her own motives impartially. Was she afraid? Was it true that she did not dare? And long after she had gone to bed, and sleep would not come, she continued thus to catechize herself.

As Hal Colby burst into the bunk-house and slammed the door behind him the sudden draft thus created nearly extinguished the single lamp that burned upon an improvised table at which four men sat at poker. Bull and Shorty, Texas Pete and one called Idaho sat in the game.

"I raise you ten dollars," remarked Idaho, softly, as the lamp resumed functioning after emitting a thin, protesting spiral of black soot.

"I see that an' raise you my pile," said Bull, shoving several small stacks of silver toward the center of the table.

"How much you got there?" inquired Idaho, the others having dropped out.

Bull counted. "There's your ten," he said, "an'

here's ten, fifteen, twenty-five—" He continued counting in a monotone. "Ninety-six," he announced. "I raise you ninety-six dollars, Idaho."

"I ain't got ninety-six dollars," said Idaho. "I only got eight."

"You got a saddle, ain't you?" inquired Bull, sweetly.

"An' a shirt," suggested Texas Pete.

"My saddle's worth three hundred an' fifty dollars if it's worth a cent," proclaimed Idaho.

"No one ain't never said it was worth a cent," Shorty reminded him.

"I'll cover it an' call you," announced Bull. "I don't want your shirt, Idaho, it's full o' holes."

"What you coverin' it with?" asked Idaho. "I don't see nothin'."

Bull rose from the table. "Wait a second," he said, and stepped to his blankets where he rummaged for a moment in his war-bag. When he returned to the table he tossed a small buckskin bag among his silver.

"They's five hundred dollars' worth of dust in that," he said. "If you win we kin weigh out what's comin' to you over at the office tomorrow mornin'."

Hal Colby looked on—an interested spectator. The others fell silent. Texas Pete knit his brows in perplexity.

"Let's see it," demanded Idaho.

Bull picked up the bag, opened it and poured a

stream of yellow particles into his palm. "Satisfied?" he inquired.

Idaho nodded.

"What you got?" demanded Bull.

Idaho laid four kings on the table, smiling broadly.

"Four aces," said Bull, and raked in the pot.

"Why didn't you raise him?" demanded Shorty.

"I just told you I didn't want his shirt," said Bull, "an' I don't want your saddle, neither, kid. I'll keep the money—it ain't good fer kids like you to have too much money—but you keep the saddle."

"I'm goin' to turn in," said Shorty, pushing back and rising.

"You'd all better turn in an' give someone eise a chance to sleep," said the foreman. "What with your damn game an' Pete's singin' a feller ain't got no more chance to sleep around here than a jack-rabbit. Why don't you fellers crawl in?"

"Crawl in! Crawl in!" exclaimed Texas Pete. "Crawl in! Crawl out! By gollies, I got another verse!

"The boss he crawls out then, all shaky an' white,
From under the bar where he's ben sittin' tight.
'Now set out the pizen right pronto, you coot,'
The stranger remarks, 'Or I shore starts to shoot,
I only ben practicin' so far,' says he;
'A bar-keep er two don't mean nothin' to me.
Most allus I has one fer breakfast each day——
I don't mean no harm—it's jest only my way.'"

CHAPTER IX

LILLIAN MANILL

"YOU sent fer me, Miss?" asked Bull, as he stepped into the office the following morning, his hat in his hand, his chaps loose-buckled about his trim hips, his two big six-guns a trifle forward against the need for quick action, the black silk handkerchief falling over the blue shirt that stretched to his deep chest, and his thick, black hair pushed back in an unconscious, half pompadour.

From silver-mounted spurs to heavy hat band he was typical of the West of his day. There was no item of his clothing or equipment the possession of which was not prompted by utilitarian considerations. There was ornamentation, but it was obviously secondary to the strict needs of his calling. Nothing that he wore was shabby, yet it all showed use to an extent that made each article seem a part of the man, as though he had been molded into them. Nothing protruded with stiff awkwardness —even the heavy guns appeared to fit into accustomed hollows and become a part of the man.

The girl, swinging about in her chair to face him, felt a suggestion of stricture in her throat, and she felt mean and small and contemptible as she looked into the eyes of the man she knew loved her and contemplated the thing she was about to do; yet she did not hesitate now that she had, after a night of sleepless deliberation, committed herself to it.

"Yes, I sent for you, Bull," she replied. "The stage was held up again yesterday as you know. Mack won't be fit for work again for a long time and I've got to have someone to guard the bullion shipments—the fellow who came down with it yesterday has quit. He said he was too young to commit suicide."

"Yes'm," said Bull.

"I don't want you to take any chances, Bull—I would rather lose the gold than have—you hurt."

"I won't get hurt, Miss."

"You don't mind doing it?" she asked.

"O' course I'm a puncher," he said; "but I don't mind doin' it—not fer you. I told you once thet I'd do anything fer you, Miss, an' I wasn't jest talkin' through my hat."

"You don't do everything I ask you to, Bull," she said, smiling.

"What don't I do?" he demanded.

"You still call me Miss, and I hate it. You're more like a brother, Bull, and Miss sounds so formal." It must have been a woman who first discovered the art of making fire.

A shadow of pain crossed his dark countenance. "Don't ask too much of me, Miss," he said quietly as he turned on his heel and started for the doorway. "I go up to the mine today, I suppose?" he threw back over his shoulder.

"Yes, today," she said, and he was gone.

For a long time Diana Henders was troubled. The assignment she had given Bull troubled her, for it was a tacit admission that she gave credence to Colby's suspicions. The pain that she had seen reflected in Bull's face troubled her, as did his parting words and the quiet refusal to call her Diana. She wondered if these had been prompted by a feeling of pique that his love was not returned, or compunction because of a guilty knowledge that he had betrayed her and her father.

Hal Colby had told her that morning of the bag of gold dust Bull had displayed in the poker game the night before, and that troubled her too, for it seemed to bear out more than anything else the suspicions that were forming around him—suspicions that she could see, in the light of bits of circumstantial evidence, were far from groundless.

"I won't believe it!" she said half aloud. "I won't believe it!" and then she went for a ride.

All the men had left but Hal Colby and Texas Pete when she reached the corrals; but she did not feel like riding with Hal Colby that morning and so she rode with Texas Pete, much to that young man's surprise and rapture.

The days dragged along and became weeks, the stage made its two trips a week, the bullion shipments came through regularly and safely and there were no holdups, and then one day Maurice B. Corson and Lillian Manill arrived. The stage took the Bar Y road that day and pulled up before the gate of the ranch house just as Diana Henders and Hal Colby were returning from a trip to the West Ranch. Diana saw Lillian Manill for the first time in her life. The eastern girl was seated between Bill Gatlin, the driver, and Bull. All three were laughing. Evidently they had been enjoying one another's company.

Diana could not but notice it because it was rarely that Bull laughed. It was Bull who stepped to the wheel and helped her to alight.

Maurice B. Corson emerged from the inside of the coach, through the windows of which Diana could see three other passengers, two of whom she recognized as the Wainrights, and then she dismounted and ran forward to greet her cousin, a handsome, dark haired girl of about her own age.

Bull, still smiling, raised his hat to Diana. She nodded to him, briefly. For some reason she was vexed with him, but why she did not know. Bull and Colby ran to the boot and dragged off the Corson-Manill baggage, while Lillian presented Corson to Diana. Corson was a young man—a typical New Yorker—in his early thirties.

"Git a move on there, Bull," shouted Gatlin, "or they'll think I ben held up agin."

"I reckon The Black Coyote's gone out o' business, fer a while," said Colby, shooting a quick look at Diana.

Instantly the girl's loyalty was in arms, "He's afraid to try it while Bull's guarding the gold," she said.

"How much longer you goin' to keep me on the job?" asked Bull, as he clambered to the seat of the already moving coach. "Mack looks pretty all-fired healthy to me."

"Just another week or two, Bull," Diana shouted after him as the stage careened away at full gallop.

"Isn't he wonderful!" exclaimed Miss Manill. "A real cowboy and the first one I ever talked to!"

"Oh, there are lots of them here," said Diana, "just as nice as Bull."

"So I see," replied Lillian Manill, smiling frankly at Hal Colby, "but Bull, as you call him, is the only one I've met."

"Pardon me!" exclaimed Diana. "This is Mr. Colby, Miss Manill."

"Oh, you're the foreman—Mr. Bull told me—how exciting!"

"I'll bet he didn't tell you nothin' good about me," said Colby.

"He told me about your heroic defense of Diana and my poor uncle," explained Lillian.

Colby flushed. "If it hadn't ben fer Bull we'd all 'a' ben killed," he said, ashamed.

"Why, he didn't tell me that," exclaimed the girl. "He never said he was in the battle, at all."

"That is just like Bull," said Diana.

They were walking toward the house, Diana and Colby leading their ponies, and the two Easterners looking interestedly at the various buildings and corrals over which hung the glamour of that irresistible romance which the West and a cattle ranch always hold for the uninitiated—and for the initiated too, if the truth were but known.

"It is just too wonderful, Mr. Colby," Lillian confided to the big foreman walking at her side; "but doesn't it get awful lonesome?"

"We don't notice it," he replied. "You know we keep pretty busy all day with a big outfit like this and when night comes around we're ready to turn in—we don't have no time to git lonesome."

"Is this a very big outfit, as you call it?" she asked.

"I reckon they ain't none much bigger in the territory," he replied.

"And to think that you are foreman of it! What a wonderful man you must be!"

"Oh, it ain't nothin'," he assured her, but he was vastly pleased. Here, indeed, was a young lady of discernment.

"You big men of the great out-doors are always so modest," she told him, a statement for which he could find no reply. As a matter of fact, though he had never thought of it before, he realized the justice of her assertion, and fully agreed with her.

She was looking now at the trim figure of her

cousin, walking ahead of them with Corson. "How becoming that costume is to Diana," she remarked; "and I suppose she rides wonderfully."

"She shore does—an' then some," he assured her.

"Oh, how I wish I could ride! Do you suppose I could learn?"

"Easy, Miss. It ain't nothin', oncet you know how."

"Do you suppose someone would teach me?" She looked up at him, archly.

"I'd be mighty proud to larn you, Miss."

"Oh, *would* you? How wonderful! Can we start right away, tomorrow?"

"You bet we can; but you can't ride in them things," he added, looking ruefully at her New York traveling costume.

She laughed gaily. "Oh, my! I didn't expect to," she cried. "I am not such a silly as that. I brought my habit with me, of course."

"Well, I suppose it's all right," he said politely; "but you don't have to bring no habits to Arizony from nowheres—we mostly have enough right here, such as they be—good an' bad."

Again her laugh rang out. "You big, funny man!" she cried. "You are poking fun at me just because you think I am a tendershoe—trying to make me believe that you don't know what a riding habit is. Aren't you ashamed of yourself—teasing poor little me?"

They were passing the bunk-house at the time, where the boys, having scrubbed for supper, were squatting about on their heels watching the newcomers with frank curiosity. After they had passed Shorty gave Texas Pete a shove that sent him sprawling on the ground. "Say," he said, "did you see them pants?"

"I shore did," replied Pete, "but you don't have no call to knock me down an' git my ridin' habit all dusty, you gosh-dinged tendershoe, jest because a guy blows in with funny pants on."

"Did you see the mug on Colby?" inquired Idaho. "He don't know a ridin' habit from the cigarette habit."

"I reckon he thought she was confessin' a sin," said Texas Pete.

"Oh, them pants! Them pants!" moaned Shorty, rocking to and fro on his heels, his long arms wound around his knees. Shorty was six feet three and thought that Kansas City was on the Atlantic seaboard.

Corson's keen, quick eyes were taking in the salient features of their immediate surroundings as he walked at Diana's side toward the two-story adobe ranch house, on two sides of which a broad, covered veranda had been built within recent years. He saw the orderly, well kept appearance not only of the main buildings, but of the corrals, fences and outbuildings as well. Everything bespoke system and excellent management. It was evidently a well-ordered plant in smooth running condition. He thought of it in terms of Eastern factories and found it good.

"You keep things up well here," he said to Diana Henders. "I want to compliment you."

"Thank you," she replied. "It was something that Dad always insisted upon, and of course I have carried out all his policies since his death."

"What are these buildings—they look like cement, but of course you wouldn't have that out here. The freight on it would make the cost prohibitive."

"They are adobe," she explained, "just big, clay bricks dried in the sun."

He nodded in understanding. "Nothing much very fancy about the architecture," he commented, laughing. "The only attempt at ornamentation is that sort of parapet on the roof of the house, with the loop-holes in it, and that doesn't add much to the looks of the place."

Diana thought that his criticisms were in rather poor taste, and there was something about them that vaguely suggested the air of a man viewing for the first time a property that he had only recently acquired—something proprietorial that she inwardly resented. Outwardly she was polite.

"You would think that it added a lot to the place," she told him, "if you should ever chance to be here when the Apaches stage a raid—it was never intended to be ornamental."

He sucked in his breath with a whistling sound. "You don't mean," he exclaimed, "that they are so bad you have to live in a fortress?"

"They haven't been on the warpath in any considerable numbers for a long time," she assured him; "but that parapet has been used more than once since the house was built, and there is always the chance that it may come in handy again. It may not be beautiful from this side, but I can tell you that it looks mighty good from the other side when there are sneaking Apaches skulking behind every out-house. I know, because I've viewed it under those conditions."

"You think there is any great danger?" he asked her, looking about nervously.

"There is always danger," she replied, for she saw that he was afraid and a spirit of mischief prompted her to avenge his indelicate criticisms of the home she loved. "It is only a matter of weeks, you know," she reminded him, "since Dad was killed by Apaches."

Corson appeared worried and his further scrutiny of the house as they approached it was influenced by other than artistic architectural considerations.

"I see you have heavy shutters at all the windows," he said. "I suppose you have them closed and fastened every night?"

"Oh, my, no!" she cried, laughing. "We never close them except for dust storms and Indians."

"But suppose they come unexpectedly?"

"Then we stand a chance of getting dust or Indians in the house."

"I think you had better have them closed nights while Miss Manill is here," he said. "I am afraid she will be very nervous."

"Oh, your rooms are on the second floor," she replied, "and you can lock them all up tight — possibly you'll get air enough from the patio. The nights are always cool, you know, but I'd feel stuffy with all the shutters closed."

"We'll see," was all he said, but there was something about the way he said it that she did not like. In fact, Diana Henders was sure that she was not going to like Mr. Maurice B. Corson at all.

As they sat down to supper an hour later Lillian Manill looked inquiringly at her cousin. "Where is Mr. Colby?" she asked.

"Over at the cook-house eating his supper, I suppose," replied Diana.

"Don't he eat with us? He seems such a nice fellow."

"He is a nice fellow," replied Diana, "but the boys would rather eat by themselves. Women folks would take away their appetites. You have no idea how we terrify some of them."

"But Mr. Colby seemed very much at ease," insisted Lillian.

"Hal is different, but the very fact that he is foreman makes it necessary for him to eat with the other men — it is customary."

"Mr. Bull seemed at ease too, after I got him started," continued Lillian. "He isn't much of a talker, but he didn't seem a bit afraid of me."

"Bull is not afraid of anything," Diana assured her; "but if you got him to talk at all you must exercise a wonderful power over men. I can scarcely ever get a dozen words out of him."

"Well, I guess I've got a way with men," said Lillian, complacently.

"I'm afraid that you will find that Bull is not very susceptible," said Diana, with just the vaguest hint of tartness.

"Oh, I don't know," replied the other; "he has promised to teach me to ride and shoot."

Diana ate in silence for several minutes. She was wondering already if she were going to like her cousin. But then, of course she was—how silly of her to think she was not, she concluded.

"I met an old friend on the stage today," remarked Corson, presently.

Diana raised her eyebrows politely. "How nice," she said.

"Yes, it was. Haven't seen him for a couple of years. Nice chap, Jefferson Wainright. Fraternity brother. Of course I was years ahead of him, but I used to see him when I'd go down to Cambridge for the games. His governor's a nice old chap, too, and got a wad of the long green."

"So he has told us," said Diana.

"Oh, you know them? They didn't mention it."

"I have met them. Mr. Wainright tried to buy the ranch."

"Oh, yes, I believe he did mention something of the kind. Why didn't you sell it to him?"

"His offer was too low, for one reason, and the other is that I do not care to sell my interest."

Corson and Miss Manill exchanged a quick glance that escaped Diana.

"How much did he offer you?" asked Corson.

"Two hundred and fifty thousand dollars."

"Why, that seems a very fair price," said Corson.

"It is ridiculous, Mr. Corson," replied Diana, "and if you are at all familiar with Mr. Manill's business you know it as well as I."

"I am very familiar with it," replied the New Yorker. "In fact, from your remarks I imagine that I am much more familiar with it than you."

"Then you know that the cattle interests alone are worth three times that amount, without considering the mine at all."

Corson shook his head. "I am afraid that way out here you are too far from the financial center of the country to have a very comprehensive grasp of values. Now, as a matter of fact, the bottom has dropped out of the live-stock market. We'll be lucky if we make expenses for the next year or so, and it probably never will come back to what it was. And as for the mine, that, of course, is about done. It won't pay to work it a year from now. If we could get two hundred and fifty thousand dollars for this business we'd be mighty lucky; but I doubt if old Wainright would renew that offer—he's too shrewd a business man."

Diana Henders made no reply. She was wondering just how much Maurice B. Corson did know about the live-stock market and the mine. She was inclined to believe that he knew a great deal more than his remarks concerning them would indicate.

At the same hour Mary Donovan's boarders were gathered about her table. She had other guests this evening in addition to her regular clientele. There were the Wainrights, and Bull was there for supper and breakfast as was usual when the bullion came down from the mine.

It was not a gay company. Mack Harber and Jim Weller looked with suspicion on Bull, an attitude that would have blossomed into open and active hostility could they have gained the support of Gum Smith; but Gum was not searching for trouble. He glowered at his plate and hated Bull. Wildcat Bob inhaled soup and hated Gum Smith.

The Wainrights scarcely raised their eyes from the business of eating for fear of the embarrassment of meeting those of the man who had run the elder Wainright off the Bar Y Ranch—an occurrence which rankled horribly in the breasts of both. Bull, taciturn as usual, ate in silence with something of the mien of a lion feeding among jackals. Mary Donovan hovered in the doorway. Bull laid down his spoon, drank a glass of water and rose from the table.

"Sure an' won't ye have another helpin' o' puddin' now, Bull?" urged Mary.

"No, thanks, Mrs. Donovan," he replied, "I'm plumb full." He walked past her into the kitchen and out the back door. An almost audible sigh of relief rose from the remaining guests.

"I reckon he thinks he owns the shack," commented Jim Weller apropos of Bull's exit through the sacred precincts of Mary Donovan's kitchen.

"Sure, he could have it fer the askin', the fine b'y he is," shot back Mary. "Him a-goin' out to fetch in wood fer me while the loikes o' ye, Jim Weller, what ain't fit to black his boots, sits here and makes re-marks about him, ye lazy whelp!" Mr. Weller subsided.

The meal over, the guests departed with the exception of Mack Harber, Jim Weller, and the Wainrights who had congregated on the veranda.

"You don't seem to like the fellow they call Bull," remarked the younger Wainright to Weller.

"I didn't say I didn't like him an' I didn't say I did," replied Weller, noncommittally.

"Well, I don't like him," said Mack, vehemently. "I wouldn't like my grandmother if she shot me in the belly."

"You mean that he shot you?" asked Wainright.

"The Black Coyote shot me, an' if Bull ain't The Black Coyote my name's McGinnis."

"You really think that he has been pulling off these holdups?" demanded the elder Wainright.

"I ain't the only one what thinks so," replied Mack. "Every one, 'most, thinks so, an' ef we had a decent sheriff that feller'd be behind the bars where he belongs, er strung up to a cottonwood in Hell's Bend. 'Pears to me like Gum was either in on the deal er afeared of Bull."

"Gum's afeared of every one," said Weller.

"Well," remarked Jefferson Wainright, Sr., "when we come over on this side o' the hills I calc'late as how things air goin' to be a heap sight different. There won't be no more o' this here funny gunplay stuff. I'm a-goin' to run all o' these would-be bad men out o' the country."

"You figgerin' on comin' over here?" asked Mack.

"I certainly am. I'm a-goin' to buy the whole Bar Y out-fit."

"The Hell you is!" exclaimed Mack. "I heard that Miss Di wouldn't sell it to you."

"She ain't got nothin' to say about it. I'm a-goin' to buy it from the man that's runnin' that outfit now, an' he's a mighty good business man, too."

"Who's that—Colby?"

"No, Colby nothin'—it's Mr. Corson of Noo York. He's handlin' all o' John Manill's interests an' he just come here today with Manill's daughter. We come over on the stage with them. I was tellin' Corson of the fine airs that chit of a Henders girl puts on, but things is goin' to be different now. Corson's goin' to close out the estate an' the holdin's here is as good as sold to me already."

CHAPTER X

WILDCAT BOB GOES COURTING

BULL sat in a corner of The Chicago Saloon watching the play at the faro table. It was too early to go to bed and he was not a man who read much, nor cared to read, even had there been anything to read, which there was not. He had skimmed the latest Eastern papers that had come in on the stage and his reading was over until the next shipment of gold from the mine brought him again into contact with a newspaper. Then we would read the live-stock market reports, glance over the headlines and throw the paper aside, satisfied. His literary requirements were few.

A man who had drunk not wisely but too well lurched up to him.

"Have a drink, stranger!" he commanded. It was not an invitation.

"Ain't drinkin'," replied Bull, quietly.

"Oh, yes, you be," announced the hospitable one. "When I says drink, you drinks, see? I'm a bad man, I am. Whoopee!" and drawing a six-shooter he commenced firing into the floor at Bull's feet.

Suddenly a large man enveloped him from the rear, held his gun hand aloft and dragged him away into an opposite corner, where, to the accompaniment of a deluge of lurid profanity, he counselled him to greater discretion.

"Why you blankety, blank, blank, blank!" he cried. "You tryin' to commit sewerside? Don't you know who that is, you blitherin' idjit?" then he whispered something in the other's ear. The effect was electrical. Thc man seemed sobered instantly. With staring eyes he looked across the room at Bull.

"I'm goin' to git out o' here," he said, "he might change his mind."

"I cain't see yit why he didn't bore ye," agreed his friend. "You better go an' apologize."

Slowly the pseudo bad man crossed the room toward Bull, who had not moved sufficiently to have changed his position since the man had first accosted him. The man halted in front of Bull, a sickly grin on his bloated countenance.

"No offense, pardner. Jest had a drop too much. No offense intended. Jest jokin'—thet was all—jest jokin'."

Bull eyed him intently for a moment. "Oh, yes," he said presently, "I remember you now—you're the flannel mouth what got gay with ol' Wildcat a coupla months ago. Did you ever return that window sash you took with you? I hearn Gum was powerful cut up about that window sash." Not the shadow of a smile crossed Bull's face. "I warn't there, but I hearn all about it."

The other flushed, attempted some witty repartee

that fell flat, and finally managed to make his escape amid a roar of laughter from the nearer card players and spectators who had overheard the brief dialogue.

Bull rose. "Goin'?" asked an acquaintance.

"I reckon so. Good night."

"Good night, Bull."

The man stepped out into the clear, star-lit night. Involuntarily he turned and looked toward the northeast in the direction of the Bar Y ranch. Diana was there. For a long time he stood motionless gazing out across the arid, moon-bathed level that stretched away to her loved feet. What emotions played behind the inscrutable mask of his face? Who may say?

As he stood there silently he heard voices coming from between The Chicago Saloon and *Gum's Place —Liquors and Cigars.*

"He's in there now," said one. "I kin see him. If there weren't so tarnation many fellers at the bar I c'd git him from here."

"You better come along afore you git in more trouble than you got the capacity to handle," urged a second voice.

"Thas all right. I know what I'm doin'. There cain't no dried up ol' buffalo chip like thet run me out o' no man's saloon an' get away with it, an' thas all they is to thet."

"Well, I'm goin' home," stated the second voice. "I know when I'm well off."

"You go home. After I shoot the ears offen this Wildcat Bob party I'm comin' home, too."

"You go to shootin' any ears offen Wildcat Bob an' you won't need no blankets where you're goin'."

"Thas-so? Well, here goes—you better stay an' see the fun."

"I'm goin' now while I got the chanct," said the other, and Bull heard him coming from the side of the building. The former stepped quickly back into the doorway of The Chicago Saloon and an instant later he saw the large man who had dragged his friend from him a few minutes before pass up the street at a rapid walk. Then Bull looked from his place of concealment, just in time to see another figure emerge from between the buildings and enter Gum's Place.

Bull was close behind him. The door was open a crack. He saw that the other had advanced into the room a few feet and was standing behind one of the rough columns that supported the second story. Across the room, at the far end, Wildcat Bob had just set down his whiskey glass upon the bar, wiped his beard on his sleeve, and turned away toward the tables where the gambling was in progress. For a moment he would be alone, with only the rough rear wall behind him.

Bull saw the stranger raise his six-gun to take deliberate aim. He was too far away to reach him before he pulled the trigger and it would do no good to warn the Wildcat. There was but a single alternative to standing supinely by and watching old Wildcat being shot down in cold blood by a cowardly murderer.

It was this alternative that Bull adopted. As the smoke rose from the muzzle of his gun the stranger threw his hands above his head, his weapon clattered to the floor, and he wheeled about. His eyes alighted upon Bull standing there, grim faced and silent, the smoking six-gun in his hand.

Suddenly the wounded man gave voice to a shrill scream. "He done it!" he cried, pointing at Bull. "He done it! The Black Coyote done it! He's killed me!" and with these last words the body slumped to the floor.

Bull stood facing them all in silence for just a moment. The whole room full of men and women were staring at him. Then he slipped his gun into its holster and advanced into the room, a faint smile on his lips. He walked toward Wildcat Bob.

"That hombre was after you, Bob," he said. "He was drunk, but I couldn't stop him no other way. He's the feller you chased through the window that time."

Gum Smith hurried to the rear of the bar. Then he leaned over it and pointed a finger at Bull. "Yo-all's undah arrest!" he cried. "Yo-all's undah arrest fo murder."

"Go kick yourself through a knot-hole!" advised Bull. "Ef I hadn't got that hombre he'd a-got Bob. They wasn't nothin' else to do."

"Yo-all hearn what he called him, didn't yo?" yelled Gum. He pointed at first one and then another. "Ah depatize yo! Ah depatize yo!" he cried. "Arrest him, men!"

No one moved, except Wildcat Bob. He came and stood beside Bull, and he drew both his long, heavy guns with their heavily notched grips.

"Any one what's aimin' to take this boy, why, let him step up," said Wildcat Bob, and his watery blue eye was fixed terribly upon the sheriff.

"Ah want yo-all to know thet when Ah depatizes yo, yo-all's depatized," shrilled Gum. "Yo hearn what the corpse called him. Ain't that enough? Do yo duty, men!"

One or two of the men, friends of Gum's, moved restlessly. Bull, sensing trouble, had drawn both his weapons, and now he stood beside the Wildcat, his steady gray eyes alert for the first hostile move.

"Don't none o' you gents go fer to start nothin'," he advised. "You all seen what happened. You know I couldn't a-done nothin' else, an' as fer what thet drunken bum called me ef Gum thinks I'm The Coyote why don't he step up an' take me? I ain't a honin' fer trouble, but I don't aim to be the subject o' no postmortem neither."

"Do yo-all surrendah, then?" demanded Gum.

"Don't try to be no more of a damn fool than the Lord made yuh, Gum," advised Wildcat Bob. "You know thet if this here boy ain't The Black Coyote you don't want him, an' ef he is The Black

Coyote you wouldn't never git outen behind thet bar ef you was to try to take him. Fer my part I don't believe he is, an' I got two ol' pea-shooters here what thinks the same as I does. What do you think, Gum?"

"Well," said the sheriff after a moment's deliberation, "Ah reckon as mebby the corpse was mistook. Hev a drink on the house, gents!"

As Bull and Wildcat Bob entered the office of The Donovan House Mary Donovan espied them through the open doorway of her sitting room and called to them.

"Come in an' have a drop o' tay wid me before yese go to bed," she invited, and as they entered she scrutinized Wildcat Bob with a stern eye. Evidently satisfied, her face softened. "I know they ain't run out o' whiskey in Hendersville," she said, "so I reckon ye must o' run out o' money, Wildcat."

The little old gentleman reached into his pocket and drew forth a handful of silver, which he displayed with virtuous satisfaction.

"The saints be praised!" exclaimed Mary Donovan. "Ye've money in yer pocket an' yer home airly an' sober! Be ye sick, Wildcat Bob?"

"I've re-formed, Mary—I ain't never goin' to tech another drop," he assured her, solemnly.

"Ye've not had a drink the avenin'?" she demanded.

"Well—" he hesitated, "you see——"

"Yis, I see," she snapped, scornfully.

"But, Mary, I only had one little one—you wouldn't begrudge an old man one little nightcap?"

"Well," she consented, relenting, "wan little one wouldn't do no harrm. I wouldn't moind one mesilf."

Wildcat Bob reached for his hip pocket. "I was thinking that same thing, Mary, and that's why I brung one home fer yuh," and he drew forth a pint flask.

"The divil fly away wid ye, Wildcat Bob!" she cried, but she was smiling as she reached for the flask.

Bull rose, laughing. "Good night!" he said, "I'm going to turn in."

"Have a drop wid us before ye go," invited Mary.

"No thanks, I've quit," replied Bull. A moment later they heard him mounting the stairs to his room.

"He's a good b'y," said Mary, wiping her lips and replacing the cork in the bottle.

"He is that, Mary," agreed Wildcat, reaching for it.

There was a period of contented silence.

"It's a lonesome life fer a widdy-lady, that it is," remarked Mary, with a deep sigh.

Wildcat Bob moved his chair closer, flushed at his own boldness, and fell to examining the toe of his boot. Mary rocked diligently, her red hands folded in her ample lap, keeping an eye cocked on the Wildcat. There was another long silence that was broken at last by Mrs. Donovan.

"Sure," she said, "an' it's funny ye never married, Bob."

Bob essayed reply, but a mouthful of tobacco juice prevented. Rising, he walked into the office, crossed that room, opened the front door and spat copiously without. Returning to the room he hitched his chair closer to Mary's, apparently by accident, as he resumed his seat.

"I—" he started, but it was evidently a false start, since he commenced all over again. "I—" again he paused.

"You what?" inquired Mary Donovan with soft encouragement.

"You—" said Wildcat Bob and stuck again. Inward excitement evidently stimulated his salivary glands, with the result that he was again forced to cross to the outer door. When he returned he hunched his chair a bit closer to Mary's.

"As ye was about to remark," prodded Mary.

"I—I——"

"Yes," said Mary, "Go on, Bob!"

"I was just a-goin' to say that I don't think it'll rain tonight," he ended, lamely.

Mary Donovan placed her hands upon her hips, pressed her lips tightly together and turned a withering glance of scorn upon Wildcat Bob—all of which were lost upon him, he having again returned to whole-souled consideration of the toe of his boot, his face suffused with purple.

"Rain!" muttered Mary Donovan. "Rain in Arizony this time o' year? Sure, an' ye mane ye thought it wouldn't shnow, didn't ye?" she demanded.

Wildcat Bob emitted only a gurgle, and again silence reigned, unbroken for long minutes, except by the creaking of Mary's rocker. Suddenly she turned upon him.

"Gimme that flask," she said.

He handed it over and she took a long drink. Wiping the mouth of the bottle with the palm of her hand she returned it to him. Then Wildcat Bob took a drink, and the silence continued.

The evening wore on, the flask was emptied and midnight came. With it came Gum Smith, reeling bedward. They watched him stagger across the office floor and heard him stumbling up the stairs. Mary Donovan arose.

"Be off to bed wid ye," she said. "I can't be sittin' here all night gossipin' wid ye."

He, too, arose. "Good night, Mary," he said, "it's been a pleasant evenin'."

"Yis," said Mary Donovan.

As Wildcat Bob climbed the stairs toward his room he was mumbling in his beard. "Doggone my hide!" he said. "Ef I'd jest had a coupla drinks I mout a-done it."

"Sure," soliloquized Mary Donovan, as she closed the door of her bedroom, "it's not so dum funny after all that the ould fool nivir was married."

CHAPTER XI

"RIDE HIM, COWBOY!"

LILLIAN MANILL awoke early and viewed the brilliant light of the new day through the patio windows of her room—the outer windows were securely shuttered against Indians. She stretched languorously and turned over for another nap, but suddenly she changed her mind, threw off the covers and arose. It was a hideously early hour for Lillian Manill to arise; but she had recalled that there was to be a riding lesson after breakfast and Diana had explained to her that the breakfast hour was an early one. Dressing, she selected a tailored walking suit—she would change into her riding habit after breakfast—for she wanted to stroll about the yard a bit before breakfast, and she knew that this new walking suit was extremely fetching.

A few minutes later as she stepped into the yard she saw signs of activity in the direction of the horse corrals and thither she bent her steps. Texas Pete, who was helping the chore boy with the morning feeding, saw her coming and looked for an avenue of escape, being in no sense a lady's man and fully aware of the fact; but he was too late—there was no avenue left, Lillian Manill being already between him and the bunk-house. So he applied himself vigorously to the pitch fork he was wielding and pretended not to see her, a pretense that made no impression whatever upon Lillian Manill. She paused outside the bars and looked in.

"Good morning!" she said.

Texas Pete pretended that he had not heard.

"Good morning!" she repeated in a louder voice.

"Mornin'," replied Pete, pulling at the brim of his hat and immediately resuming the fork. He wished she would move on. The horses were fed and there was no other excuse for him to remain in the corral, but in order to reach the bunk-house he must pass directly by this disconcerting person. Diana he did not mind—he was used to Diana, and aside from the fact that he was madly in love with her she caused him little embarrassment or concern except upon those few occasions when he had attempted to maintain an extended conversation with her. Dr. Johnson would have found nothing in Pete's conversational attainments to have aroused his envy.

Pete continued feeding the horses. He fed them twice as much as they could eat in a day, notwithstanding the fact that he knew perfectly well they were to be fed again that evening; but finally he realized that he could defer the embarrassing moment no longer and that the girl had not left. He stuck the fork viciously into the hay stack and crossed the corral. He tried to appear unconcerned and to pass her by without looking at her, but in both he failed—first because he was very much concerned and second because she placed herself directly in his path and smiled sweetly at him.

"I don't believe I had the pleasure of meeting you last night," she said. "I am Miss Manill—Miss Henders' cousin."

"Yes'm," said Pete.

"And I suppose you are one of the cow-gentlemen," she added.

Pete turned suddenly and violently purple. A choking sound issued from his throat; but quickly he gained control of himself. Something in that remark of hers removed instantly all of Texas Pete's embarrassment. He found himself at once upon an even footing with her.

"No'm," he said, "I hain't one o' the cow-gentlemen—I'm on'y a tendershoe."

"I'm sure you don't look it," she told him, "with those leather trousers with the fleece on. But you ride, don't you?" she added quickly.

"I ain't larned yit," he assured her.

"Oh, isn't that too bad! I thought of course you were a wonderful equestrian and I was going to ask you to teach me to ride; but you'd better come along after breakfast and we'll get Mr. Colby to teach us both."

"I reckon he wouldn't like it," explained Pete. "You see I'm in his afternoon ridin' class. He don't take nothin' but ladies in the mornin'."

"Oh, does he teach riding regularly?"

"My, yes, that's what he's here fer. He's larnin' us all to ride so's we kin go out on hosses an' catch the cows 'stid o' havin' to hoof-it."

"I thought he was foreman," she said.

"Yes'm, but that's one of his jobs—larnin' cow-gentlemen to ride."

"How interesting! I've learned so much already and I've only been in Arizona since day before yesterday. Mr. Bull was so kind and patient, answering all my silly little questions."

"I reckon Bull could answer most any question," he told her.

"Yes, indeed; but then he's been here in Arizona so long, and had so much to do with the development of the country. Why, do you know he planted all the willows along that funny little river we followed for so long yesterday—miles and miles of them?"

"Did he tell you that?" inquired Texas Pete.

"Yes, isn't it wonderful? I think it shows such an artistic temperament."

"There's more to Bull than I ever suspected," murmured Texas Pete, reverently.

A sudden, clamorous, metallic din shattered the quiet of the cool Arizona morning. The girl gave a little scream and sprang for Texas Pete, throwing both arms about his neck.

"O-o-h!" she cried; "what is it—Indians?"

"No'm," said Pete, striving to disengage himself, for he saw the malevolent eyes of several unholy cow-gentlemen gloating upon the scene from the doorway of the bunk-house. "No'm, that ain't Injuns—that's the breakfast bell."

"How silly of me!" she explained. "Now I suppose I must be going. I'm so glad to have met you, Mr.——"

"My name's Texas Pete."

"Mr. Pete, and I do hope you learn to ride quickly. I am sure we could have some lovely excursions, picnicking among the beautiful hills. Oh, wouldn't it be divine—just you and I, Mr. Pete?" and she let her great, lovely eyes hang for a moment on his in a fashion that had turned more sophisticated heads than Texas Pete's.

When she had gone and Pete was making his way toward the cook-house he ran his fingers through his shock of hair. "By gollies!" he muttered. "The outside o' her head's all right, anyway."

As he entered the cook-house Shorty seized him and threw both arms about his neck. "Kiss me darlin'!" he cried. "I ain't had a single kiss before breakfast."

"Shet up, you long-legged walrus," replied Pete, grinning, as he shoved the other aside.

He ate in silence despite the gibes of his companions, who quickly desisted, realizing the futility of attempting to arouse Texas Pete's ire by raillery. He was quick enough of temper and quicker still with his guns when occasion warranted; but no one could arouse his anger so long as their thrusts were shod with fun.

"Lookee here, cook," he called promptly to that individual; "you're the best eddicated bloke in this bunch o' long-horns—what's a questreen?"

"Somethin' you puts soup in," replied the cook.

Texas Pete scratched his head. "I thought all along that I didn't like her," he muttered, "an' now I knows it."

Diana Henders greeted her guests with a cheery smile and a word of welcome as they entered the dining room for breakfast. "I hope you slept well," she said.

"Oh, I did," exclaimed Lillian Manill. "I never knew a thing from the time my head touched the pillow until broad daylight this morning. I had a perfectly wonderful night."

"I didn't," said Corson, and Diana noticed then that he looked tired and haggard. "What happened last night?" he asked.

"Why, nothing, that I know of," replied Diana. "Why do you ask?"

"Have you seen any of your men this morning—or any of the neighbors?" he continued.

"I have seen a couple of the men to talk with—we have no neighbors."

"How many women are there on the place?" he went on.

"Just Lillian and I."

"Well, something terrible happened last night," said Corson. "I never spent such a hideous night in my life. It's funny you didn't hear it."

"Hear what?" asked Diana.

"That woman—my God! I can hear her screams yet."

"Oh, Maurice! what do you mean?" cried Miss Manill.

"It was about midnight," he explained. "I had been rather restless—just dozing a little—when all of a sudden the dogs commenced to bark and then a woman screamed—it was the most awful, long-drawn, agonized wail I ever heard—some one must have been torturing her. I'll bet the Indians were out last night and the first thing you know you'll hear about a terrible massacre. Well, it stopped all of a sudden and pretty soon the dogs commenced to yap again—there must have been fifty of 'em—and then that woman shrieked again—I'll hear that to my dying day. I don't think you ought to let any of the men go away today until you find out just what happened last night. The Indians may just be waiting for 'em to go and then they'll rush down on us and kill us all."

A faint smile had slowly curved Diana's lips and brought little wrinkles to the corners of her eyes.

"What you smiling about, Miss Henders?" demanded Corson. "If you'd have heard that woman you wouldn't feel like smiling—not for a long time."

"That wasn't a woman you heard, Mr. Corson—they were coyotes."

He looked at her blankly. "Are you sure?" he asked, presently.

"Of course I'm sure," she told him.

Corson breathed a sigh of relief. "I'd like to believe it," he said. "I'd sleep better tonight."

"Well, you can believe it, for that is what you heard."

"I'd hate to be caught out after dark by 'em," he said. "A pack of fifty or a hundred such as there was last night would tear a fellow to pieces in no time."

"They are perfectly harmless," Diana assured him, "and the chances are that there were no more than two or three of them—possibly only one."

"I guess I heard 'em," he insisted.

"They have a way of sounding like a whole lot more than they really are."

He shook his head. "I guess I know what I heard."

"I'll have to show that cook of yours how to make coffee," remarked Corson a few minutes later.

Diana flushed. "I suppose we don't get the best coffee out here," she said, "but we are accustomed to it and learn to like it first rate. I think Wong does the best he can with what he has to do with."

"Well, it won't hurt him any to learn how to make coffee," said Corson.

"He has been with us a great many years and is

very faithful. I think he would be terribly hurt if a stranger criticised his coffee," said Diana.

"Maurice is very particular about his food," said Miss Manill. "It is really an education to hear him order a dinner at Delmonico's, and the way he does flay the waiters if everything isn't just so. I always get such a thrill—you can see people at the nearby tables listening to him, and whispering to one another."

"I can imagine," said Diana, sweetly, but she did not say just what she could imagine.

Corson swelled visibly. "Call the Chink in, Miss Henders," he said, "and I'll give him a lesson now—you might learn something yourself. Way out here, so far from New York, you don't get much chance, of course. There's really nothing quite like the refining influences of the East to take the rough edges off of people."

"I think I prefer to speak to Wong privately and in person, if I find it necessary," said Diana.

"Well, just so I get some decent coffee hereafter," said Corson, magnanimously.

Lillian Manill, having finished her breakfast, rose from the table.

"I'm going to put on my riding habit now, Maurice," she said. "Go out and tell Mr. Colby to wait for me."

Diana Henders bit her lip, but said nothing as Corson rose and walked toward the door. He was garbed in a New York tailor's idea of the latest

English riding mode, and again Diana bit her lip, but not in anger. Corson, setting his hat jauntily over one eye, stalked into the open and down toward the corrals where the men were saddling up for the day's work.

He lighted a big, black cigar and puffed contentedly. As he hove in sight work in the corral ceased spontaneously.

"My Gawd!" moaned Texas Pete.

"Who left the bars down?" inquired Idaho.

"Shut up," cautioned Colby. "That feller's likely to be boss around here."

"He won't never boss me," said Shorty, "not with thet funny hat on. I wonder could I crease it," and he reached for his gun.

"Don't git funny, Shorty. They's friends o' Miss Henders," whispered Colby. "It'd only make her feel bad."

He could not have hit upon a stronger appeal to these men. Shorty lowered his hand from the butt of his gun and almost at once work was resumed. When Corson joined them he could not have guessed that he was the object either of ridicule or pity, though he was—of both.

"Say, Colby," he said. "Saddle up a couple of safe horses for Miss Manill and me, and wait around until she comes out. I want you to give her a few lessons in riding."

"Did Miss Henders say that it would be all right?" he asked. "You know the work is pretty well laid out an' we ain't got none too many hands."

"Oh, that's all right, my man," Corson assured him. "You'll be safe to do anything that I say. I'm handling Miss Manill's interests and looking after everything in general until the estate is closed. Just trot along and saddle up a couple of horses, and see to it that they're gentle. I haven't ridden for a number of years, although I was pretty good at it when I was a boy."

Hal Colby eyed Mr. Maurice B. Corson for a long minute. What was transpiring in his mind it would have been difficult to guess from the expression on his face; though what should have been going on within the convolutions of his brain the other men knew full well, and so they lolled around, their faces immobile, waiting for the fun to begin, but they were doomed to disappointment, for there was no gunplay—Colby, they thought, might have at least "made the dude dance." Instead he turned away without a word to Corson, gave some final directions for the day's work, swung into the saddle and rode toward the office, utterly ignoring the Easterner's instructions. Corson flushed angrily.

"Here you, one of you men," he snapped, turning toward the punchers, most of whom had already mounted their ponies, "I want two horses saddled immediately—one for Miss Manill and one for me."

Silently, ignoring him as completely as though he had not existed, the riders filed out of the corral past him. At a little distance they drew rein, waiting for Colby.

"I've saw gall before," remarked Texas Pete in an undertone, "but thet there dude tenderfoot's got more'n a brass monkey."

"If he don't c'ral thet jaw o' his pronto," growled Shorty, "I ain't a-goin' to be responsible fer what happens — I cain't hold myself much longer."

"I wouldn't a-took what Colby did," said Idaho.

"Some blokes'll take a lot to hold their jobs," said Shorty.

"They c'n hev mine right now," stated Texas Pete, "ef I gotta take thet dude's lip."

"Here comes the boss now," said Idaho. "She'll settle things, durn her pretty little hide," he added affectionately.

Diana had stopped just below the house to listen to Colby, whom the men could see was talking earnestly to her.

"Look here, Di," he was saying, "I want to know ef I gotta take orders from thet tin-horn lawyer feller. Is he boss round these diggin's, or is you?"

"Why, I supposed I was, Hal," she replied, "though I must admit that there appears to be a suspicion of doubt on the subject in Mr. Corson's mind. What has he said to you?"

Colby told her, repeating Corson's words as nearly as he could, and the girl could not suppress a laugh.

"Oh, I reckon it's funny, all right," he said, testily, "but I don't see the joke—hevin' a paper-collared cracker-fed dude like that-un callin' me 'my man' an' orderin' me to saddle up a hoss fer him, right in front o' all the boys. 'Trot along,' he says, 'an' saddle up a couple o' hosses, an' see to it thet they're plumb gentle.' My Gawd, Di! you don't expect me to take thet sort o' jaw, do you?"

Diana, by this time, was frankly in tears from laughter, and finally Colby himself was unable to longer repress a smile.

"Don't mind him, Hal," she said, finally. "He is just one of those arrogant, conceited, provincial New Yorkers. They are mighty narrow and disagreeable, but we've got to put up with him for a short time and we might as well make the best of it. Go and ask Willie to saddle up two horses for them, and be sure that the one for Miss Manill *is* plumb gentle." She accompanied her last instructions with the faintest trace of a wink.

Colby wheeled his pony and loped off to the corral, where he imparted the boss's orders to the chore boy, Willie, lank, raw-boned and pimply. Willie, who always thought of himself as Wild Bill, swaggered off to catch up the two ponies, grinning inwardly as he roped Gimlet for Mr. Maurice B. Corson.

Corson, seeing Diana approaching, had gone to meet her. He was still red and angry.

"Look here, Miss Henders," he exclaimed.

"You've got to tell these fellows who I am. I asked them to saddle up a couple of horses and they absolutely ignored me. You tell them that when I give orders they are to be obeyed."

"I think it will be less confusing if the orders come from me, Mr. Corson," she replied. "It is never well to have too many bosses, and then, you see, these men are peculiar. They are unlike the sort of men you have apparently been accustomed to dealing with. You cannot talk to them as you would to a Delmonico waiter—unless you are tired of life, Mr. Corson. They are accustomed to me—we are friends—and they will take orders from me without question, so I think that it will be better all around if you will explain your wants to me in the future. Colby told me what you wanted just now and the horses are being saddled."

He started to speak and then, evidently reconsidering, caught himself with a palpable effort. "Very well," he said, presently, "we'll let it pass this time."

Together they walked toward the corral where Willie was saddling a quiet, old horse for Miss Manill. Beside him stood Gimlet with drooping head and dejected mien.

"Which one is for me, sonny?" demanded Corson.

Wild Bill glanced up in sullen scorn, eyed Mr. Corson for a brief moment and then jerked a soiled thumb in the direction of Gimlet.

"What! that old crow-bait?" exclaimed the New Yorker.

"You said you wanted a gentle hoss," explained Colby, lolling in his saddle nearby, "an' Gimlet won't pitch."

"I don't want to ride a skate," growled Corson. "When I'm on a horse I want to know I'm on something."

"You'll know you're on Gimlet," Colby assured him, sweetly, "he ain't so dumb as he looks. Jest stick your spurs into him an' he'll act quite lively."

"All right," said Corson, glumly; "tell him to hurry—I see Miss Manill coming now."

There were others who saw her coming, too. Texas Pete was only one of them.

"By gollies!" he exclaimed. "Look what's got loose!"

Lillian Manill was approaching jauntily, clothed in a black riding habit, with a long, voluminous skirt, a man's collar and tie and black silk hat, with a flowing veil wound around it. Shorty eyed her for a long minute, then he let his gaze wander to Mr. Corson.

"It wouldn't never be safe fer me to go to New York," he confided to Idaho. "I'd shore laugh myself to death."

By the time Miss Manill joined the group the two horses were saddled and Willie had led them out of the corral.

"Mercy!" exclaimed Miss Manill. "Haven't

you a side-saddle? I could never ride one of those horrid things."

"I'm sorry," said Diana, "but we haven't one. I doubt if there is a side-saddle in the county. I think you can work it though, if you will put your leg around the horn. Next time I'll fix you up with a skirt like mine and then you can ride astride."

"Are you sure the horse is perfectly safe?" inquired Lillian. "I'll have to have a few lessons before I can ride one of those bouncing ones. Oh, Mr. Colby, good morning! Here I am all ready for my first lesson."

Her eyes took in the punchers grouped a few yards away. "I see you are going to have quite a class this morning. Mr. Pete told me, though, that you taught the cow-gentlemen in the afternoon."

Colby shot a quick glance at Pete, who had just been overcome by a violent fit of coughing, and knowing Texas Pete, as he did, grasped the situation at once.

"Oh, I had to give up the afternoon class," he told her, "after I found they was a few like *Mr.* Pete who wouldn't never larn to ride."

"Isn't that too bad," she said, politely. Then she turned toward Corson. "I think you'd better try it first, Maurice. I'll watch how you do it."

"All right," said he. "It's been a long time since I have ridden, but I guess it'll come back to me quick enough. I might be able to give you a few pointers at that."

He walked up to Gimlet's off side and took hold of the saddlehorn, neglecting the reins, which Willie still held. Gimlet eyed him sadly. When he essayed to place a foot in the stirrup the pony sidestepped rapidly in the opposite direction.

"You'd better mount from the other side, Mr. Corson," advised Diana. "These horses arc not broken to work with from the off side."

"I knew all along he was a damn Injun," remarked Idaho.

"An' you better take the reins, you may need 'em," supplemented Willie, who, at bottom, had a kind heart and shrank from bloodshed.

Corson walked to the near side of Gimlet, gathered the reins loosely in his right hand, stuck a foot into the stirrup, took hold of the horn with both hands and pulled himself laboriously into the saddle. Gimlet stood quietly.

"Giddap!" said Mr. Corson, but Gimlet moved not.

"Throw the hooks into him!" shouted Willie, gleefully.

"Why don't the old skate go?" demanded Corson, shaking the reins.

"Use your spurs!" called one of the cowboys. "That's what you bought 'em fer, ain't it?"

Mr. Corson used his spurs. The result was electrical, galvanizing Gimlet into instant and surprising action—action which glowingly elucidated the derivation of his name. He wheeled dizzily round and round upon the same spot, and with lightning rapidity.

Mr. Corson's funny hat flew off. He clawed at the horn in intervals that he was not clawing at the loose reins in a mad effort to gather them. Then Gimlet bolted. He ran for some hundred yards, stopped and commenced wheeling again. Mr. Corson lost a stirrup. Then he let go both reins and seized the horn with two hands.

"Stop him!" he yelled. "Stop him! Whoa! Whoa!"

"Rip him open!" shrieked Willie. "Spur him in the eyes!"

"Ride him, cowboy!" yelled Idaho.

Again Gimlet bolted and this time Mr. Corson commenced to slip dangerously to one side. A hundred-yard sprint back to where he had started and Gimlet paused to wheel once more. It was the end. Mr. Corson spun off, alighting on his back. He rolled over with surprising agility and on hands and knees crawled rapidly away from this man eater that he was sure was pursuing him. But Gimlet was only standing dejectedly, with drooping ears.

Corson came to his feet. The men about him—rough fellows with none of the finer sensibilities of New Yorkers—were laughing rudely.

"It was a put-up job," he spluttered. "It was a put-up job. You'll suffer for this, Colby! You told me that animal was gentle."

"I told you he wouldn't pitch, mister!" snapped Colby. "An' he didn't pitch."

Miss Manill had started back toward the house. "I think I'll not ride this morning," she said.

CHAPTER XII

CORSON SPEAKS

"'COME here!' he yells then to the rest o' us boys,
'Step up to the fun'ral an' don't make no noise
The while we inter all the barb-wire what's here,
After which we'll dispose o' the seegars an' beer.'"

sang Texas Pete. "Hello! See whose came!"

Bull entered the bunk-house with a grin and a nod. "Still singin' I see, Pete," he said. "Ain't you finished thet one yit?"

Two weeks had slipped by since the arrival of Corson and Miss Manill. Bull had just been relieved from duty as bullion guard and was only now returning to the home ranch. In the weeks that he had brought the gold down from the mine there had been no holdup—The Black Coyote or Gregorio had not once been seen.

"How's everything?" asked Bull.

"So-so," replied Texas Pete.

"Where's Colby? I gotta report to him."

"Up at the house—he eats there now."

Bull made no comment. He thought he understood why Hal Colby ate at the house. One day soon, doubtless, he would sleep there, too, as master.

"This Manill heifer got stuck on him an' insists

on his eatin' there," explained Pete. "Things ain't ben the same since them two shorthorns hit the diggin's. The boss she looks tired and worried all the time an' sadlike. I reckon she ain't got no more use fer 'em then the rest o' us."

"Is Colby gone on this Manill girl?" asked Bull.

"I dunno. Sometimes I reckons he is an' sometimes I reckons he ain't. Looks like as if he wern't quite sure which side his bread was buttered on an' he's waitin' to find out."

Bull busied himself arranging his blankets on his old bunk, working in silence. Texas Pete eyed him surreptitiously. There was a troubled look in Pete's eyes. Presently he coughed nervously. The two men were alone in the bunk-house.

"Say, Bull," Pete finally broke the silence, "you an' me's ben good pals."

Bull looked up from the work of folding his tarpaulin. "Who said we ain't?" he inquired.

"Nobody ain't said we ain't," Pete assured him.

"Then what's eatin' you?"

"It's only just what everybody's sayin', Bull," said Pete. "I thort you'd orter know about it."

"What?"

"Thet you an' The Black Coyote air the same feller. Not thet it makes any difference with me. I ain't askin' whether you air or whether you ain't. I'm just a-tellin' you fer your own good."

Bull smiled one of his slow smiles. "If I wasn't I'd say so, wouldn't I?" he asked.

"I reckon you would."

"An' if I was I'd say I wasn't, wouldn't I?"

"I reckon you would," assented Pete.

"Then what the hell's the use o' sayin' anything?" he demanded. "And 'specially when I don't give a damn what they think."

Pete shook his head. "I dunno," he said.

Bull started for the doorway. "I'm goin' up to the house to report to Colby," he said.

"Look out thet Manill heifer don't git her grubhooks on you," cautioned Pete.

In the office he found Diana Henders writing a letter. She looked up with a little start as she heard his voice.

"Oh, Bull!" she cried, "I'm so glad you're back."

"Thanks, Miss. I come up to report to Colby, but I see he ain't here."

"He's in the living-room with Mr. Corson and Miss Manill," she told him.

"I reckon I'll see him later then." He started to leave.

"Don't go, Bull," she said. "I want to talk with you. Please sit down."

He walked toward her and lowered himself into the big easy chair that had been her father's. His movements were like those of a lion—silent, powerful and yet without stealth.

For the first time in weeks the sense of loneliness that had constantly oppressed her vanished. Bull was back! It was as if a big brother had come home after a long absence—that was why she was so glad to see him. Her heart forgot the thing that her reason had been practically convinced of—that Bull was the bandit of Hell's Bend—that it was Bull who had been robbing her father and her for months—that it was Bull who had shot Mack Harber.

She only knew that she felt relief and safety when Bull was near. Nearly everyone feared him—many hated him. Could they all be wrong? Could she alone be right in believing in him?—as her heart did against the wise counseling of reason.

"Yes, Miss?" he said, interrogatively.

"The Wainrights are trying to buy the ranch again, Bull," she said, "and Mr. Corson seems to favor the idea."

"Do you want to sell?" he asked.

"No, I do not; but the worst of it is the price they want to accept—two hundred and fifty thousand dollars for all our holding—ranch, cattle and mine. They are bringing all kinds of pressure to bear on me. Mr. Corson says I must either buy them out or agree to the sale. I haven't the cash to buy them out and they won't take my notes."

"Don't sell, Miss, at that price, an' don't sell at all if you don't want to—they can't force you to sell."

"But they make it so unpleasant for me, and

Mr. Corson is always telling me that the bottom has fallen out of the live stock business and that the new vein in the mine doesn't exist."

"The live stock business is all right, Miss. It wasn't never better, an' as fer the new vein that's all right too. I was scratchin' around a little bit myself while I was up there these past six weeks. The gold's there all right. The trouble is you ain't got the right man up there—that new superintendent looks to me like a sharper. Did you know the Wainrights was up there often?"

"No! really?"

"Yes, an' that superintendent is thick as thieves with 'em."

"He has no business to permit them on the property."

"He does though," said Bull, "but he raised thunder when he found I'd been snootin' around the workings. I don't like that hombre, Miss."

"Everybody seems to be against me, Bull, and it's so hard to know what to do, now that Dad's gone. Mr. Corson and my cousin are nagging at me all the time to agree to sell. Sometimes I am almost determined to just to get rid of them."

"If you want to git rid o' them, Miss, that's easy," said Bull. "All you gotta do is say so an' I'll run 'em off the ranch an' outta the county. I wouldn't like nothin' better."

"I thought you had taken quite a fancy to my cousin, coming in on the stage," said Diana.

"The only rope she could ever have on me, Miss, is that she's your cousin," replied Bull, and she knew that he meant it. "If you want me to run 'em out of the country, say the word, an' I'll start 'em in ten minutes—an' keep 'em on the jump, too."

"I'm afraid that wouldn't do, Bull," she said, smiling.

"I don't see why not," he replied.

Just then, Hal Colby entered the room. He nodded to Bull.

"You back?"

Bull took no notice of a question so obviously foolish.

"How long you ben back?" continued Colby.

"'Bout half an hour."

"Why didn't you report?" Colby was vexed. The easy familiarity of Bull's attitude, stretched comfortably as he was in Mr. Henders' chair, and in pleasant converse with Diana, galled him.

"Ain't you got eyes?" inquired Bull. "Cain't you see me sittin' here reportin' to my boss?"

"You're supposed to report to me," snapped Colby.

"I'm apt to do lots of things I ain't supposed to do," Bull told him, softly.

"I reckon most everybody knows that, too," said Colby, meaningly.

"Come!" cried Diana. "Don't you boys quarrel—I have troubles enough now. Bull was looking for you, to report, when he came up here," she told Colby. "He asked for you."

"Why didn't he say so, then? I got some work for him an' I ben expectin' him all day."

"Well, I'm here," said Bull. "What do you want me to do?" His voice, unlike Colby's, carried no trace of anger, if he felt any.

"Cramer wants off a few days an' I want you to go over to the West Ranch an' look after the hosses 'til he comes back. They's some colts over there that needs to be rid—Cramer'll tell you all they is to do."

"When do you want me to go?"

"Tonight—that'll give Cramer a chance to git an early start in the mornin'."

"All right," said Bull, rising. "Good night, Miss."

"Good night, Bull. I may ride over while you're at the West Ranch. I've been intending to look the place over for a month or more. Cramer said we needed some new corrals."

He nodded and left the room.

"I don't see how you kin be decent to a feller what's ben robbin' you an' your dad fer months," said Colby, after Bull had left. "'Er mebby you don't believe it even now?"

"I know it looks suspicious, Hal; but it's so hard to believe it of Bull. I hate to believe it. I almost don't believe it. You are hard on him because you don't like him."

"Didn't I tell you he was one of my best friends —you know that—till I got wise to his game. I ain't a-wantin' no rattle snake like thet as no friend o' mine."

Diana sighed and rose wearily from her chair. "I'm going up to wash for supper," she said.

She had been gone but a moment when Corson entered the office.

"Well," he asked, "has she changed her mind?"

"I didn't say nothing about the matter to her," replied Colby. "It wouldn't have done no good after what I hearn Bull a-tellin' her just afore I come in the room."

"What was that?" demanded Corson.

"He was a-tellin' her not to sell, an' furthermore he offers to run you an' Miss Manill outta the country if she gives the word."

"What did she say to that?" Corson's voice showed indications of nervousness.

"Oh, she wouldn't stand fer that, o' course; but he's a dangerous feller to have around her. He's got too damn much influence over her."

"I wish we could get rid of him," said Corson. "It seems funny that he isn't arrested, when everyone knows he's The Black Coyote."

"He'll run his neck into a noose one o' these days," replied Colby.

"But in the meantime he may spoil this deal with Wainright," said Corson, "and I've got my heart set on that. I want to get out of this damned country. It gives me the willies. Too many Indians, and coyotes, and irresponsible kids with fire arms—it isn't safe."

"I don't see why you are so anxious to sell now," said Colby. "You can get more if you half try."

"That would mean going back to New York. There isn't any capital out here. Wainright is a find, pure and simple. I can't chance taking the time to arrange a deal back East—I don't know what Miss Henders would be up to out here. What Miss Manill wants to do is get some ready money out of it quick and get out. I guess there's only one thing to do and that's to spring my last card on the girl. I'd rather have done it an easier way, but she's so damn stubborn she's forcing me to it."

"To what?" asked Colby.

Corson leaned close to him and whispered for several minutes into his ear.

When he was through Colby leaned back in his chair and whistled. "You don't mean it!" he exclaimed.

"Wainright is coming over to Hendersville on the stage tomorrow and I want to get this matter settled with the Henders girl so that I can have something definite to say to him. I think she's coming around all right now that she is commencing to realize that the mine's about played out and that the cattle business isn't much better. Of course it don't make much difference what she thinks about it except that she could make it mighty unpleasant around here if she wanted to."

"She shore could make it unpleasant fer you and Wainright ef she wanted to," agreed Colby, "an don't fool yourself that she thinks the business ain't worth nothin'. Ef you had her thinkin' so today, Bull's give her something new to think about since he was here."

"Hows that?" demanded Corson.

"I hearn him tellin' her he'd ben diggin' 'round in the mine while he was up there an' that he knows the new vein's rich as all get-out, an' he told her the cattle business was all right, too. I reckon she'll believe him afore she will you."

Corson bit his lip. "That settles it!" he exclaimed. "I've fooled around long enough. I'm going to tell her tonight."

Outside the bunk-house some of the men were washing for supper. Inside, Bull was rolling and roping his bed preparatory to moving to the West Ranch after the evening meal.

"What yuh doin'?" demanded Texas Pete. "Yuh ain't quit?"

"Goin' over to the West Ranch—Cramer's gettin' off fer a spell," explained Bull.

"Looks like they weren't crazy fer your company here," remarked Pete.

Bull shrugged his shoulders and went on with the business of half-hitches, to the final knot, after which he tossed the bed-roll onto his bunk.

"I shouldn't think you'd stay on, Bull," said Texas Pete. "Let's pull our freight. I ain't never ben to Calyforny—hev you?"

The ex-foreman shook his head. "I got my own reasons fer stayin' on a spell yet, Pete," he said.

Pete said nothing more on the subject. Bull's answer to his suggestion that they leave the country troubled him, however. It was not Diana Henders who was keeping Bull, of that Pete was certain, because Hal Colby had long since as much as admitted that he, Colby, was engaged to marry the dainty boss.

It wasn't because of any love he had for the job, either—Texas Pete knew that—for Colby had never made Bull's job any too easy since the former had become foreman, and Bull was not staying because he loved Colby. It was true that he never spoke a derogatory word concerning him, nor once had he criticized his methods as foreman, but Texas Pete knew as well as though Bull had told him that the latter had no use for the foreman.

What was it, then, that was keeping Bull? Texas Pete's loyalty to his friend made it difficult for him to harbor the only answer that his knowledge of events permitted him to entertain; but that answer to the question persisted in obtruding itself upon his consciousness.

If Bull was, after all, The Black Coyote he could not work to better advantage as a bandit than while in the employ of the Bar Y outfit, where he could easily obtain first-hand knowledge of every important bullion shipment.

"By gollies!" soliloquized Texas Pete, "I don't give a durn ef he be, but I'll be durned ef I believe it yit!"

At the house Hal Colby was talking earnestly to Lillian Manill in the sitting room. Supper had not yet been served, Corson had gone to his room to clean up and Diana had not yet come down.

"Look here, Lill," Colby was saying. "I don't like the way Corson's treatin' Di. I think a heap o' thet little girl an' I don't want to see her git the worst of it."

Lillian Manill reached up and encircled his neck with her arms. "I thought you were all over that, Hal," she said. "You've been telling me how much you love me, but how do you expect me to believe it if you're always thinking of her and not ever considering my interests. You want her to have all the property and you don't want me to have any. You don't love me!"

"Yes, I do, Lill—I'm crazy about you," he insisted.

"Then act like it," she advised him, "and quit siding with her all the time. I'm going to be a rich girl, Hal, and we can have a mighty good time after we're married, if you don't go and make a fool of yourself and try to keep me out of what rightly belongs to me."

"I ain't always so durned sure you're goin' to

marry me," he said gloomily. "You've ben pretty thick with thet feller Corson, an' he's sweet on you —enny fool c'd tell thet."

"Oh, pshaw!" exclaimed Lillian Manill, laughing lightly; "why, old Maurice is only like a big brother to me. Now give me a kiss and tell me that you won't let Diana or anyone else steal all our money." She drew his face down to hers and their lips met in a long kiss.

When they separated Colby was panting heavily. "Gawd!" he exclaimed huskily. "I'd commit murder fer you."

In the shadows of the hall stood Maurice B. Corson, scowling darkly upon them through the partially opened door-way. Presently he coughed discreetly and a moment later entered the room, where he found Lillian idly turning sheets of music at the piano, while Colby was industriously studying a picture that hung against the wall.

Corson accosted them with a pleasant word and a jovial smile, and a minute later Diana Henders entered the room and the four went in to supper. The meal, like its predecessors for some weeks, was marked by noticeable constraint. The bulk of the conversation revolved about the weather, about the only thing that these four seemed to have in common that might be openly discussed, and as Arizona summer weather does not offer a wide field for discussion the meals were not conspicuous for the conversational heights attained. Nor was this one any exception to the rule. When it was nearly over Corson cleared his throat as is the habit of many when about to open an unpleasant subject after long deliberation.

"Miss Henders," he commenced.

Hal Colby arose. "I gotta see Bull before he leaves," he announced hastily, and left the room.

Corson started again. "Miss Henders," he repeated, "I have a painful duty to perform. I have tried to work in harmony with you, but I have never met with any cooperation on your part, and so I am forced to reveal a fact that we might successfully have gotten around had you been willing to abide by my judgment in the matter of the sale of the property."

"And what fact is that?" asked Diana, politely.

"We will get to it presently," he told her. "Now, my dear young lady, your father's death has left you in very unfortunate circumstances, but, of course, as is natural, Miss Manill wants to do what she can for you."

"I am afraid that I do not understand," said Diana. "Lillian and I have suffered equally in the loss of our fathers and our uncles, and together we have inherited the responsibilities of a rather large and sometimes cumbersome business. I am sure that we wish to help one another as much as possible—I as much as she."

"I am afraid that you do not understand, Miss Henders," said Corson, solemnly. "By the terms of your uncle's will everything would have gone to your father had he survived Mr. Manill, but he did not. Your father made a similar will, leaving everything to your uncle. So you see, Miss Henders!" Corson spread his palms and raised his brows in a gesture of helplessness.

"I must be very dense," said Diana, "for I am sure I do not know even yet what you are driving at, Mr. Corson."

"It is just this," he explained; "your father left everything to your uncle—your uncle left everything to his daughter. It is very sad, Miss Henders—Miss Manill has grieved over it a great deal; but the law is clear—it leaves you penniless."

"But it is not what was intended and there must be another will," exclaimed Diana. "Uncle John and Dad both wished that, when they were gone, the estate should be divided equally between their lawful heirs—half and half. Dad left such a will and it was his understanding that Uncle John had done likewise—and I know he must have for he was the soul of honor. Their wills were identical—Dad has told me so more than once. They had such implicit confidence in one another that each left everything to the other with the distinct understanding that eventually it all was to go to the heirs of both, as I have explained."

"I do not doubt that your father left such a will, if you say he did; but the fact remains that Mr. Manill did not," said Mr. Corson, emphatically.

"But you shall not want, Miss Henders. Your cousin will see to that. She has already authorized me to arrange for an annuity that will keep you from want until you are married—we thought best not to continue it beyond that time for obvious reasons."

"You mean," asked Diana, dully, "that I have nothing? That I am a pauper—that even this roof under which I have lived nearly all my life does not belong, even in part, to me—that I have no right here?"

"Oh, please, don't say that, dear!" exclaimed Lillian Manill. "You shall stay here just as long as you wish. You will always be welcome in my home."

"*My home!*" Diana suppressed a sob that was partially grief and partially rage. The injustice of it! To take advantage of a technicality to rob her of all that rightly belonged to her. She was glad though that they had come out into the open at last—why had they not done so before?

"Of course," said Corson, "as Miss Manill says, you are welcome to remain here as long as the property is in her hands, but, as you know, we have received an advantageous offer for it and so it is only fair to tell you that you might as well make your plans accordingly."

"You are going to sell to Wainright for two hundred and fifty thousand?" asked Diana.

Corson nodded. Diana rose and walked the

length of the room, then she turned and faced them. "No, you are not going to sell, Mr. Corson, if there is any way in which I can prevent it. You are not going to steal my property so easily. Why have you been attempting all these weeks to persuade me to agree to a sale if you knew all along that I had no interest whatsoever in the property?" she demanded suddenly.

"That was solely due to a desire on our part to make it as easy as possible for you," he explained, suavely. "Your cousin would have given you half the purchase price rather than have had to tell you the truth, Miss Henders; but you have forced it upon us. She desires to sell. It is her property. You alone stood in the way. You have been your own worst enemy, Miss Henders. You might have had one hundred and twenty-five thousand dollars had you not been stubborn—now you must be content with whatever Miss Manill sees fit to allow you in the way of an annuity."

Diana squared her shoulders as she faced them. "Miss Manill shall give me nothing—I will not accept as a gratuity what rightfully belongs to me. If you think, Mr. Corson, that you are going to take my property away from me without a fight, you are mistaken," and she wheeled about and started for the doorway.

"Wait a moment, Miss Henders!" cried the New Yorker. "I am a lawyer and I know how expensive litigation is. Such a case as you contemplate, and I take it for granted that you purpose taking the matter to court when you say 'fight,' might drag on for years, wasting the entire property in attorneys' fees and legal expense, so that neither of you would get anything—I have seen such things happen scores of times.

"Now, let us rather compromise. We were willing to make you a gift of half the purchase price immediately on the consummation of the sale to Mr. Wainright. That offer is still open. It is extremely fair and generous and if you will take my advice you will accept it."

"Never!" snapped Diana.

Corson and Lillian sat in silence listening to Diana's foot-falls as she ascended the stairs. Presently they heard her door close, then the girl turned upon Corson. "You poor sucker, you!" she exclaimed. "What do you think you are, offering her a hundred and twenty-five thousand when we don't have to give her a cent!"

"Don't be a hog, Lill," advised the man. "We'll get enough, and if we can save a lot of trouble we'd better let her have the hundred and twenty-five. You can't tell what these people out here'll do.

"Take that Bull fellow, for instance—he's already offered to run us out of the country if she says to. Look what he did to old man Wainright, for instance. Why, say, there are a lot of her friends here that would think no more of shooting us full of holes than they would of eating their

Sunday dinners, if she just so much as hinted that she thought we were trying to do her out of anything.

"And we'll be getting plenty, anyway—you and I each get a third and Wainright gets the other third—and that mine alone is worth millions. Why, we could afford to give her the whole two hundred and fifty thousand dollars if she'd agree to the sale."

"I'm not so keen as you on giving my money away," replied Lillian.

"Your money, hell," he replied. "You wouldn't have anything if it wasn't for me, and as for that measly little hundred and twenty-five thousand, why, it'll cost us all of that to square these people around here before we get through with it—I've promised Colby ten thousand already, and say, speaking of Colby, I saw you two in the sitting room before supper. You got to lay off that business—you're getting too thick with that fellow to suit me. You belong to me," he added suddenly and fiercely.

"Oh, come on, Maurice, don't be silly," replied Lillian. "You told me to get him on our side. How did you suppose I was going to do it—by making faces at him?"

"Well, you don't have to go too far. I heard you telling him what you two would do after you were married. You may be a good little actress, Lill, but that kiss you gave him looked too damn realistic to suit me. I'm not going to have you running off with him after you get your mitts on a little money."

"Say, you don't think I'd marry that rube, do you?" and Lillian Manill burst into peals of laughter.

Colby found Bull in the bunk-house.

"Bull," he said, "I wish you'd ride up Belter's tomorrer an' see how the water's holdin' out."

"Listen, Bull," said Texas Pete, "I got the rest of it:

"An' so we lines up at the bar, twelve or more;
The boss tries to smile, but he caint, he's so sore.
The stranger says: 'Pronto! you durn little runt.'
Jest then we hears some one come in at the front,

"An' turnin' to look we see there in the door
A thin little woman — my gosh, she was pore! —
Who lets her eyes range til they rest on this bloke
With funny ideas about what was a joke.

"She walks right acrost an' takes holt o' his ear.
'You orn'ry old buzzard,' she says, 'you come here!'
He give us a smile thet was knock-kneed an' lame,
An', 'Yes, dear, I'm comin'!' he says, an' he came."

CHAPTER XIII

THE NECKTIE PARTY

WHEN Diana Henders left the dining room after hearing Corson's explanation of her status as an heir to the estate of her father and uncle she definitely severed relations with the two whom she now firmly believed had entered into a conspiracy to rob her of her all. The following day she ate her meals in the kitchen with Wong to whom she confided her troubles. The old Chinaman listened intently until she was through, then he arose and crossed the kitchen to a cupboard, a crafty smile playing over his wrinkled, yellow countenance.

"Me fixee—me no likum," he said, as he returned with a phial of white powder in his hand.

"O, Wong! No! No!" cried the girl, grasping instantly the faithful servitor's intent. "You mustn't do anything so horrible as that. Promise me that you won't."

"All lightee—jest samee you say," he replied with a shrug, and returned the phial to the cupboard.

"I'm going away tonight, Wong," she told him, "and I want you to promise me that nothing like that will happen while I am away and that you will stay until I return. There is no one else I could trust to look after the house."

"You clomee backee?"

"Yes, Wong, I'm going to Hendersville tonight so that I can catch the stage for Aldea in the morning. I am going to take the train for Kansas City and consult some of Dad's friends and get them to recommend a good lawyer. You'll take care of things for me, Wong?"

"You bletee blootee!"

That afternoon she sent for Hal Colby and told him what Corson had said to her. Colby seemed ill at ease and embarrassed.

"I'm mighty sorry, Di," he said, "but I don't see what you kin do about it. If I was you I'd accept half the purchase price. They got you dead-to-rights an' you won't make no money fightin' 'em."

"Well, I won't accept it, and I'm surprised that you'd advise me to."

"It's only fer your own good, Di," he assured her. "It ain't Lillian's fault that your uncle done your dad outen the property. You cain't blame her fer wantin' what was left to her an' I think it was mighty pretty of her to offer to split with you."

"I don't," she replied, "and I think there is something behind that offer that is not apparent on the face of it. I am going to find out, too. I'm going to Kansas City to hire a lawyer and I'll want the buck-board and one of the men to drive me to town after supper tonight."

"I'm plumb sorry, Di, but Corson an' Lillian have took the buck-board to town already."

"Then I'll go on Captain," she said. "Please have him saddled for me right after supper."

She packed her traveling dress and other necessary articles in a small bag that could be tied to a saddle, leaving on her buckskin skirt and blouse for the ride to town, and after supper made her way to the corral after waiting a few minutes for Captain to be brought to the house and rather wondering why Hal had neglected to do so.

To her surprise she discovered that Captain had not even been saddled, and was, as a matter of fact, still running in the pasture a mile from the house. She went to the bunk-house to get one of the men to catch him up, but found it deserted. From there she walked to the cook-house, where she found only the cook setting bread for the morrow.

"Where are all the men?" she asked.

"They's a dance to Johnson's tonight an' some of 'em went there," he told her. "The rest went to town. Idaho, Shorty an' Pete went to the dance."

"Where's Hal?"

"I reckon he went to town—I ain't seen him since this arternoon some time."

"Did Willie go too?"

"No'm, he's here sommers—hey, Willie! You Willie!"

Willie appeared from the outer dusk. "Oh, Willie," said Diana, "won't you please catch Captain up for me and saddle him?"

"You ain't goin' to ride tonight all alone, be you?" he asked.

"I've got to get to town, Willie, and Hal forgot to tell anyone to ride with me," she explained.

"Well, I'll go along with you," said Willie. "I'll have the hosses saddled pronto," and off he ran.

Ten minutes later they were in the saddle and loping away through the rapidly falling night toward town.

"I can't understand how Hal happened to let all the boys go at the same time," she said, half musingly. "It was never done before and it isn't safe."

"Bull wouldn't never have done it," said Willie. "Bull was a top-notch foreman."

"You like Bull?" she asked.

"You bet I do," declared Willie, emphatically; "don't you?"

"I like all the boys," she replied.

"Bull wouldn't never have left you here alone at night. He set a heap o' store by you, Miss." Willie was emboldened to speak freely because of the darkness that would cover any sudden embarrassment he might feel if he went too far. The same darkness covered Diana's flush—a flush of contrition that she harbored a belief in Bull's villainy.

Before they entered Hendersville they became

aware that something unusual was going on in town. They could hear the hum of excited voices above which rose an occasional shout, and as they rode into the single street they saw a hundred figures surging to and fro before Gum's Place. A man stood on the veranda of the saloon haranguing the crowd.

"This business has gone fer enough," he was saying as Diana and Willie paused at the outskirts of the crowd. "It's high time we put a end to it. You all knows whose 'a' doin' it as well as I do. What we orter do is ride out 'n git him tonight—they's a bunch o' cottonwoods where he is right handy an' we got plenty o' ropes in the cow-country. Whose with me?"

Two score voices yelled in savage assurance of their owners' hearty cooperation.

"Then git your bronchs," cried the speaker, "an' we'll go after him an' git him!"

Diana saw that the orator was Hal Colby. She turned to one of the men who was remaining as the majority of the others hastened after their ponies.

"What is it all about?" she asked. "What has happened?"

The man looked up at her, and as he recognized her, pulled off his hat awkwardly. "Oh, it's you, Miss Henders! Well, you see, the stage was held up ag'in today an' Mack Harber was kilt—it was his first trip since he was wounded that time. It was the first trip, too, since Bull quit guardin' the gold, an' a lot o' the fellers has got it in their heads thet it's Bull as done it."

"'Tain't no sech thing!" cried a little old man, near-by, "'tain't Bull."

The speaker was Wildcat Bob. "I don't like to think so neither," said the first man; "but it shore looks bad fer him—the fellers is all het up. There ain't one in thet crowd but what would lynch his gran-maw ef he had another drink, an' they sure hev had plenty—Gum's ben settin' 'em up in there fer a coupla hours on the house. Never did see Gum so plumb liberal."

"He's aimin' to get someone else to go after The Black Coyote," said Wildcat Bob, "or he wouldn't be so doggone liberal with his rot-gut—he couldn't git up enough nerve ef he drunk a whole distillery."

"You think they really intend to lynch Bull?" asked the girl.

"They ain't no two ways about it, Miss," said the man she had first accosted. "They're aimin' to do it an' I reckon they will. You see they're pretty sore. Mack tried to put up a little fight an' this Black Coyote feller bored him plumb between the eyes. Then he takes the gold, cuts all the hosses loose from the stage an' vamooses. Thet's why we didn't hear of it 'til just a bit ago, cause they didn't have no way to git to town only hoofin' it."

Already the avenging mob was gathering. They came whooping, reeling in their saddles. Not one of them, sober, would have gone out after the ex-foreman of the Bar Y, but, drunk, they forgot their fear of him, and Diana knew that they would carry out their purpose.

They were going to lynch Bull! It seemed incredible, and yet, could she blame them? Knowing him as she did she had herself half admitted the truth of the rumor of his guilt before this, the latest outrage, that seemed to fix the responsibility beyond peradventure of a doubt. For the six weeks that Bull had guarded the bullion there had been no holdup, and now on the very first stage day after he had been relieved the depredations had been renewed.

She recalled the fact that he had been seen with Gregorio on the very afternoon of a previous hold-up; she recalled the blood upon his shirt that same day—the day that Mary Donovan had fired upon the bandits; she thought of the bag of gold dust that he had displayed at the bunk-house. There seemed no possible avenue of escape from a belief in his guilt.

The yelling avengers were milling around in a circle in front of Gum's Place, firing off their guns, cursing, shouting. The sheriff appeared on the veranda and raised his hand for silence.

"Ah'm sheriff yere," he said, "an as an ahm of the law Ah cain't permit yo-all to go fer to lynch nobody, but Ah can an' do invite yo-all in to hev a drink on the house befo' yo go."

There was a wild shout of approval and a

scramble for room at the tie rail. Those who lost out rode their ponies into the saloon, and as the last of them disappeared, Diana, who had lost sight of Willie in the jostle and excitement of the past few minutes, turned her pony about and rode back in the direction from which she had come.

Just beyond the last house she turned abruptly to the left—the Bar Y ranch lay to the right—urged Captain into a lope and started off through the darkness toward the west. Presently she struck a well-defined trail and then with a word and a touch of her spurs she sent Captain into a run. Swiftly the wiry animal sprang through the night while the beating of his mistress' heart kept time to the rapid fall of his unshod hoofs.

What was she doing? Was she mad? A dozen times Diana Henders repeated those questions to herself, but the only answer was a monotonous cadence that beat upon her brain, reasonless, to the accompaniment of Captain's flying hoofs:

They shall not kill him! They shall not kill him! They shall not kill him!

Constantly she listened for sounds of the coming of the lynching party, though she knew that she had sufficient start to outdistance them completely, even had Captain not been the fleet and powerful runner that he was. It was ten miles to the West Ranch from Hendersville and the Captain made it in thirty minutes that night.

Diana threw herself from the saddle at the gate

and crawled through the bars, leaving Captain on wide stretched feet and with nose to ground blowing after his hard run, knowing that he would not move from the spot for some time. She hastened to the darkened cabin and pounded on the door.

"Bull!" she cried. "Bull!" but there was no answer. Then she opened the door and entered, fumbling around for a table she found it and matches, striking one. The cabin, a one room affair, was empty. Her ride for nothing! Bull was away, but they would hide in the brush and wait for him to come back and then they would shoot him down in cold blood, and he would never have a chance for his life. If she only knew where he had gone, she might ride out and meet him; but she did not know.

Wait! There was one chance! If he was The Black Coyote he would doubtless come in from the north or the northeast, for in the latter direction lay Hell's Bend, the scene of his many holdups.

But it wasn't Bull—it couldn't be Bull—Bull, of all the men in the world, could never have robbed her, or killed her messenger.

Slowly she returned to Captain, standing with heaving sides and dilated nostrils. The animal staggered a bit as she mounted, but at a touch of the rein he turned and walked out into the sage brush toward the north. She rode for a quarter of a mile and then she reined in her mount and called the man's name aloud.

There was no reply and she turned to the east and rode in that direction for a while, now and then calling "Bull!" her voice sounding strange and uncanny in her own ears. In the distance a coyote yapped and wailed.

She turned and rode west to a point beyond the cabin and then back again, establishing a beat where she might hope to intercept the returning Bull before he reached the danger of the ambush. At intervals she called his name aloud, and presently she halted frequently to listen for the coming of the lynchers.

It was a matchless Arizona night. The myriad stars blazing in the blue-black vault of infinite space cast their radiance softly upon vale and height, relieving the darkness with a gentle luminosity that rendered distant objects discernible in mass, if not in form, and because of it Diana saw the black bulk of the approaching horsemen while they were yet a considerable distance away, and, seeing them, dared not call Bull's name aloud again.

The mob rode silently now—a grim and terrible shadow creeping through the darkness to lay bloody hands upon its prey. A quarter of a mile from the cabin it halted while its members dismounted and, leaving a few to hold the horses, the balance crept stealthily forward on foot.

Diana, too, had dismounted, knowing that she would be less conspicuous thus, and was leading Captain over a circuitous trail toward the north and east. The girl knelt and placed an ear to the ground.

Faintly, as though at a great distance, she heard the rhythmic pounding of a horse's hoofs. He was coming—loping through the night, Bull was coming—all unconscious of what awaited him there in the darkness. He was riding to his death. She hastened forward a short distance and listened again. If the sounds should be plainer now she would be sure that he was coming from the north-east.

The self-appointed posse crept toward the cabin and according to a general plan imparted to them by Colby, separated into two sections and surrounded it, finally worming their way close in on hands and knees, taking advantage of the cover of the sage to shield them from the sight of the man they believed to be there, then Colby arose and walked boldly to the door. Knocking, he called Bull's name aloud. There was no response.

"Hey, Bull!" cried Colby again, in a friendly voice, "it's Hal." Still no reply. Colby pushed the door open and entered. Of all the motley crew that followed him he alone had the courage to do the thing he was doing now. He struck a match and lighted a candle that stood on the rude table, embedded in its own grease in the cover of a baking powder can.

A brief survey of the interior showed him that it was untenanted. He extinguished the light and returned to his party where word was passed around that they were to remain quietly in hiding where they were until the quarry came.

In the meantime a lone horseman had thrown himself from a half-spent pony in the Bar Y ranch yard and seeing a light in the cook-house had burst in upon the astonished cook. "What in all tarnation's the matter of ye, Wildcat Bob?" he demanded.

"Where's Bull?" asked the little old man.

"Reckon he's over at the West Ranch—leastways there's were he's supposed to be, why?"

"Warn't they a gang o' the boys jest here lookin' for him?"

"No."

A burst of lurid profanity filled the room as Wildcat Bob explained just how he felt and what he thought of himself.

"They set out to lynch Bull," he explained finally, "an' I supposin' o' course thet he was here got away ahead o' 'em, an' now, ding-bust my ornery ol' carcass, like as not they already got him over at the West Ranch. Where's the rest o' the boys? Where's Texas Pete? You don't reckon thet critter's with Colby, do you?"

"Not by a long shot," replied the cook. "He'd stick up fer Bull ef he massacreed the whole durn county. So'd Shorty an' Idaho, but they ain't none o' 'em here—they's all down to Johnson's to a dance."

"Well," said Wildcat Bob, "I done my best, which same ain't no good. Ef I hed a hoss instead o' a hunk o' coyote fodder I'd try to git to the West Ranch in time, but I reckon they ain't no chanct now. Howsumever I'll do the best I kin. So-long!" and he was gone.

A half hour later his horse fell dead a mile north of Hendersville while his rider was taking a short cut straight across country for the West Ranch. It was a warm and lurid Wildcat Bob who plodded through the dust of Hendersville's lone thoroughfare and stopped at the veranda of The Donovan House some time later to be accosted by one of a group gathered there in semi-silent expectancy.

"The saints be praised!" exclaimed Mary Donovan. "Is it a banchee or is it not?"

"It's worse," said Bill Gatlin, the stage driver; "it's Wildcat Bob—walkin'."

"Did they git the poor b'y?" demanded Mary, whereat the little old gentleman burst forth anew with such a weird variety of oaths that Mr. Jefferson Wainright, Jr., could feel the hot flush that mounted to his ears fairly scorching his skin.

"Ef I ever gits a-hold o' the blankety, blank, blank thet loaned me that blankety, blank, blank ewe-necked, ring-boned, spavined excuse fer a cayuse I'll cut his heart out," announced Wildcat Bob in a high falsetto.

Finally Mary Donovan inveigled the facts from him. "Ye done well, Bob, thet ye did," she assured him. "Shure an' how was yese to know thet he wasn't at the home ranch."

"I shouldn't think you'd care if they did hang a bandit and murderer," declared Mr. Jefferson Wainright, Jr.

"Who in hell told you to think, you durn dude?" screamed Wildcat Bob, reaching for his gun.

Mr. Wainright sought the greater safety of the office, tipping over his chair and almost upsetting Mary Donovan in his haste. "Don't shoot!" he cried. "Don't shoot! I meant no offense."

Wildcat Bob would have followed him within, but Mary Donovan caught him around the waist and pushed him into a chair. "Be ca'm, Robert," she soothed him.

As Diana arose to her feet after listening close to the ground for the second time she was assured by the increased loudness of the sounds she had heard that the lone rider was rapidly approaching from the northeast and in that direction she again led Captain, intending to mount once more as soon as she had reached what she considered a safe distance from the cabin and the hidden watchers encircling it. She had forged ahead for about five minutes when the way dipped into a shallow swale in which the sage brush grew to greater size.

Here would be a good place to remount, and with this intention crystallized she wound downward among the scattered brush toward the bottom, when, rounding a particularly high bush, she came suddenly face to face with a man leading a horse.

"Stick 'em up!" whispered the man in a low voice, presenting an evil looking six-gun at the pit of her stomach.

"Oh, Bull!" she cried in low tones, for she would have known his voice among thousands.

"You?" he cried. "My gawd, Miss, what are you doin' here?"

"They have come to lynch you, Bull," she told him. "There are forty or fifty of them lying in the brush around your cabin now. They say that you held up the stage and killed Mack Harber today."

"And *you* came to warn me?" His voice sounded far away, as though, groping for a truth he could not grasp, he spoke half to himself.

"You must go away, Bull," she told him. "You must leave the country."

He paid no attention to her words. "I seen a light flash fer a minute in the shack," he said, "an' so I reckoned I'd hev a look around before I come too close. Thet was why I was walkin' when I hearn you. I was just a-goin' to leave Blazes here an' go ahead an' scout aroun' a bit. Mount up now an' I'll take you home."

"No," she said, "you get away. I can get home all right—I only have to go to town. I'm stopping at Mary's tonight."

"I'll ride with you," he insisted.

She knew him well enough to know that he would never let her ride to town alone through the night and so she mounted as he did and together they followed the swale which ran in the general direction of Hendersville.

"You say you're stoppin' at Mary's?" he asked.

"Just for tonight. I'm taking the stage for Aldea in the morning. I'm going to Kansas City to consult a lawyer. They are trying to take the property away from me, Bull," and then she told him all that had transpired since yesterday.

"You don't need a lawyer, Miss," he told her. "What you need is a two-gun man, only you don't *need* him, 'cause you got one already. You go back to the ranch an' come mornin' there won't be airy dude or dudess to try to put their brand on nothin' thet belongs to you."

"Oh, Bull, don't you understand that you mustn't do anything like that?" she cried. "It would only make things worse than they are now. Wong wanted to poison them."

"Good ol' Wong!" interjected Bull.

"But we can't make murderers of ourselves just because they are wicked."

"It ain't murder to kill a rattlesnake," he reminded her.

"But promise me that you won't," she urged.

"I wouldn't do nothin' you didn't want done, Miss," he said.

They were nearing town now and could see the

lights plainly, shining through the windows and doorways. "You'd better go now, Bull," she said.

"Not 'til I get you in town safe," he replied.

"But I'm safe now—it is only a little way, and I'm afraid they might get you if you came in."

"Shucks, they won't git me now thet I know they're after me," he replied. "Say, Miss," he exclaimed suddenly, "you ain't asked me ef it was me kilt Mack."

She drew herself up proudly. "I'll never ask you, Bull," she said.

"But you wouldn't hev come out to warn me ef you'd thought it," he suggested.

She was silent for a moment, and then: "Yes, I would, Bull," she said in a very little voice.

He shrugged his shoulders. "As I told Pete, ef I had done it or ef I hadn't done it, I'd say I hadn't, so what's the use o' wastin' breath; but I shore appreciates what you've done, Miss."

"And you will go away?" she asked.

"No'm, I'll stay here. I reckon you need me, Miss, from what you've told me, so I'll hang around a spell. I'll ride over to the ranch o' nights now an' then. Ef you happen to hear a meadow-lark settin' up late after dark you'll know it's me."

"But I'm afraid they'll get you, Bull, if you stay in the country. They're terribly angry," she warned him.

"They won't be so keen to find me after they're sobered up a bit," he said, with a smile. "Colby's the only one thet's got the nerve to go agin' guns single-handed."

"I don't see why he hates you so," she said. "I used to think that he liked you."

"Then all I got to say, Miss, is thet you must be plumb blind," said Bull.

Diana was evidently not so blind as he thought her, for she flushed deliciously.

"Now you must turn back," she said. They were almost in town.

"I will, because they mustn't see you ridin' in with me," he replied.

She reined in her horse and held out her hand to him. "Good-bye, Bull," she said.

He took her slim hand in his and pressed it strongly. "Good-bye—Diana!" said Bull.

She spoke to Captain and moved off toward the little town and the man sat there in the darkness watching her retreating form until it was hidden behind a corner of The Donovan House.

CHAPTER XIV

BULL SEES COLBY

BULL turned Blazes' head toward the northeast and rode off slowly in the direction of Coyote Canyon near the head of which there was a wild and almost inaccessible country just east of Hell's Bend Pass. There was water there and game for himself, with year round pasture for Blazes.

As he rode he hummed a gay little air, quite unlike the grim, taciturn Bull that his acquaintances knew, for Bull was happy—happier that he had been for months.

"An' to think," he mused, "thet she rode out there all alone to warn me. An' once she said to me, 'Bull,' says she, 'I don't love any man, Bull, thet way; but if ever I do he'll know it without my tellin' him. I'll do something thet will prove it—a girl always does.'

"Thet's what she says—them's her very words. I ain't never fergot 'em an' I ain't never goin' to—even ef I don't believe it. It was just her good heart that sent her out to warn me—she'd a-done as much fer any of the boys."

When Diana reined in before those assembled on the veranda of The Donovan House she was greeted by a gasp of astonishment from Mary Donovan.

"Diana Henders, child!" she exclaimed. "What are ye doin' here this time o' night? Sure an' I thought ye had gone back to the ranch, after hearin' ye was in town airlier in the av'nin'."

Diana dismounted without making any reply and tied Captain to the rail in front of the hotel. As she mounted the steps to the veranda the younger Wainright rose, politely. Corson and the elder Wainright nodded, the latter grunting gruffly. Lillian Manill pretended that she did not see her.

"I am going to stop here tonight, Mrs. Donovan," said Diana to the proprietress, "that is if you have room for me."

"An' if I didn't I'd be after makin' it," replied the latter.

"I wonder if you'd mind putting Captain up for me, Bob," said Diana, turning to the Wildcat, and as the old man stepped from the veranda to comply with her request, Diana turned and entered the office, followed by Mary Donovan.

"May I have a cup of tea, Mrs. Donovan?" asked the girl. "I feel all fagged out. This evening has been like a terrible nightmare."

"You mane about poor Bull?" asked Mary.

Diana nodded.

"They ain't back yit," said Mary; "but I suppose they got him, bad 'cess to 'em."

Diana came close to the older woman and whispered. "They didn't get him. I just saw him—he brought me to the edge of town."

"Now, the Lord be praised for that!" ejaculated Mary Donovan, "for shure an' if it's guilty he is I'll not be after belavin' it at all, at all."

"It looks pretty bad for him, Mrs. Donovan," said Diana, "but even so I can't believe it of him either—I won't believe it."

"An' no more don't yese, darlin'," advised Mary Donovan, "an' now make yersilf comfortable an' I'll have ye a cup o' tay in no time."

As her hostess left the sitting room by one doorway, Jefferson Wainright, Jr., appeared in the other which opened from the office, his hat in his hand.

"May I have just a word with you, Miss Henders?" he asked.

The girl nodded her assent, though none too cordially, and Wainright entered the little sitting room.

"I can't begin to tell you, Miss Henders," he commenced, after clearing his throat, "how badly I feel over this matter that Mr. Corson has explained to us. There isn't any question, of course, about the unfairness and injustice of it; but the fact remains that the law is the law, and I don't see how you are going to get around it by fighting them."

"It is a matter, Mr. Wainright, that I do not care to discuss with you," said Diana, rising.

"Wait a minute, Miss Henders," he begged. "That wasn't exactly what I wanted to discuss with you, though it has a bearing on it. There is a way out for you and it was that I wanted to talk over.

Your father was a wealthy man—you have been accustomed to everything that money could buy in this country. To drop from affluence to penury in a single day is going to be mighty hard for you, and it is that I want to save you from."

"It is very kind of you, I am sure," she told him, "but I cannot see how you, of all people, can help me, for your own father is a party to this whole transaction."

"I think you are a bit hard on him," he said. "You surely cannot blame him for wanting to drive as good a bargain as possible—he is, first and last, a business man."

Diana only shrugged her shoulders.

"Now, as I said," continued Mr. Wainright, "there is a way for you to continue to have, not only the luxuries you have been accustomed to, but many more, and at the same time to retain the Bar Y Ranch."

She looked up at him questioningly. "Yes!" she said, "and how?"

"By marrying me, Miss Henders. You know I love you. You know there is nothing I would not do for you. There is no sacrifice that I would not willingly and gladly make for you. I would die for you, dear girl, and thank God for the chance."

Diana Henders' lip curled in scorn. "It seems to me that I heard you make that very assertion once before, Mr. Wainright, and in those self-same words—the night before you ran away, like the coward you are, and left us at the mercy of the Apaches.

"If you had half the courage that you have effrontery, the lion would appear a mouse by comparison. Please, never mention the subject to me again, nor is there any reason why you should ever address me upon any subject. Good night!"

"You'll regret this," he cried as he was leaving the room. "You see if you don't. You might have had one friend, and a good one, on your side—now you haven't any. We'll strip you to the last cent for this, and then you'll marry some ignorant, unwashed cow-puncher and raise brats in a tumble-down shack for the rest of your life—that's what you'll do!"

"An do yuh know what you'll do?" demanded a squeaky voice behind him.

Jefferson Wainright, Jr., turned to see Wildcat Bob glaring at him from the center of the office floor. The young man turned a sickly hue and glanced hurriedly for an avenue of escape, but the Wildcat was between him and the outer doorway and was reaching for one of his terrible guns.

With a half-stifled cry Wainright sprang into the sitting room and ran to Diana. Seizing her he whirled the girl about so that she was between him and the Wildcat's weapon.

"My God, Miss Henders, don't let him shoot me! I'm unarmed—it would be murder. Save me! Save me!"

His screams brought his father, Corson, Lillian Manill and Mary Donovan to the room, where they saw the younger Wainright kneeling in abject terror behind Diana's skirts.

"What's the meanin' of all this?" yelled the elder Wainright.

"Your son insulted me—he asked me to marry him," said Diana. "Let him go, Bob," she directed the Wildcat.

"Gosh-a-mighty, Miss!" exclaimed the old man in an aggrieved tone, "yuh don't mean it, do yuh? Why, I just ben honin' fer a chanct to clean up this here whole bunch o' tin-horns an' now that I got an excuse it don't seem right to let it pass. By cracky, it ain't right! 'Tain't moral, that's what it ain't!"

"Please, Bob—I've got trouble enough—let him go."

Slowly Wildcat Bob returned his gun to its holster, shaking his head mournfully, and Jefferson Wainright, Jr., arose and sneaked out of the room. As his party returned to the veranda the young man's father was growling and spluttering in an undertone, but Wildcat Bob caught the words "law" and "sheriff."

"What's thet?" he demanded in his high falsetto.

The elder Wainright cringed and stepped rapidly through the doorway. "Nothin'," he assured the Wildcat. "I didn't calc'late to say nothin' at all."

It was almost morning when the weary and now sobered members of the necktie party returned to town. Gum Smith and several others, among whom was Wildcat Bob, met them in the street.

"Git him?" demanded the sheriff.

"No," replied Colby, "an' I don't savvy it neither—someone must o' put him wise; but I got some evidence," and he drew a worn leather pouch from his shirt. "Here's one o' the bullion bags that was took from the stage yesterday—I found it under his blankets. He may o' ben there an' saw us comin', but thet ain't likely 'cause we snuk up mighty keerful—someone must o' put him wise."

"Ah wondeh who-all it could o' ben," wondered Gum Smith.

As the crowd was dispersing Wildcat Bob caught sight of Willie among them.

"Hey, thar, you!" he called. "What was you doin' with thet bunch—I thought you claimed to be a friend o' Bull's."

"Course I am," maintained Willie, stoutly; "but I hain't never seed no one hanged."

A few hours later Diana Henders left on the stage for Aldea and after she had departed Corson and Lillian Manill drove back to the ranch, taking the Wainrights with them, while Hal Colby trotted along beside them. He had not seen Diana before she left, nor had he made any effort to do so.

"We might save a right smart o' trouble if we

could get everything fixed up before she gets back, Corson," the elder Wainright was saying.

"The government patent to the land as well as Manill's will are in the New York office," replied Corson. "I've sent for them. They ought to be along now any time. I rather expected them on yesterday's stage—they certainly must come in on the next and I imagine she won't get back for a week at least—that will give us three days. Then we'll all go to Aldea, have the papers drawn up there, you turn the money over to us and Miss Manill and I can get away for New York on the train that night—I've had all of this damn country I want."

Hal Colby, fortunately for his peace of mind, did not overhear the conversation. It outlined an entirely different plan from that which Lillian Manill had explained to him only the preceding day —a plan which included a hasty wedding and a long honeymoon, during which the Bar Y foreman would taste the sweets of world travel in company with a charming and affectionate bride.

"You're goin' to leave me here to run all the risk, eh?" demanded Wainright, Sr.

"Oh, there's no risk now that that Bull fellow is out of the way," Corson assured him.

"I wish I was sure he was out o' the way," said Wainright, dubiously. "I don't like that fellow a little bit."

"He'll never show up again," said Corson, confidently, "and anyway, just as soon as I get to New York I'll look up a good man to represent me here, and I'm going to pick the toughest one I can find in New York, too."

"I'm afraid I'm buyin' a heap o' trouble with that one-third interest o' mine," said Wainright, scratching his head.

"But look what you're going to get out of it," Corson reminded him. "I'll bet we take a million out of that mine in the next year."

Back at the ranch Colby was met by a scowling trio—Texas Pete, Shorty and Idaho. "Where's Bull?" demanded Texas.

"How should I know?" replied Colby, gruffly. "When was I elected his nurse-girl?"

"You went out after him with a bunch o' drunken short-horns last night," accused Shorty. "You know whether you got him or not."

"They didn't git him," said Colby, shortly.

"It's a damn good thing fer you, Colby, thet they didn't," said Texas Pete, "an' another thing—we wants our time. We ain't a-aimin' to work under no pole-cat no more."

"I reckon we kin git along without you," retorted Colby, ignoring the insult. "You kin come back in a week fer your checks—the boss ain't here."

"Then we'll stay 'til she is," said Pete.

"Suit yerselves," replied Colby, as he turned and walked away.

The routine of the ranch moved in its accustomed

grooves as the days passed, though there was noticeably absent the spirit of good-fellowship that marks the daily life of a well-ordered cow outfit. A little coterie, headed by Texas Pete, herded by itself, in the vernacular of the West, while the remaining punchers grouped themselves about the foreman.

Mealtimes, ordinarily noisy with rough but good-natured badinage, had become silent moments to be gotten through with as rapidly as possible. There was a decorous restraint that was far too decorous, among these rough men, to augur aught of good. It revealed rather than veiled the proximity of open hostilities.

There was one topic of conversation that was eschewed particularly. It would have been the steel to the flint of prejudice which lay embedded in the powder of partisanship. Bull's name was never mentioned when the factions were together.

The stage came again to Hendersville on the third day after Diana's departure. It brought mail for the ranch, but the vaquero who had been sent from the Bar Y for it tarried longer at *Gum's Place—Liquors and Cigars*—than he had intended, with the result that it was well after supper and quite dark before he delivered it to the office.

As he approached the yellow rectangle of the open office door it may have been the light shining in his eyes that prevented him seeing the figure of a man beneath the darkness of the cottonwoods that surround the house, or the horse, standing as silently as its master, fifty feet away—a blazed face chestnut with two white hind feet.

The vaquero entered the office, where Corson was sitting in conversation with the two Wainrights, and laid the mail upon the table. The New Yorker picked it up and ran through it. There was a bulky letter addressed to him, which he opened.

"Here's what we've been waiting for," he said, glancing quickly through two enclosures and laying them aside to peruse the accompanying letter.

The man beneath the shadows of the cottonwoods moved closer to the open office doorway, keeping well out of the yellow shaft of lamp-light.

Bull had not come down to the Bar Y from his hiding place in Coyote Canyon for the purpose of spying upon Corson. He had hoped against hope that Diana might return on the day's stage, for he wanted a word with her. He knew that she could not have made the trip to Kansas City and return in so short a time, but then she might have changed her mind at Aldea and given up the trip. It was on this chance that he had come down out of the mountains tonight.

Diana had not returned—he had convinced himself of this—but still he tarried. These were her enemies. It could do no harm to keep an eye on them. He did not like the proprietorial airs of Corson, sitting there in "the old man's" easy chair, and as for the Wainrights, they too seemed much more at home than suited Bull. His hand caressed the butt of a six-gun affectionately.

"Hell!" exclaimed Corson, explosively. "The addle-brained idiot!"

"What's the matter?" inquired the elder Wainright.

Corson was in the midst of the letter. He shook it violently and angrily in lieu of anything more closely representative of its writer.

"The chump has dug up some papers that we don't want—we don't want 'em in Arizona at all. He's a new man. I thought he had good sense and discretion, but he hasn't either. He's sendin' 'em out here by registered mail.

"If anything happens to them, if they fall into the Henders girl's hands our goose is cooked. He says they 'put a new aspect on the situation' and that 'he knows I'll be delighted to have them.' They surely will put a new aspect on the situation, but I don't want 'em—not here.

"If I'd had any sense I'd have destroyed them before I left New York; but who'd have thought that they weren't safe right in my own office. I'd be delighted to have him—by the neck. Lord! suppose they're lost now! They should have been here with this other mail."

"If it's registered stuff it may have been delayed just enough to miss the stage at Aldea by one train," suggested Wainright. "If that is the case it'll be along by the next stage."

"What were the papers?" demanded the elder Wainright, suspiciously.

Corson hesitated. He realized that he had been surprised by his anger into saying too much.

"Perhaps I overestimate their value," he said. "They might not do any harm after all."

"What were they?" insisted Mr. Wainright.

"Oh, they were reports that show the tremendous value of the new vein in the mine," lied Corson, glibly.

Wainright sank back in his chair with a sigh of relief. "Oh, if that's all they was we don't need to worry none about them," he said. "We as good as got the place now. We'll drive over to Aldea tomorrer and fix things up, eh?"

"I think I'll wait for the next mail," said Corson. "Those reports might not do any harm, but I'd rather be here when they come and see that no one else gets hold of them."

"Mebby you're right," assented Wainright. He arose, yawning, and stretched. "I calc'late to go to bed," he said.

"I think I'll do the same," said his son. "I hope Miss Manill is feeling better by morning."

"Oh, she'll be all right," said Corson. "Just a little headache. Good night! I'm coming along too."

They lighted lamps, blew out the one in the office, and departed for their rooms. The man in the shadows turned slowly toward his horse, but he had taken only a few steps when he halted listening.

Some one was approaching. He glanced through the darkness in the direction of the sounds which came out of the night along the pathway from the bunk-house. Stepping quickly behind the bole of a large tree, Bull waited in silence. Presently he saw dimly the figure of a man and as it came nearer the star-light revealed its identity.

It was Colby. Like himself, Colby waited in the shadows of the trees—waited silently, watching the dead black of the office windows. The silence was tangible, it was so absolutely dominant, reigning supreme in a world of darkness. Bull wondered that the other did not hear his breathing. He marvelled at the quietness of Blazes—even the roller in his bit lay silent. But it could not last much longer—the horse was sure to move in a moment and Colby would investigate. The result was a foregone conclusion. There would be shooting.

Bull did not want to shoot Colby—not now. There were two reasons. One however would have been enough—that Diana Henders was thinking of marrying this man.

And then the silence was broken. Very slightly only was it broken. A suspicion of a sound came from the interior of the house, and following it a dim light wavering mysteriously upon the office walls, growing steadily brighter until the room was suddenly illuminated.

From where he now stood Bull could not see the interior of the office, but he knew that some one carrying a lamp had come down the stairway, along the hall and entered the office. Then he saw Colby move forward and step lightly to the veranda and an instant later the office door swung open, revealing Lillian Manill in diaphanous negligee.

Bull saw Colby seize the girl, strain her to him and cover her lips with kisses. Then the girl drew her lover into the room and closed the door.

With a grimace of disgust Bull walked to Blazes, mounted him and rode slowly away. Now there was only one reason why he could not kill Colby yet.

CHAPTER XV

"NOW, GO!"

IT WAS Wednesday again. Four horses, sweat streaked, toiled laboriously to drag the heavy coach up the north side of Hell's Bend Pass. It was a tough pull even with a light load—one that really demanded six horses and would have had six in the old days—and today the load was light. There was but a single passenger. She sat on the driver's box with Bill Gatlin with whom she was in earnest discussion.

"I tell you I don't believe he did it," she was saying. "I'll never believe that he did it, and I'm mighty glad that he got away."

Gatlin shook his head. "There ain't no one got a better right to say that than you has, Miss," he said, "fer 'twas your gold as was stole, an' your messenger as was shot up; but nevertheless an' howsum-ever I got my own private opinion what I'm keepin' to myself thet it was Bull all right as done it."

"I'd just like to see this Black Coyote once," said the girl. "*I'd* know if it was Bull or not."

"They ain't no chanct today, Miss," Gatlin told her. "They ain't no gold shipment today, unless I'm mighty mistook."

"Don't he ever make a mistake?" asked the girl.

"Never hain't yet, Miss."

Diana relapsed into silence, her thoughts reverting to her interview with the Kansas City attorney. He had not held out very roseate hopes. By means of litigation—long and expensive—she might, after a number of years, get a small portion of her father's share of the business. She had better take a cash settlement, if she could get one, he thought. A hundred and twenty-five thousand dollars in the hand would be much better, in his opinion, than a long-drawn-out law suit that could be nothing better than an expensive gamble with the odds against her.

"But I won't! I won't! I won't be robbed," she ejaculated beneath her breath.

"How's that, Miss?" inquired Bill Gatlin. "Was you speakin' to me?"

"I must have been thinking aloud," she said, smiling. "What a long pull this is, Bill!"

"We're nigh to the summit," he replied, pulling in his team to breathe them for a moment.

On the shoulder of Wagon Mountain overlooking the south stretch of Hell's Bend Pass road two men sat their horses amidst a clump of chaparral that effectually hid them from the road, though they could see nearly its entire length from the summit to the gap at the bottom. Presently one of them spoke.

"Here it comes," he said. He was a swarthy,

powerfully built Mexican, somewhere in his thirties, Gregorio, the bandit.

His companion was adjusting a black silk handkerchief across his face in such a way as to entirely hide his features. There were two small holes cut in the handkerchief opposite its wearer's eyes which, through them, were fixed upon the stage as it topped the pass and started downward upon its rapid and careening descent toward the gap and Hendersville.

"Come," said Gregorio, and wheeled his horse about.

His companion's mount moved suddenly before the handkerchief was finally adjusted and as the man reached for his reins the thing fell away from his face, revealing it. It was Bull.

A second attempt was more successful and then the men rode down the sheer mountain-side, keeping just below the crest upon the south side and hidden from the view of the driver and the passenger upon the stage. Their horses moved with extreme care and without haste, for the way was precarious, occasionally requiring that the horses sit upon their haunches and slide for short distances until they found footing again further down. The riders seemed unperturbed either by the dangers of the descent or fear of being late at their rendezvous, suggesting habitude with the work in hand. In a dense growth of scrub just above the gap they tied their horses, continuing on foot.

The stage lumbered downward, rocking from side to side. Diana held tight and said nothing. She had ridden with Bill Gatlin before, many times. He glanced at her out of the corner of an eye.

"This ain't nothin'," he said, as though in answer to a remonstrance on her part. Diana knew what was coming. She had heard it many times. "No, siree," continued Bill, "this ain't nothin'. Why, you'd orter ben with me one night when I was on the Denver run in the ol' days, afore the railroads spiled the country. The trail crossed plumb over the top of a mountain. 'Twarn't no road. 'Twarn't nothin' but a trail. I hed the ol' stage plumb full an' passengers a-hangin' onto the boot. It was pitch dark—the doggonest, darkest night I ever see. Couldn't see airy wheel-horse. Only ways I knowed I hed any horses was when their shoes struck fire on the stony parts o' the road. Jest afore we struck the top o' the mountain they was the worst cloud-bust I ever did see. Them horses had to swim the last hundred rods to the top o' thet mountain, an' the ol' stage was bobbin' aroun' so on the waves thet eight of the passengers got sea-sick.

"But thet wa'n't nothin'. When we come to the top I found the road'd ben all washed away. They wa'n't no more road 'n a jack-rabbit; but I was a-carryin' the mail, jest like I be now an' I hed to git through. It was a high mountain an' tolably steep, but not no trees, so I see there wa'n't only one thing to do an' thet was to go down road or no road, so right there on the top o' thet mountain I threw the leather into 'em an' headed 'em fer Denver an' down we goes faster'n ever I rid afore or since, the wheelers a-jumpin' to keep out o' the way o' the stage an' the leaders a jumpin' to keep out o' the way o' the wheelers.

"Well, sir, we was a-goin' so fast thet the fust thing I knowed the friction hed melted the nut offen the nigh front wheel an' away went thet wheel hell-bent-fer-election down the mountain, but it couldn't keep up with the stage an' purty soon it was left behind, but the stage was a-goin' so fast thet it never missed thet wheel at all. An' purty soon off came the off rear wheel, an' thet wheel couldn't keep up, though I could see it was doin' its best outen the corner o' my eye.

"Well, sir, 'twa'n't long afore tother hind wheel come off, but we was goin' about twict as fast now as when the fust wheel come off an' that ol' stage jest skimmed along on one wheel a dinged sight smoother an' it ever done on four. When we were about to the bottom off come the last wheel an' then thinks I fer sure we gotta quit an' we ain't to Denver yit, but we'd got so much mo-mentum by this time thet the last wheel didn't make no more difference then the others.

"Them horses jest drug thet stage out behind them like a comet does its tail an' on we went streakin' down thet mountain an' five mile out onto the flat afore the stage hit the ground an' then, o' course, we hed to stop. It was too bad. I tell you I felt plumb sore. I hadn't never ben off schedule sence I took the run.

"Then, all of a suddint, says one o' the passengers, 'Look back yender, Bill,' says he. 'Look what's comin'!' An' I looked an' there come them four wheels a-tearin' across the flat straight fer us. Well, to make a long story short, they peters out right beside the stage an' with the help o' the passengers an' some extra nuts we got 'em back on where they belonged an' pulled into Denver two hours ahead o' time. But I tell you, Miss, thet was some ride. I'd hate to hev to take it again. Why——"

"Hands up! Put 'em up!"

The stage had slowed down for the rough road through the gap, when two men with muffled faces stepped before the leaders, covering the driver and his lone passenger with wicked looking six-guns.

Diana Henders sat as one turned to stone, her eyes fixed upon the tall, fine figure of the leading highwayman. A little gust of wind moved the handkerchief that covered his face so that she saw, or she thought that she saw, a scar upon the square chin. She was not afraid. It was not fear—physical fear that held her motionless—it was worse than that. It was the paralyzing terror of the heart and soul. Was it Bull? Could it be Bull?

But, dear God, could she be mistaken in the familiar lines of that figure—every movement, every gesture proclaimed the numbing truth? He had not spoken. She was glad of that, for she wanted something upon which to hang a doubt. The second man had given the brief commands. That he was Gregorio she had no doubt.

"Throw down the mail pouch," he commanded, and Bill Gatlin threw it down.

The taller man took it and went to the rear of the stage, out of sight. Five minutes later Gregorio commanded them to drive on. That was all. The thing had not consumed six minutes, but in that brief time the structure of Diana's life had been shaken to its foundations. A new, a terrible truth had engulfed her—a truth that should have up-borne her upon a wave of exaltation and happiness now dragged her down into the vortex of a whirlpool of self-loathing and misery.

They rode on in silence for a few minutes, Bill Gatlin cracking his long whip above the ears of the leaders, galloping smoothly over a comparatively level road.

"Doggone!" he said presently. "It's gettin' too almighty reg'lar to suit me, though I reckon as how I mought git lonesome if I wasn't held up oncet in a while; but you hed your wish, Miss—you got to see The Black Coyote, all right, and now what do you think? Is it or isn't it Bull?"

Diana Henders bit her lip. "Of course it was not Bull," she said.

"Looked powerful like him to me," said Gatlin.

As they drew up in front of The Donovan House the usual idlers came forth to learn what new element this, their sole link to civilization, had infused into their midst. They greeted Diana none the less cordially because she was the only passenger and the stage had brought no new interest to Hendersville.

"Held up agin," announced Bill. "Some on you better go an' tell Gum—he might want to deputize some one."

Immediately the crowd was interested. They asked many questions.

"They wa'n't much to it," said Bill Gatlin. "Bein' as how they wa'n't no gold he took the mail. I reckon if you was lookin' fer any letters you won't git them."

A man from the Bar Y spoke up. "Thet New York feller up to the ranch was lookin' fer a important piece o' mail," he said. "He sent me down special to git it."

"Hey, what's this?" demanded another, peering into the interior of the coach. "Here's yer mail bag, Bill, a-lyin' right in here." He dragged it out and exhibited to the others.

"They's somethin' wrong with it—it's ben cut open," said another, pointing to a slit in the leather. Then the postmaster came up and rescued the sack. The crowd followed him to the general store in which the post-office was conducted. Here the postmaster, assisted by the crowd, went through the contents of the sack.

"Course I cain't tell what's missin'," he said, "only they ain't no registered letter fer Mr. Corson."

Diana Henders had gone immediately into The Donovan House as quickly as she could clamber from the stage after it had come to a stop, and Mary Donovan had taken her into the privacy of her sitting room for the cup "o' tay" that Diana had been looking forward to for the past couple of hours. Here she told the motherly Irish woman the details of her trip to Kansas City and the quandary she was in as to what procedure to follow in her future dealings with Corson.

"If I had anything to fight with, I'd fight," she exclaimed; "but I'm all alone—even the law seems to be on their side, against justice."

"Shure, an' it's not all alone ye are," Mary Donovan assured her. "What wid all the friends ye have that would fight fer ye at the drop o' the hat. Faith, they'd run thim tin-horns out o' the country, an' ye give the word."

"I know," assented the girl, "and I appreciate what the boys would do for me, but it can't be done that way. Dad always stood for law and order and it wouldn't do for me to sponsor illegal methods."

"Ye've got to fight the divil wid fire," said Mary.

Diana made no reply. She sat sipping her tea,

her expression one of troubled sadness, but she was not thinking of those who would take her property from her nor of their unfair methods. Mary Donovan was moving about the room tidying up.

Diana set her empty cup upon the rickety center table which supported an oil lamp, a bible, a red plush photograph album and a gilded conch shell, and sighed. Mrs. Donovan glanced at her out of the corner of an eye and guessed shrewdly that there was something more than New Yorkers troubling her. Presently she came and stood in front of the girl.

"What is it, mavourneen?" she asked. "Be after tellin' Mary Donovan."

Diana rose, half turned her head away and bit her lower lip in an effort to hide or suppress a short, quick intaking of the breath that was almost a gasp.

"The stage was held up again today," she said, mastering herself and turning, wide eyed, toward the older woman. "I saw them—I saw them both."

"Yis!" said Mary Donovan.

"But it wasn't—it wasn't he! It wasn't, Mary Donovan!" and Diana, throwing herself upon the broad, motherly bosom, burst into tears, through which she gasped an occasional, "It wasn't! It wasn't!"

"Shure, now, it wasn't," soothed Mary, "an' the first wan that'll be after sayin' it was'll wish he'd nivir bin born, an' even if it was, Diana Henders, there's many a good man's gone wrong an' come right again.

"Why, look at that ould fool Wildcat Bob! They do be sayin' he was a road agent his-self thirty year ago an' he's killed so many men he's lost count o' 'em, he has; but now look at him! A quiet an' paceable ould man, an' a good citizen whin he ain't full o' barb-wire, which ain't often."

Diana dried her tears through a smile. "You're very fond of Bob, aren't you?" she asked.

"Run along wid ye, now!" exclaimed Mary Donovan, smiling coyly.

"I think Bob would make you a good husband," continued Diana, "and you really need a man around here. Why don't you marry him? I know he's anxious enough."

"Marry him, indade!" sniffed Mary. "The ould fool's stricken dumb ivery time he's alone wid me. If iver he's married it is, it's the girl that'll be havin' to pop the question."

They were interrupted by a rap on the sitting-room door. It was the vaquero from the Bar Y who had come down for the mail.

"Bill Gatlin told me you was here, Miss," he said. "Do you want me to tell Colby to send the buckboard down for you?"

"I left Captain here, thanks," replied Diana, "and as soon as I change my clothes I'll ride back to the ranch."

"Shall I wait fer you?" he inquired.

"No, thanks. I don't know how long I'll be," she told him; "but if Pete is there you might ask him to ride out and meet me."

A half hour later Diana rode out of Hendersville on Captain along the winding, dusty road bordered by interminable sage and grease-wood that stretched off in undulating billows of rolling land to the near mountains on the north and away to the south as far as the eye could reach where the softened outlines of other mountains rose, mysterious, through the haze. The low sun cast long shadows toward the east, those of herself and her mount transformed into a weird creature of Brobdingnagian proportions mincing along upon preposterous legs.

The inhabitants of a prairie-dog village watched her approach with growing suspicions, scampering at last to the safety of their catacombian retreat—all but a single patriarch and two owls, who watched her from the safe proximity of burrow mouths until she had passed.

Drear and desolate the aspect of the scene, perhaps, but to Diana it was home, and a tear came to her eye as she thought that in a day or a week she might be leaving it forever. Her home! And they were driving her away from it—stealing it from her—her home that her father had built for her mother—that he had planned that Diana should have after he had gone. The wickedness of it! The injustice! That was what rankled—

the injustice! She dashed away the tear with an angry gesture. She would not be dispossessed! She would fight! Mary Donovan was right. It was no sin to fight the devil with fire.

It was at this moment that she saw a horseman approaching her from the direction of the ranch. Her eyes, long accustomed to keen observation and to vast expanses, recognized the man minutes before his features were discernible, and a little cloud crossed her brow. It was not Texas Pete, as she had hoped, but Hal Colby. Perhaps it was for the best. She would have to see him sometime, and tell him. As he approached her she saw that there was no welcoming smile on his face, which wore a troubled expression. But his greeting was cordial.

"Hello, Di!" he cried. "Why didn't you let me know you was comin' today?"

"There was no way to let you know, of course," she replied. "You might have guessed that I would be back as soon as I could."

"Tom jest got in from town an' told me you was comin'. I hurried out to head you off. You don't want to come to the ranch now, it wouldn't be no ways pleasant for you."

"Why?" she demanded.

"The Wainrights is there for one thing," he said, drawing rein in front of her.

She set her firm little jaw and rode around him. "I am going home," she said.

"I wouldn't be foolish, Di," he insisted. "It'll

only make more trouble. They as good as got the place now. We can't fight 'em. It wouldn't get us nowheres.

"Lemme see what I kin get 'em to do fer you. They're willin' to give you enough to live decent on if you're reasonable, an' I'll git the most I kin fer you; but if you go to fightin' 'em they won't give you nothin'."

"They'll never give me anything," she cried. "I'd never accept anything from them, but I'll take and keep what's mine, and my friends will help me."

"You'll only git yourself an' your friends in a peck o' trouble," he told her.

"Listen, Hal—" she hesitated, stumbling a little over the speech she had been rehearsing. "There is something I want to say to you. You asked me to marry you. I told you that if you would wait a little while I thought that I could say yes. I can't say yes, Hal, ever, for I don't love you. I'm sorry, but the only fair thing to do was tell you."

He looked a bit crestfallen and disconcerted, for, though he had realized that it would be poor policy to press his suit now that she was penniless, it injured his pride to be told that he could not have won her in any event, and suddenly came the realization that, money or no money, he wanted her very much. His infatuation for Lillian Manill was revealed in all its sordidness—it was not love. All the money in the world, all the clothes in New York, would not make Lillian Manill as desirable as Diana Henders.

Colby was a crude, uneducated man, yet he discerned in Diana Henders a certain quality, far beyond his powers of analysis, that placed her in a sphere to which Lillian Manill and her kind might never hope to aspire. He knew now that he wanted Diana Henders for herself and Lillian Manill for her money and for that coarse, feminine attraction that certain types of women have for coarse men.

He lived in a more or less lawless country and a more or less lawless age, so it is not strange that there should have crept into his mind the thought that he might possess them both. Naturally it would be only the part of good business to possess lawfully the one with the money. It was only the flash of a thought, though, and he quickly put it aside.

"I'm plumb sorry, Di," he said; "but of course you know your own business."

That was all he said, but he did a great deal of thinking and the more he thought the more he realized how much he wanted her now that she seemed least accessible. His face wore an expression such as Diana Henders had never seen upon it before—he was not the laughing, good-natured Hal that she had liked very much and almost loved. There was something almost sinister about him, and she wondered if being disappointed in love had this effect upon men.

"How is everything at the ranch since I've been away?" she asked presently.

"So-so," he replied. "Some o' the hands want to quit. They're waitin' 'til you come, to git their checks."

"Who are they?"

"Pete, Shorty an' Idaho," he replied. "They'd a-ben the fust to be let out after the change come, anyhow, so it don't make no difference."

"You planned to stay on as foreman?" she asked.

"Shore! Why not? I got to work for someone, don't I?"

She made no reply and they rode on in silence toward the ranch. He had given up trying to dissuade her. Let them do their own dirty work, he thought. As they neared the ranch a horseman emerged from the yard and came toward them at a run amidst a cloud of dust that obscured the ranch and all else behind him. It was Texas Pete. He brought his horse to its haunches beside her and wheeled the animal about on its hind feet.

"I jest got in, Miss," he said, "an' Tom told me you had sent word in that I was to meet you. I'm plumb sorry I was late."

Each man ignored the other as completely as though he had not existed.

"I understand you want to quit, Pete," said the girl; "you and Shorty and Idaho."

Pete looked down, shamefacedly. "We was a-aimin' to," he said.

"I wish you'd come up to the office and bring Shorty and Idaho with you when we get home," she said. "I want to talk with you."

"All right, Miss."

The three finished the ride in silence. Diana dismounted with them at the corral and leaving her horse for Pete to unsaddle walked toward the office. As she approached the doorway she saw that there were several people in the room and when she crossed the threshold found herself face to face with Corson, Lillian Manill and the two Wainrights. Corson nodded and he and the younger Wainright rose.

"Good evening, Miss Henders," said Corson; "back safely, I see."

She ignored his greeting and stood for a moment silently eying them through narrowed lids. Her wide brimmed sombrero sat straight and level above slightly contracted brows. A tendril of hair waved softly over one temple where it had escaped the stiff confinement of the heavy hat, but it did not tend to soften the light in those cold, steady eyes, reflecting the bitterness of her resentment toward these four.

About her hips a cartridge filled belt supported a heavy gun—no toy such as women sometimes effect, but a .45, grim and suggestive. Its grip was shiny with usage and the blue was worn from the steel in places.

"I know little about law, Mr. Corson," she said,

without prelude. "I have lived almost all my life a long way beyond either the protection or the menace of law. We do not bother much about it out here; but we understand moral right perfectly. We know what justice is and we have our own ways of enforcing it. We have similar ways of protecting our just rights, as well.

"These means I intend to invoke against you, all of you, who have come here with the intention of robbing me of what is rightly mine. Though I owe you no consideration it is my duty to warn you that our methods in such matters are usually sudden and always unpleasant.

"I shall give you, Mr. Corson and Miss Manill, an hour to leave the premises—the buckboard will be ready then. Mr. Wainright and his son have five minutes, as they have no excuse whatsoever for being here. Now, go!"

CHAPTER XVI

COMMON CRIMINALS

AN AMUSED smile curled Mr. Corson's unpleasant mouth. Mr. Wainright, Sr., bobbed to his feet, though through no belated urge of chivalry. Lillian Manill rose languidly, pretending to suppress a simulated yawn with the backs of her white fingers. Young Mr. Wainright shuffled uneasily from one foot to the other.

"I am afraid, Miss Henders," said Corson, "that you do not quite grasp the situation. You ——"

"It is you who fail to grasp it, Mr. Corson," snapped Diana, "and please remember that you have only an hour in which to pack."

Corson dropped his suavity. "See here," he exclaimed, "I've fooled along with you as much as I'm going to. You're the one who's going to get off this place. You haven't a right on earth here. You don't own a stick or a stone, a hoof or a tail, the length or breadth of the Bar Y. Now you go and go quick or you'll land in jail, where you belong for the threats you've made. I imagine you'll learn something about law then."

"How come?" inquired a voice from the doorway and simultaneously three figures appeared upon the veranda. "You sent for us, Miss, and here we are," continued Texas Pete.

"An' I reckon we arriv about the right time fer the party," opined Shorty.

"I craves the first dance with that dude with the funny pants," said Idaho, staring at Corson.

"Boys," said Diana, "these people are trying to rob me of the ranch, the mine and all the cattle. I have given Mr. Corson and Miss Manill an hour to leave the premises. Idaho, I wish that you would see that they get away on time, and drive them, or better, have Willie drive them, to town. Mr. Wainright and his son had five minutes in which to leave, Shorty. They have wasted three of them. Can you help them to get away on schedule?"

"Whee!" wheed Shorty. "Watch my smoke—and their dust. Fan yerselves, gents," and he sprang into the room, circling the Wainrights to come upon them from the rear, true to the instincts of the cowman.

The elder Wainright had arguments upon his tongue—you could see them in his eye, paradoxical as it may sound—but he permitted them to expire, voiceless, and took to his heels, followed closely by his son. Jefferson Wainright, Sr., had been run off the Bar Y upon another occasion and he had not relished the experience. He moved now with great rapidity and singleness of purpose in the direction of the corrals, his son at his heels and Shorty inconveniently close behind.

To Mr. Wainright's partial relief Shorty had as yet indulged in no target practice, but it might come at any moment. Sympathetic perspiration streamed down the red face of Wainright, of Worcester blankets. He almost breathed a sigh of relief when he reached the corrals, but a sudden thought froze him with terror. They could not have more than a minute left. It would be impossible to hook up their team in that time. As he climbed through the bars he tried to explain that impossibility to Shorty.

"Ride 'em, then," admonished their escort.

"But we have no saddles," expostulated the younger Wainright.

"No," agreed Shorty, "you ain't got nothin' but a minute an' you won't have thet long. I commences shootin' when the minute's up—an' I ain't a-goin' to shoot fer fun. I ben a-waitin' fer this chanct fer months."

Frantically the Elder Wainright dragged a reluctant broncho by the halter, got him outside the corral and struggled to clamber to his back. It was an utter failure. Then he seized the rope again and tugging and pulling started for the gate. His son, more successful, had succeeded in mounting the other animal, and as he trotted past his father he whacked that gentleman's unwilling companion on the rump with the bight of his halter rope. The effects were thrilling and immediate. The broncho leaped forward, upset Mr. Wainright, galloped over him and dashed out the gate into the vast, unfenced immensity.

"Five seconds!" announced Shorty.

Mr. Wainright scrambled to his feet and started after the broncho. He passed through the Bar Y gate behind his son and heir with one second to spare. Disgusted, Shorty slipped his gun back into its holster.

"Now keep goin'," he told them, "an' don't never nary one of you come back."

"Gosh ding it!" he soliloquized as he walked back toward the office, "I wisht she'd only a-gave 'em four minutes."

He was suddenly confronted by Colby, running and out of wind. "What you ben doin'?" demanded the foreman. "I jest seen the tail end of it from the cook-house winder. Wot in 'ell do you mean by it, anyhow, eh?"

Shorty eyed him up and down insolently. "I ain't got no time fer you, Colby," he said. "I'm gettin' my orders from the boss. If she tells me to run any ornery critters offen the ranch I'm here to run 'em off, sabe?"

"You mean Miss Henders told you to run the Wainrights off?" demanded Colby.

"I reckon you ain't deef," and Shorty continued his way toward the office. Colby followed him. He found Texas Pete and Idaho standing in the room. Diana was seated in her father's easy chair.

"What's the meaning of this business, Di?" demanded Colby. "Did you tell Shorty to run the Wainrights off?"

"I ran them off, Hal," replied the girl. "I only asked Shorty to see that they went. I have told Mr. Corson and Miss Manill to go, too. Idaho will see that they get to town safely."

"You must be crazy!" exclaimed Colby. "They'll have the law on you."

"I am not crazy, Hal. I may have been a little blind, but I am far from crazy—my eyes are open now, open wide enough for me to be able to recognize my friends from my enemies."

"What do you mean?" he demanded, noting the directly personal insinuation.

"I mean, Hal, that any of my men who would contemplate working for those people after they had robbed me can't work for me. Pete has your check. He is acting foreman until Bull returns." Her chin went up proudly as she made the statement.

Colby was stunned. He took the check in silence and turned toward the door, where he stopped and faced her. "Bull won't never come back," he said, "'less it's with a halter round his neck."

The other three men looked toward Diana for an intimation of her wishes, but she only sat silently, tapping the toe of a spurred boot upon the Navajo rug at her feet. Colby turned once more and passed out into the gathering dusk.

A half hour later Wild Bill, otherwise and quite

generally known as Willie, jogged dustily townward with Maurice B. Corson, Lillian Manill and their baggage. Halfway there they overtook the Wainrights, the elder riding the single horse, which his son had given up to him, while the younger plodded along in the powdery dust. Corson told Willie to stop and take them both into the buck-board.

"Not on your life," said Willie. "I gits my orders from the boss an' she didn't say nothin' about pickin' up no more dudes. Giddap!"

Later that evening a select gathering occupied a table at one side of Gum's bar-room. There were the Wainrights, Mr. Maurice B. Corson, Miss Lillian Manill, Hal Colby and Gum Smith. All but Gum seemed out of sorts, but then he was the only one of them who had not been run off a ranch.

"We have the law on our side, Mr. Sheriff," Corson was saying, "and all we ask is your official backing. I realize that the first thing to do is to get rid of the ruffians in her employ and then we can easily bring her to terms. The worst of them is this man Bull, but now that he is practically an outlaw it should be comparatively easy to get him.

"I have arranged for an exceptionally large gold shipment from the mine on the next stage and I have taken pains not to keep the matter too secret. The news is almost certain to reach him through the usual channels and should serve as an excellent bait to lure him into another attempted holdup of the stage.

"You can then be on hand, in hiding, with a posse and should you fail to get him alive it will be all the better for society at large if you get him dead. Do you understand me?"

"That ain't no way to go about it," interrupted Colby. "You couldn't hide nowhere within five miles o' the gap without them two hombres knowin' it. Now you just forget that scheme an' leave it to me. You an' your posse keep away from the gap. Just leave it to me."

"Ah think Hal's about right," agreed Gum Smith. "Yo-all doan' know them two. They shore is foxy. Why, jes look at all the times Ah've ben after 'em. Yo jes leave it to Hal here an' he shore'll git 'em."

"All right," said Corson, "and then we can get the other three later, some way. Lure them into town one by one an'—well, I don't need to tell you gentlemen what's necessary. Only don't forget that they're worth a thousand dollars apiece to me—if they can't bother us any more."

Worn out by the excitement of the day Diana retired to her room shortly after the lonely evening meal. She had been keyed up to a high pitch of nervous excitement for hours and now that she had relaxed the reaction came, leaving her tired and melancholy. She was almost too tired to undress and so she threw herself into an easy chair and sat with her head thrown back and her eyes closed.

The window of her room, overlooking the ranch

yard toward the corrals, was wide open to the cooling summer air. The lamp burning on her reading table cast its golden light upon her loosened hair and regular profile.

Outside a figure moved cautiously around the house until it stood among the trees beneath her window—the figure of a man who, looking up, could just see the outlines of the girl's face above the sill. He watched her for a moment and then glanced carefully about as though to assure himself that there was none other near.

Presently, faintly, the notes of a meadow-lark rose softly upon the night air. Diana's eyes flashed open. She listened intently. A moment later the brief, sweet song was repeated. The girl rose to her feet, gathered her hair quickly into a knot at the back of her head, and ran down the stairway, along the hall, into the office. She walked quickly, her heart beating a trifle wildly, to the door. Without hesitation she opened it and stepped out into the night. Below her stood a tall man with broad shoulders.

"Bull!" she exclaimed, in a low whisper.

The man swept his broad sombrero from his head. "Good evening, *Señorita!*" he said. "It is not *Señor* Bull—it is Gregorio."

Diana Henders stepped back. She had removed her belt and gun. So sure she had been that it was Bull and such confidence she had in him that she had not given a thought to her unarmed condition.

What better protection could any girl demand than just Bull!

"What do you want here, Gregorio?" she demanded.

The Mexican perceived the girl's surprise, saw her draw back, and grinned. It did not offend him that she might be afraid of him. He had become what he was by inspiring fear in others and he was rather proud of it—proud of being an outlaw, proud of being hunted by the gringoes, whom he knew held his courage and his gun-hand, if not himself, in respect.

"Do not be afraid, *Señorita,*" he said. "I was sent to you by *Señor* Bull, with a message." He held out a long, flat envelope. "You are to read it and hide it where the others will not find it. He says that you will know how to make use of it."

She took the proffered parcel. "Why did not *Señor* Bull come himself?" she asked.

"How should I know, *Señorita?*" he replied. "Perhaps he thought that you would not want The Black Coyote to come here. He knew that you recognized him today. He saw it in your eyes."

She was silent a moment as though weighing the wisdom of a reply to his statement, but she made none. "Is that all, Gregorio?" she asked.

"That is all, *Señorita.*"

"Then thank you, and good-bye. Thank *Señor* Bull, too, and tell him that his job is waiting for him—when he can come back."

Gregorio swept his hat low and turned back into the shadows. Diana entered the office and closed the door. Going directly to her room she took a chair beneath the reading-lamp and examined the outside of the envelope Gregorio had given her.

It was addressed to Maurice B. Corson! How had Bull come by it? But of course she knew—it was a piece of the mail that had come into his possession through the robbing of the stage.

The girl shuddered and held it away from her. She saw that the envelope had been opened. Bull had done that. She sat looking at the thing for a long time. Could she bring herself to read the contents? It had not been meant for her—to read it, then, would be to put herself on a par with The Black Coyote. She would be as much a thief as he. The only right and proper thing to do was to get the letter into Corson's hands as quickly as possible—she could not be a party to Bull's crime.

She laid it, almost threw it, in fact, upon the table, as though it were an unclean thing, and sat for a long time in deep thought. Occasionally her eyes returned to the letter. The thing seemed to hold a malignant fascination for her. What was in it?

It must concern her, or Bull would not have sent it to her. She would send it to Corson the first thing in the morning. Bull would not ask her to read something that did not concern her. She rose and commenced to remove her clothing. Once or twice as she passed the table she stopped and looked at the envelope and at last, in her night robe, as she went to blow out the lamp she stood for a full minute staring at the superscription. Again she argued that Bull would not have sent it to her had it been wrong for her to read it. Then she extinguished the light and got into bed.

For an hour Diana Henders tossed about, sleepless. The envelope upon the reading table haunted her. It had no business there. It belonged to Maurice B. Corson. If it were to be found in her possession she could be held as guilty as the robber who took it from the United States mail pouch. They could send her to jail. Somehow that thought did not frighten her at all.

What was in it? It must be something concerning the property they were trying to steal from her. They were thieves. One was almost justified in taking any steps to frustrate their dishonest plans.

Suddenly she recalled what Mary Donovan had said: "You've got to fight the devil with fire!" And then Diana Henders flung the covers from her and swung her feet to the floor. A moment later she had lighted the lamp. There was no more hesitation.

She took up the envelope and extracted its contents, which consisted of three papers. The first she examined was a brief letter of transmission noting the enclosures and signed by a clerk in Corson's office. The second was John Manill's will—the later will that Corson had told her did not exist. She read it through carefully. Word for word it was a duplicate of the last will her father had made, except for the substitution of Elias Henders' name as beneficiary. The clause leaving the property to their joint heirs in the event of her father's prior death followed.

Suddenly Diana experienced a sensation of elation and freedom such as had not been hers since her father's death. She could fight them now—she had something to fight with, and Lillian Manill could claim only what was legally hers.

An even division would entail unpleasant complications of administration, but at least they could not take her share from her. They might sell theirs—they might and probably would sell it to the Wainrights, which would be horrible of course, but she would stand her ground and get her rights no matter who owned the other half.

She laid the will aside and picked up the third paper. It was a letter, in her uncle's familiar handwriting, addressed to her father:

Dear El:

In the event that I go first I want to ask you to look after Lillian for me at least until she is married. Since her mother's death she has no one but me and naturally I feel not only a certain responsibility for her but a real affection that is almost paternal, since she was but a year old when I married her mother. She has never known any other father, her own having been killed before she was born. Although she knows the truth concerning her parentage I think she looks upon me as a father and if I am unable to do so I know that you will provide for her. I did not mention her in my will because our understanding included only our legal heirs, or I should say heir now, since Diana is the only one left, and as she will inherit all our property eventually I hope that you will pass this request on to her, which I shall leave attached to my will.

Affectionately,

JOHN.

Diana sat with staring eyes fixed upon the letter in her hand—and she had almost sent these papers back to Corson! She shuddered as she thought of the narrow escape she had had. Why, they were no better than common criminals!

And she was sole heir to the Bar Y! She did not think of the gold mine, or the value of the great herds and the broad acres. She thought only of the Bar Y as something that she loved—as home.

Now no one could take it away from her, and yet she was not happy. There was *a little rift within the lute*—Bull was an outlaw! And who else was there than Bull upon whom she might depend for guidance and advice in the handling of her affairs?

He was a good cattleman—her father had always said that, and had had confidence in his judgment and ability. His one fault, they had thought, had been his drinking, and this she felt, intuitively, he had overcome. Of his loyalty there had never been any doubt until the whisperings of the ugly rumors that had connected him with the robberies of the stage. These she had consistently refused to believe—even to the point of denying the evidence of her own eyes; but Gregorio had definitely confounded the remnants of her hopes.

Yet still she thought of Bull as her sole resource—even now she had confidence in him. She could not fathom the mental processes that permitted her mind to dwell upon him without loathing or contempt—but, after all, was she being influenced by the dictates of her mind? She shrank from contemplation of the alternative, yet it persistently obtruded itself upon her reveries. If her mind refused to fly to the defense of Bull, then it must be her heart that championed him. What reason would not do, love had accomplished.

She flushed at the thought and tried to put it aside, for it was impossible. It could not be that she, Diana Henders, could love an outlaw and a criminal. No, she must put Bull out of her mind forever, and with this resolve mingling with her tears she fell asleep.

CHAPTER XVII

THE BLACK COYOTE

WITH the coming of morning Diana Henders' mind had, to some extent at least, emerged from the chaos of conflicting emotions that had obstructed reasonable consideration of her plans for the immediate future. It had been her intention to ride forthwith to Hendersville and confront Corson and Lillian with the proofs of their perfidy, but now saner reflection counseled more rational procedure. The law now was all upon her side, the proofs were all in her hands. It was beyond their power to harm her. She would continue in the even tenor of her ways, directing the affairs of the ranch and mine, as though they did not exist. When they made a move she would be prepared to meet it.

She spent an hour before breakfast in the office writing diligently and then she sent for Texas Pete. When he arrived she handed him an envelope.

"Take this to Aldea, Pete," she said, "and mail it on the first eastbound train. I can't trust to the stage—it is held up too often—and, Pete, I am sending you because I know that I can trust you to get to Aldea as quickly as you can without letting anything interfere. It means a great deal to me, Pete."

"I'll git it there," said Texas Pete, and she knew that he would.

Ten minutes later she glanced through the doorway of the kitchen, where she was talking with Wong, and saw a cloud of dust streaking swiftly northward toward Hell's Bend Pass, across country in an air line. Roads and trails were not for such as Texas Pete when speed was paramount.

The day, occupied by the normal duties of the ranch, passed without unusual incident. There was no word from Corson. The next day came, brought Texas Pete back from Aldea, and went its way with the infinite procession of other yesterdays, and still no word from Corson. By this time Diana was about convinced that the New Yorker, appreciating what the theft of his letter must mean to him, had abandoned his scheme and that doubtless the stage that arrived in Hendersville today would carry him and his accomplice back to Aldea and an eastbound train.

Her mind was occupied with such satisfactory imaginings that morning when the office doorway was darkened by the figure of a man. Looking up she saw Gum Smith standing with hat in hand.

"Mo'nin', Miss," he greeted her.

Diana nodded, wondering what Gum Smith could be doing on the Bar Y, a place where he had always been notoriously unwelcome.

"Ah've came on a mos' onpleasant duty, Miss," he explained. "As sheriff o' this yere county it is mah duty to serve yo-all with notice to vacate this property by noon tomorrer, as the rightful an' lawful owners wishes to occupy same."

"You mean Mr. Corson and Miss Manill?" inquired Diana, sweetly.

"Yes, Miss, an' they hopes they won't be no trouble. They's willin' to do the right thing by yo, ef yo moves off peaceable-like an' pronto."

"Would you mind taking a note to Mr. Corson for me?" she asked. "I think I can convince him that he is making a mistake."

Gum Smith would be glad to accommodate her. He said so, but he also advised her, as "a friend of her father," to make her preparations for early departure, since Mr. Corson's patience was exhausted and he had determined to take drastic action to possess himself of the ranch, as Miss Manill's agent.

When Mr. Maurice B. Corson read that note an hour later he swore in a most unseemly manner. He did not divulge its contents to the Wainrights, but he went into executive session with Gum Smith and Hal Colby from which he did not emerge for an hour. A short time later the sheriff, accompanied by a dozen deputies, rode out of Hendersville and some time thereafter Corson, Lillian Manill and the Wainrights drove off in the latter's buckboard which Diana had sent in to them the morning after their hasty departure from the Bar Y.

The ranch was deserted that afternoon, except for a couple of laborers, the white cook at the cook-house and Wong at the residence. Texas Pete and his vaqueros were spread over a vast principality occupied with the various duties of their calling. Idaho had been left at home, in accordance with time-honored custom, to act as body guard for Diana should she wish to ride abroad, which she had wished to do, and they were both off to the southeast somewhere, in the direction of the Johnson Ranch.

It was a lazy afternoon. The air vibrated with heat. But in one corner of the kitchen, far from the stove, which was now out, there was a cool corner, or rather one less like inferno. Here stood a long table that had once graced the dining room, and upon it at full length, supine, lay Wong, asleep, his long pipe with its tiny brass bowl still clutched in one depending hand.

He was aroused by the sound of voices in the front of the house. He opened his eyes, sat up and listened. There was a woman's voice among those of men, but it was not the voice of "Mlissee Dli." Wong arose and walked toward the office. He stopped where he could observe the interior without being observed. His slanting, oriental eyes narrowed at what he saw. There were Corson and Miss Manill, the two Wainrights and Gum Smith. Corson was going through Elias Henders' desk as though it belonged to him. Presently, after having examined many papers, he evidently found what he wanted, for there was a look of relief upon his face as he stuffed them into an inside pocket of his coat after a superficial glance.

The elder Wainright was continually glancing through the doorway with an air of extreme nervousness. "You think it is perfectly safe, Sheriff?" he demanded.

"Of course it is, Wainright," snapped Corson. "We've got the law on our side, I tell you, and enough men out there to back it up. As soon as her men find we mean business they won't bother us as long as she isn't here to egg them on, and most of them would just as soon work for us anyway when they find Colby is coming back as foreman —a lot of them are his friends."

"I don't see why Colby didn't come along with us now," grumbled Wainright.

"He wanted to wait until we were settled in our ownership and then we could hire whom we pleased as foreman," said Corson. "I see how he feels about it and it will help to make him stronger with the men and with the neighbors if he hasn't taken any part in the eviction. It'll be better for us in the long run, for we are going to need all the friends we can get in the county."

"I am afraid we are," agreed Wainright. "I hope you will fire that Texas Pete and the ones they call Shorty an' Idaho the very fust thing you do. I don't like 'em."

"That's about the first thing I intend doing as soon as they get in," replied Corson. "Just now we'd better look up that damned insolent Chink and tell him how many are going to be here for dinner, or supper, or whatever they call it out here."

Wong tiptoed silently and swiftly to the kitchen, where Lillian Manill found him a moment later and imparted her orders to him.

An hour later Texas Pete rode into the ranch yard with his men. He was met at the corrals by a fellow he recognized as an habitué of Gum's Place —one Ward, by name.

"Evenin'," said Ward.

"Evenin'," replied Texas Pete. "Wotinell are you doin' here, Ward?"

"They wants you, Shorty an' Idaho up to the office."

"Who wants us?"

"Miss Henders an' the people she's sold out to."

"Sold out, hell!" exclaimed Pete.

"Go on up an' ask 'em."

"I shore will. Come on, Shorty. Idaho must be aroun' the bunk-house somewheres." The two men started for the office. At the bunk-house they looked for Idaho, but he was not there, so they went on without him. As they approached the house they saw three men lolling on the veranda outside the office door. They were not Bar Y men. Inside they saw Corson sitting at the desk. He motioned them to enter.

"Come in, boys," he said, pleasantly.

As they entered the three men behind them rose and drew their six-guns and at the same instant three others just within the office covered them with theirs.

"Put 'em up!" they were advised, and Texas Pete and Shorty, being men of discretion, put them up. While they had them up one of the gentlemen in their rear relieved them of their weapons.

"Now look here, boys," said Corson, not unpleasantly, "we have no quarrel with you and we don't want any, but you're rather quick with your guns and we took this means of insuring an amicable interview. Mr. Wainright, Miss Manill and I are now owners of the Bar Y Ranch. Miss Henders, realizing that she had no claim, has vacated the premises and turned them over to us. We shall not need your services any longer. We shall give you a month's wages and escort you as far as town, where your weapons will be turned over to you; but I want to warn you that you are not to return to the Bar Y. If you do I shall see that the law takes its full course with you."

"Where's Miss Henders?" demanded Texas Pete.

"She has left the ranch," replied Corson. "I do not know her exact plans, but I think she went directly to Aldea to take the train for the East."

"I don't know her exact plans neither," said Texas Pete, "but I know you are a damn liar.

You got the drop on me an' Shorty, an' we goes to town as you says, but if the rest that you have told us ain't straight we're comin' back agin. An' when we do it's a-goin' to be gosh-almighty onpleasant fer dudes in these parts. Sabe?"

"If you show your faces around here again you'll be shot on sight," said Corson. "We've got the men and the money to run this ranch as we see fit, and we mean business. The old, disgraceful, lawless days are about over in this county, and there won't be any place for bad-men like you two."

"No, Pete," said Shorty, "we're did fer, our time's up, they ain't no more place fer us 'an a jack-rabbit. We're a-goin' to hev a new brand o' bad-men now—the kind they raise in Noo York that wears funny pants an' robs orphants."

"Take them to town, boys," said Corson, addressing his own men, "and then come back here. You've all got jobs here on the Bar Y, and one of the first duties you have is to shoot bad-men on sight, if they show up around the ranch."

Texas Pete and Shorty turned and walked out with their escort, and shortly after, still under guard, were loping away in the direction of Hendersville.

The stage came down the pass with a load of passengers that day and among them was a lawyer from Aldea imported by Corson and Wainright to draw up the papers that would make one-third the Bar Y property Wainright's and place a hundred and twenty-five thousand dollars in the hands of Corson and Lillian Manill.

At the mine road it stopped and took on the messenger with the bullion. Then to the crack of Bill Gatlin's whip it lurched onward toward the gap. Bill was discoursing to a tender-foot who had remarked on the dry appcarancc of thc country that he had seen, stretching away as far as the eye could reach, from the summit of the pass.

"I should hate to be caught out there alone," said the young man. "I'm afraid I'd starve to death."

"Why that wouldn't be nothin'," observed Bill. "That wouldn't be nothin' at all. Why back in the seventies when I was ridin' fer the Lazy H outfit in Montana I was chasin' a critter one day when my pony stepped in a badger hole an' after turnin' three complete somersaults lights plumb on his feet an' starts across country scared stiff, which would a'ben all right ef it hadn't a'ben that the last somersault shuck me clean outen the saddle, an' by cracky it was jest my durn luck that my foot caught in the stirrup an' that ornery critter up an' drags me. He was so sceart that he never much more'n slowed up fer three days. Yes, sir, he drug me fer three days *an'* nights, an' all I hed to eat was when he drug me through a strawberry patch an' all I hed to drink was when he drug me through a river. No, sir, after thet it wouldn't seem bad at all to be left out no wheres in no country."

The tender-foot looked at Bill with deep and reverent awe, but he said nothing. The stage bumped over the uneven road, lurching drunkenly around curves. A masked man waited silently behind the boulders at the south end of the gap. He appeared nervous, turning often to glance back into the chapparal from which he had emerged a few moments before. "I wonder where in hell Gregorio is," he muttered, half aloud, "he told me last night that he would be here before me."

The stage drew nearer. Bill Gatlin reined his team to a walk at the first deep chuck-hole at the entrance to the gap. The horses moved slowly, picking their way and sometimes stumbling in the deep, dust filled cavities that made this short stretch of scarce fifty yards the most notorious piece of road within a hundred miles.

The lone highwayman could wait no longer for his accomplice—he must essay the thing alone. He stepped forward to intercept the slow-moving stage and as he did so a noise behind him attracted his attention, and a single backward glance revealed to him a masked man and the familiar habiliments of Gregorio. He breathed a quick sigh of relief, motioned to his accomplice to hurry, and moved forward with the second man now close at his heels.

Bill Gatlin and the messenger were not surprised when the two men stepped into the middle of the gap and held them up. They would not have been surprised under ordinary circumstances, but today they had been forewarned that there would doubtless be an attempted holdup on account of the unusually valuable gold shipment, which was being used as a lure to trap The Black Coyote, and they had been warned to offer no resistance since Hal Colby had agreed to take the notorious robber if the matter was left entirely in his hands without any interference whatsoever. All of which pleased Bill Gatlin and the messenger immensely, since it relieved them both of most of the danger and all the responsibility. Not only did Bill Gatlin show no surprise at the appearance of the two masked figures, but, as a matter of fact, he was already stopping his team as they appeared, and had his hands in the air almost as soon as the command left the lips of the foremost of them. As usual the Mexican kept the driver and messenger covered while The Black Coyote approached the stage to obtain the gold, but this time the second robber followed his principal more closely than had formerly been his custom. The Coyote menaced the passengers with his weapons, seeing that they kept their hands elevated, and then with Gregorio on the watch behind him he slipped both his guns back into their holsters and reached up to take the bags of gold away from the messenger.

He had placed one foot on the hub of the front wheel to raise himself to a height that would enable him to reach the precious pouches when his confederate stepped quickly toward him, shoved the muzzles of his guns into The Black Coyote's back, and ordered him to put up his hands.

"Step down and put 'em up," he said. "You're through."

"Durn my hide!" exclaimed Bill Gatlin. "Hal's pretty cute. I thought he was Gregorio all the time. He's got Bull to rights this time."

The Black Coyote stepped back from the stage, with a growl. "You dirty greaser, you," he cried. "I'll get you for this yet, Gregorio."

The latter nodded to the messenger. "Get down an' git his guns," he said, and when the man had done so, "Now yank off his mask."

The messenger jerked the black silk handkerchief from the face of The Black Coyote with a single quick movement, and then stepped back suddenly, his eyes wide with surprise. "Colby!" he ejaculated.

Bill Gatlin almost swallowed his quid of tobacco. "Well I'll be hornswaggled!" he exclaimed, and then to the second robber, "an' you was Gregorio all the time an' I mistook you fer Colby. The joke sure is on me, an' the drinks too."

"They are," agreed the second robber. He shoved one of his guns into its holster and removed his own mask.

"Well now I *will* be hornswaggled," murmured Bill Gatlin—"ef it ain't Bull!"

"Keep him covered," said Bull to the messenger, "while I get our horses."

Colby glared sullenly at Bull as the latter walked back up the road to get the horses, but he said nothing. He was still half dazed from the surprise of seeing Bull disguised as Gregorio, for even to the latter's guns Bull wore the entire outfit of the Mexican, and when Bull returned, riding Gregorio's and leading Colby's animal, The Black Coyote eyed him as though he still doubted his identity.

Bull drew rein beside him and nodded toward Colby's horse. "Climb aboard," he said. Colby mounted and Bull tossed the noose of his reata around his prisoner's neck, drawing up the slack until the honda touched the collar of the man's shirt.

"Pull yer freight, Colby," said Bull, and the two started off down the road toward Hendersville. A moment later the stage passed them.

"Want me to stay along with you in case you need any help?" called Bill Gatlin.

"I won't want no help," said Bull.

As the stage drew away from them, concealing itself in its own dust, a swarthy rider galloped up to Bull and Colby, reining in a blaze-face chestnut beside them It was Gregorio. Colby glared at the Mexican.

"You— you—" he shouted.

"Shut up, Colby," Bull interrupted him. "You got what was comin' to you. It'll learn you not to ditch a pal."

Gregorio had dismounted and was stripping off

his outer garments and Bull followed his example. As they exchanged clothing and horses they joked together over the day's work, which they considered good. Gregorio swung himself into his saddle first.

"A Dios, Señor Bull!" he cried with a wave of his hand. "Perhaps in a few days Gregorio comes out of the hills, eh?"

"I'll fix that up when I git through with this business, Gregorio," replied the American. "In the meantime just lay low."

"And I will work with you for the Bar Y Rancho?" inquired the Mexican.

"If I do, Gregorio. So-long!"

"A Dios, Señor!" and Gregorio wheeled his pony back toward the hills.

"Thet greaser's whiter'n some white men," said Bull.

When he trotted into Hendersville a few minutes behind the stage he found that already the news had spread and a crowd, gathered about the stage in front of The Donovan House, surrounded him and his prisoner.

"Durn his hide!" exclaimed one who had been foremost among the posse that had ridden forth to hang Bull only a short time before, "I knew right along 'twarn't Bull. I allus said they was something shady about thet there Colby feller."

Bull had but just drawn rein when Texas Pete and Shorty rode up, safely delivered in town by their escort and having reclaimed their guns which had been emptied of cartridges and dropped in the road at the edge of town while the escort galloped quickly out of range toward the Bar Y.

Texas Pete had no time for questions. His quick eyes took in the scene at a glance and possibly he guessed the explanation, or caught it from the comments of the crowd, but another and more important matter occupied his thoughts as he forced his pony to Bull's side.

"Have you saw anything of Miss Di?" he asked. "Is she here in town?"

"I don't know. Why?"

"She ain't on the Bar Y. Corson says she's sold out an' left fer Aldea," replied Texas Pete.

"Corson's a liar," snapped Bull. He turned toward the veranda of The Donovan House where he espied the proprietress. "Mrs. Donovan!" he called to her, "is Miss Henders in town?"

"She is not, Bull," replied Mary Donovan.

Bull turned his eyes toward the crowd until they alighted upon a man he knew who bore a decent reputation—one who was not affiliated with Gum Smith or his gang.

"Thompson," he called, "you take Colby an' keep him 'til I git back. Don't let Gum Smith git his hands on him, an' shoot Colby if he makes any funny plays. Git down offen your horse, Colby. Take him, Thompson. Come on boys!" and with Texas Pete and Shorty at his pony's heels he started on a run for the Bar Y. As they raced along, now neck and neck, Texas Pete jerked his head back in the general direction of Hendersville. "What was it all about?" he inquired.

"I jest runded up The Black Coyote," replied Bull.

"Colby?"

Bull nodded. "I ben suspicionin' him," he said, "fer a long time back, but I couldn't never call the turn on him. Then I runs onto Gregorio while I'm hidin' out up Coyote Canyon. Him an' Colby ben workin' together all along, but it seems lately the greaser's found out Colby's plannin' on double-crossin' him an' goin' south with all the swag. This was to be the last job, an' Colby fixed it someway to have a big shipment of gold today, so Gregorio an' me fixes it an' swaps clothes an' horses an' I takes the greaser's place. Colby never got onto it at all. He thinks I was the greaser plumb up to the minute I yanks off the mask."

"I thought Gregorio didn't have no use fer you, Bull," said Shorty.

"I done him a good turn a spell back." That was all he said about the fight with the Apaches in Cottonwood Canyon, where he had risked his life to save the Mexican's.

They rode on in silence for a while. The ranch buildings, nestling among their trees, were visible in the distance when Texas Pete called attention to a speck among the sage brush far to the southeast.

To an untrained eye it was scarcely appreciable.

"There's a saddled cayuse," he said. "What fer is it doin' out yender?"

Bull strained his eyes in the direction of the animal. "Looks like the L-O sorrel Idaho used to ride," he said.

"Idaho was left home with Miss Di," said Pete.

As one man the three reined toward the distant pony and with loosened reins tore over the powdery earth, bounding in and out and over the brush like so many nimble-footed jack rabbits. Blazes, outdistancing the other ponies, reached the L-O sorrel first. Bull threw himself from his saddle and kneeled beside the prostrate form of a man, half hidden in the brush. It was Idaho. As Bull lifted his head he opened his eyes. He looked at Bull in a bewildered way for a moment, the expression of his face denoting a concentrated effort to recall his mental faculties. Then Texas Pete and Shorty reined in beside him in a cloud of dust and profanity.

"Where's the boss?" demanded Pete.

"What you loafin' out here fer?" inquired Shorty.

Slowly Idaho sat up, assisted by Bull. He looked at the reins looped about his wrist. He felt of his side and brought his hand away covered with blood.

"I done the best I could," he said, "but they was too many of them."

"Where's the boss, you ornery side-winder?"

yelled Texas Pete. "Whose 'them'? What hev they done with her?"

"They was all masked," said Idaho. "I didn't know no more after they creased me. I dunno what they done with her. Help me aboard thet cayuse, you bow-legged flannel mouth, an' we'll pull our freight an' find her, 'stid o' sittin' round here listenin' to your yap."

Pete, who had dismounted, helped Idaho, almost tenderly, into the saddle.

"You better beat it fer town," he said. "You ain't much good no-how an' with a .45 between your ribs you ain't no good whatsumever."

"Shut up!" Idaho admonished him. "If I was perforated like a salt cellar I'd be wuth two o' you." He reeled a little in the saddle, but shook himself and straightened up. It was evident that he was weak from shock and loss of blood, and that he was suffering pain beside.

"You'd better go back, Idaho," said Bull. "You ain't in no shape to ride at all an' I reckon we got some hard ridin' ahead o' us."

"Go back, you damn fool," said Texas Pete, who, under the cloak of rough and almost brutal badinage, had sought to hide his real concern for his friend's welfare.

"Go chase yerselves," replied Idaho. "I'm goin' with you."

They wasted no more time in argument, but started riding a wide circle, looking for the tracks of the abductors. They found sufficient evidence to convince them that there had been upward of a dozen horsemen concerned in the work, which corroborated Idaho's statement, and that approximately half of these had ridden directly in the direction of the Bar Y, while the others had taken a southerly route. It was the latter trail they elected to follow after Bull discovered upon it the imprint of an iron shoe, and as Captain, being tender in front, had recently had his fore feet shod it was safe to assume that they had taken Diana Henders this way.

They rode fast, for dusk was already on them, and when, a short time later, it became too dark to distinguish the trail from the saddle they were often compelled to stop and dismount, and, upon several occasions, strike matches to make sure that they were still on the right track. Their progress was, therefore, necessarily slow. Toward midnight they lost the trail completely. It was there they left Idaho, too weak from loss of blood to continue.

CHAPTER XVIII

THROUGH THE NIGHT

IN a back room of The Chicago Saloon Thompson sat guard over Hal Colby, who was neatly and securely trussed and tied to a chair, in which he sat. In The Donovan House the guests were seated at dinner when Gum Smith entered and took his accustomed place. He had just come from the Bar Y and as the streets of Hendersville had happened to be deserted at the meal hour he had met no one.

"'Lo, Gum," greeted Bill Gatlin. "I reckon you hearn we got The Black Coyote."

"Ah hain't see no one sence Ah reached town," replied Smith, "but Ah knowed Colby'd git the critter," yet withall he looked a bit mystified and uneasy. "Whar be he?" he asked.

"He's safe in The Chicago," said Wildcat Bob.

"Ah reckon Ah'd better git him over to the jail," said Gum Smith.

"I reckon you'll leave him at The Chicago," replied Wildcat. "Do you know who he is?"

"Bull, o' course."

"Bull, hell—it's Colby."

Gum Smith paled, just a trifle. "They must be some mistake," he said, weakly. "Who got him?"

"Bull got him an' they ain't no mistake," said Bill Gatlin. "I knew all along 'twarn't Bull."

"Well," said Gum Smith, "The Chicago Saloon ain't no place fer a dangerous prisoner. Soon's Ah've et my victuals Ah'll take him over to the jail whar he'll be safe."

"I tells you you'll leave him at The Chicago," said Wildcat Bob.

"Ah'm sheriff o' this yere county," bawled Gum Smith, "an' nobody don't want to interfere with me in the dis-charge o' mah duties. Do yo-all hear me, Wildcat Bob?"

"I hears you, but jest like a jack-ass brayin' it don't make no impression on my onderstandin'," replied Wildcat, embellishing his remarks with lurid and descriptive profanity. He finished his meal first and went out. When Gum Smith left The Donovan House he repaired at once to his own saloon. Here he deputized a half a dozen loafers, gave each of them several drinks, and led them to The Chicago Saloon, where he demanded of the proprietor that he turn over to him, forthwith, the person of Hal Colby, otherwise known as The Black Coyote.

"He's in the back room yonder," replied the owner of The Chicago Saloon. "Ef you craves him, go git him. *I* don't want him."

In front of the door to the back room sat Wildcat Bob. His elbows were resting on his knees and from each hand dangled a .45.

"In the name o' the lawr," piped Gum Smith in his high voice, "Ah demands the pusson o' one Hal Colby."

"Git the hell outen here, you blankety, blank, blank, blank!" screamed Wildcat Bob.

"Yo-all better listen to reason, Wildcat Bob," yelled the sheriff, "or Ah'll have the lawr on yo."

Wildcat Bob, raising his voice yet higher again than that of his ancient enemy bawled out an incoherent volley of blasphemous and obscene invective. Gum Smith turned and whispered to one of his followers, who withdrew from the room with two others. Presently Gum Smith stepped to one side of the room and, pointing at the little old man sitting before the locked door, called to his remaining deputies: "Take him, men—do yore duty!"

One of the men stepped forward. Wildcat Bob whirled a gun about his forefinger and without taking aim shot the fellow's hat from his head. The three stepped back. Almost simultaneously there came the sound of the crashing of glass from the interior of the room where Colby was confined, the voice of Thompson raised in protest, and then shots. Wildcat Bob leaped to his feet and reached for the knob of the door. As he did so his back was toward the barroom for an instant and in that instant Gum Smith raised his six-shooter and fired. Without a word Wildcat Bob crumpled to the floor and lay there motionless.

Smith and his men leaped for the door. It was locked, and being a strong door, withstood their combined efforts for several minutes. When at last it gave before their assault and they stepped across the threshold they saw only the body of Thompson sprawled upon the floor in a pool of blood. The Black Coyote was gone.

Surrounded by masked men, her escort shot from his horse, Diana Henders realized only too well the gravity of her situation and though she recognized no individual among those who had lain in ambush for her she guessed well enough that they acted under orders from Corson. Her note to him revealing the fact that she knew the entire truth concerning his duplicity and was in possession of the papers that proved it beyond peradventure of a doubt, had, she guessed, prompted the desperate adventure in which he pitted all against all. So suddenly had the masked riders come upon them from the bed of a dry wash that they had had them covered before either could draw, yet Idaho, true to the unwritten code of his calling and his time, had invited death by drawing in the face of their levelled guns in defense of a woman. Had he been alone, or with another man, his hands had gone up the moment he had realized that the odds were all against him, and one of them had gone up, but it had carried a six-gun with it, and he had been shot out of his saddle for his chivalry, and left for dead upon the parched ground as his assailants galloped off toward the south with Diana.

Night fell and yet the men kept on, two riding ahead of Diana Henders and four behind. They rode rapidly, not sparing their horses, and from both their haste and the direction of their way the girl guessed that they were making a try for the border. Once in the mountains they were forced to a slower gait, and around nine o'clock they halted for a brief rest where there was water for both the horses and their riders.

At first Diana had attempted to question them relative to their intentions, but they would not tell her where they were taking her and at last silenced her with oaths and threats. Nor did they remove their masks until darkness equally as well hid their features from her. This and their almost unbroken silence convinced her that her abductors were men who feared recognition and therefore must have been recruited in the neighborhood.

A shrewd guess suggested that an habitue of *Gum's Place—Liquors and Cigars*—would have recognized them all. The abduction had therefore been engineered or at least connived in by the sheriff, and this line of reasoning but corroborated what was already a foregone conclusion that it had been done at Corson's behest.

What their purpose with her she could not guess. It might be but a plan to remove her temporarily to some hidden spot where she might not further interfere with the plans of the New Yorker, or it might easily have a more sinister purpose. She knew that Corson would never be safe in possession of the Bar Y property while she lived and she did not believe that he was fool enough not to appreciate that fact; but would he dare to have her done away with? She wondered.

It was after midnight when they crossed the summit, at a point where there appeared not the slightest vestige of a trail, and dropped down a dangerous and rocky declivity into a wooded canyon. A dozen times the girl's life was in jeopardy—her only safeguard the agility and sure-footedness of Captain. A half hour later the canyon widened into a little pocket in the mountains and here they stopped again. Through the gloom of the deep gorge her eyes finally distinguished the outlines of a small cabin.

The men dismounted. "Get down," said one of them to Diana, and when she had done so the fellow took her by the arm, with a gruff, "Come along!" and led her toward the shack. He pushed open the door and told her to enter. Following behind her, he struck a match, revealing a single room, rudely furnished with a table, a few benches and a couple of cots, all constructed in rustic fashion from branches of the trees which grew about the place. On the table was a candle holder and a candle, which the man lighted. At one end of the room was a blackened fireplace above which a long shelf supported a few small boxes and cans. On pegs, flanking the fireplace, were crude cooking utensils—a frying pan, a stew pan and a coffee pot, while a larger kettle, for heating water, squatted in the ashes of the dirty hearth.

The other men came in presently. All were masked again. One of them took the kettle and went out, returning shortly with water. Another brought wood and then a third set about preparing a meal. They had brought some flour and bacon with them. There were baking powder, salt, pepper and sugar in the cans upon the mantel shelf, together with one of coffee and another of tea.

The aroma of cooking food awoke Diana to a realization of the fact that she was hungry. Her situation, while grave, had not as yet reached a point that she might consider dangerous. The attitude of the men had been determined, albeit somewhat nervous, yet never at any time actually menacing. What they had done had evidently been accomplished under orders from some person or persons who were taking no active part in the actual abduction—who were not even present when the thing was done nor now that they had reached this hiding place in the mountains.

Diana Henders was more or less familiar with these southern hills and she knew that she never had been in this spot before. What an ideal place it would be to commit and effectually hide all traces of a crime! She put such unpleasant thoughts from her and turned her attention to the bacon sizzling upon the hearth the while it filled the room with its delicious aroma. She was given a portion of the food and, seated upon one of the rude cots, devoured it ravenously. Her fears, of what ever magnitude they might be, had not spoiled her appetite, nor did she show in any other outward manner that she was afraid, either of her abductors or contemplation of the fate that awaited her.

The meal over, one of the men arose and left the cabin. From the monosyllabic conversation that ensued she gathered that he had been sent back along their route to a point where he could act as sentinel and thus safeguard them from surprise. They did not appear to expect pursuit, but took this precaution, evidently, in accordance with orders previously received, or a plan prearranged.

After the meal the men smoked for a while and then, one by one, lay down upon the rough boards to sleep, so disposing themselves that the girl could not approach either the door or the single window without disturbing one or more of them. The last man blew out the candle before he lay down. Diana Henders stretched herself at length upon the rough branches that formed the bottom of one of the cots and tried to sleep. How long she lay awake she did not know, but eventually she fell into a light slumber, from which she was awakened about three in the morning by the sound of horses' feet on the ground outside the cabin. Then she heard men's voices, speaking in subdued tones. A sudden premonition seized her—rescue was at hand! She heard the door open and immediately two of the men upon the floor awoke and sat up.

"Who's that?" demanded one.

"Me," replied one of the newcomers. "The rest o' you fellers wake up—we got to get outta here." He stepped to the table, struck a match and lighted the candle. In its first flare Diana recognized his figure as that of the man who had gone out after the meal to act as guard along the trail—the man with him was Hal Colby.

"Put out that light, you damn fool!" cried one of the awakened sleepers. "Do you want this girl to reco'nize us all?" The light went out, quickly. Hal Colby stepped across the room to her side.

"Everything's all right, Di," he said. "I've come for you."

The other man was speaking to his fellows. "They's someone on our trail—Colby passed them on the cut-off. He'd ben ridin' behind 'em fer an hour. He says they's three o' 'em. We gotta git out." Hastily the men rose and sought their horses. Colby took Diana by the arm.

"Come!" he said. "I'll get you out o' here."

"Why should I want to get out when someone is coming to take me away from these men?" she demanded.

"But I'm here—I'll take you out, Di. Come, we must hurry."

She shook her head. "No! I shall stay here."

"They won't let you—they'll take you along. You had better come with me. I am your friend."

"You cannot be a friend of their's and mine, both."

He took her by the arm again. "Come! This is no time for fooling."

She struggled to free herself and when he attempted to drag her forcibly she struck him in the face with a clenched fist.

"You—!" he cried, applying a vile epithet to her. "You'll come, damn you," and he picked her up and carried her out into the waning night.

Most of the men had found their horses and mounted. "Where's her horse?" demanded Colby of one of them, and when it was led forward he threw her roughly into the saddle and with her own reata he bound her there. Then he mounted his own animal and, leading her's, started down the rough and wooded gorge toward the South.

A few miles away three men drew rein upon a ridge. "We've lost the damn trail agin," muttered Texas Pete, sourly.

Bull sat erect upon Blazes, his head thrown far back, his nostrils dilated.

"What you lookin' up yender fer?" demanded Shorty. "The trail thet bunch o' short-horn's on don't lead to heavin."

"Smell it?" asked Bull.

"What?"

"Wood smoke! They's a east wind. Come on!" He rode blindly through the darkness, trusting to the instinct and the eyesight of his horse, toward the east and the fire from which that tenuous suggestion of wood smoke emanated. Where there was fire there should be man—thus reasoned Bull.

A half hour later the three slid and rolled with their horses down the steep side of a gorge into a cup-like opening in the hills and before them, in the growing dawn, they saw a mean, weatherworn shack. From the crumbling chimney a thin wisp of smoke arose into the still air, to be wafted gently westward after it had topped the summit of the canyon walls. They hid their horses among the trees and the under-brush and crept stealthily toward the building from three sides. Bull was the first to come into the open and as he did so he stood erect and sprang toward the doorway of the building, bursting into the interior with two guns ready in his hands. The place was empty. Embers smouldered upon the dirty hearth. A greasy frying pan lay upon the floor at one side, a kettle half filled with warm water upon the other. There was the odor of cigarette smoke in the air of the single room.

"They ben here, but they's gone," said Bull as his two friends joined him.

"They ain't ben gone long," said Shorty.

They found the trail leading down the canyon

and followed it, while a few miles ahead Colby and Diana with the six masked men debouched upon the wide flat at the foot of the hills. Here they halted.

"One o' you fellers swap horses with the girl," commanded Colby, "and then you all circle back to the west an' north an' hit the high spots fer Hendersville. Here, Grift, you take her horse."

"How come?" demanded Grift.

"Why to lead the folks back at Hendersville offen the trail, o' course," replied Colby. "You'll tell 'em you found her horse tother side o' the West Ranch an' they'll look there 'til the cows comes home."

Grift, satisfied with this explanation, dismounted and took Diana's horse, after which she was bound to the one he had quitted.

"Now beat it!" said Colby. "I'll take care o' the girl," and he started off toward the south, while the others turned westward.

"I reckon I fooled 'em," remarked Colby when the others were out of hearing.

Diana made no reply.

"Them three hombres is trailin' you, Di," he continued, "an' they'll be jest wise enough to foller Captain's tracks. I reckon I fooled 'em fine. Grift never would o' swapped horses ef he'd a-knowed what my reason was."

Diana said nothing. She did not even look at him. They rode on in silence then for some time.

"Look here, Di," he exclaimed finally. "You might as well come down offen your high horse. You're mine now an' I'm a-goin' to keep you—as long as I want you. I'm rich now. I'll git all the money I wants from Lillian, but you're the one I love—you're the one I want and you're the one I'm a-goin' to have. After I gits all o' Lillian's money I'll quit her an' you an' me'll do some travelin', but in the meantime I gotta marry her to git the money. Sabe?"

"Cur!" muttered Diana, shuddering.

"Well, ef you wants to belong to a cur, call me one," he said, laughing, "'cause you're goin' to belong to me after today. You won't never want to go back then. You thought you'd turn me down, did you? You wanted that dirty damn bandit, didn't cha? Well, you won't never git him. If he isn't follerin' you with the three thet's behind us he won't never catch up to us this side o' the border, an' after that he couldn't never find us in a hundred years. If he is with them he'll foller the Captain's hoof-prints until he catches up with 'em an' then that bunch o' bad-uns'll shoot him full o' holes. I guess maybe I wasn't foolin' the whole bunch on 'em, eh?"

Diana Henders looked her unutterable contempt and loathing. Colby fell silent after a bit, seeing that it was impossible to draw the girl into conversation. Thus they continued on for miles. Suddenly, from far away toward the north, came, just barely audible to their ears, faintly the sound of distant fire arms.

Bull and his pals had come upon the six. There had been no preliminary—no questions asked. The three had but put spurs to their horses and overtaken the fleeing abductors, who, their work done, had no desire to enter into an argument with anyone. The moment he thought that he was within safe range Bull had opened up with a single gun, and at the first shot a man had tumbled from his saddle. It was a running fight from then on until but a single one of the six remained. Holding one hand far above his head he reined in his jaded mount, at the same time letting his gun fall to the ground. Bull drew up beside him.

"Where's Miss Henders?" he demanded.

"I don't know nothin' about her—I ain't seen her."

"You lie," said Bull, in a low voice. "You're riding her horse now. Where is she? I'll give you five seconds to answer before I send you to hell."

"Colby taken her—South—toward the border," cried Grift, and Bull wondered, for he had left the man safely in Hendersville.

"You take thet horse home, Grift," said Bull, "to the Bar Y. Ef you've lied to me about Miss Henders, or ef thet horse ain't in a Bar Y corral when I gets back, I bore you. Sabe?"

Grift nodded.

"Now beat it," said Bull, and reined about toward the South.

Again the hard, pitiless grind commenced. Beneath a scorching sun, over blistering alkali flats, the three urged their weary horses on.

"You gotta make it, Blazes. You gotta make it," whispered Bull in the ear of his pony. "She cain't be much ahead, an' there ain't nothin' can step away from me an' you, Blazes, forever. We'll catch up with 'em some day."

CHAPTER XIX

"TELL ME THAT YOU LOVE ME!"

IT was ten o'clock that morning before Bull, Texas Pete and Shorty picked up Colby's trail and by that time the man and his unwilling companion were a good four hours ahead of them. On tired horses, through the heat of a blazing Arizona day, it seemed hopeless to expect to overhaul their quarry before night had fallen and by that time Colby would have crossed the border. Not however that that meant much to the three who pursued him, to whom international boundary lines were of no more practical import than parallels of latitude or isothermal lines.

Before noon they were obliged to stop and rest their horses at a water hole that afforded a brackish but refreshing drink for the three jaded animals. In the mud at its border they saw the fresh tracks of Colby's pony and Diana's. It was evident that they had stopped here for a considerable time, which, in truth, they had, so positive was Colby that he had thrown their pursuers off the track, leading them into a gun fight with a superior force that might reasonably have been expected to have accounted for them to the last man.

Five minutes was all the rest that the pursuers

allowed their horses. Once again they were in the saddle. "Lookee yender!" exclaimed Texas Pete, pointing toward the south. "Ef it ain't rainin' there I'm a siwash."

"It's about a month too early for the rains," said Bull, "but it shore is rainin'—rainin' like hell. Look at thet lightnin'. Say, if they ain't crossed Salee's Flats yet they won't never git acrost, not while thet rain lasts."

"'N' if they has crossed we won't never catch 'em," said Shorty.

"I'll catch 'em ef I hev to ride plumb to hell an' it takes me a hundred years," said Bull.

The rain struck Colby and Diana at the northern edge of the Flats. It came in driving sheets and sometimes in solid masses that almost crushed them. It came with deafening reverberations of Titanic thunder and vivid, almost terrifying, displays of lightning. It was bad where they were, but Colby knew from experience of the country that in the low hills at the upper end of the Flats it was infinitely worse—that there there had been a cloud burst. He put spurs to his horse and dragging Diana's into a gallop urged them both to greater speed, knowing that if he did not cross the wash in the center of the Flats within a few minutes he might not cross it again for days. When they reached it three feet of turbid water tumbled madly down the narrow bed between the precipitous clay walls. The man found a steep path that stock had made for crossing when the bed of the wash was dry and urged his horse downward. The force of the current almost swept the animal from its feet, but with wide spread legs it stemmed the torrent, while Colby, taking a few turns of the lead rope around his horn, dragged Diana's pony through in safety after him. At the top of the bank the man turned and looked toward the north and then down at the rising flood.

"If this rain holds out they won't nothin' more cross here fer a spell," he said, smiling. "In ten minutes she'll be plumb full. We kin take it easier now."

He started off again, but now at a walk, for he knew that there was no longer need for haste, if there had been before, which he had doubted. The horses, cooled and refreshed by the rain, would have been equal to a spurt now, but none was necessary, and so they came after a mile to the dim outlines of an adobe house showing through the driving downpour, directly ahead. Colby rode close to the door, and leaning from his saddle, pounded upon it. There was no reply.

"I reckon we'll stop here a while," he said, dismounting.

He opened the door and looked in. The place was deserted. In rear of it was an open shed for stock and to this they rode. Colby helped Diana from her horse, removed the saddles and bridles from the animals and tied them beneath the shed, then he led the girl to the house, her arms still bound by her reata. There was no chance that she could escape now, so the man removed her bonds.

"We'll rest here a few hours an' give the horses a chance, then we'll hit the trail. We gotta find a place where we kin feed, my belly's wrapped around my back-bone. Let's be friends, Di. You might as well make the best of it. You cain't blame a feller fer lovin' you, an' I ain't so bad—you might a-done a lot worse." He came toward her and raised his hand as though to place it on her arm.

"Don't touch me!" She drew back with an appreciable shudder of revulsion.

He laughed. "You'll feel better after a while," he said. "We're both too dog tired to be very good company. I'm goin' to get in a little sleep. You'd better do the same; but I'll have to tie you up again unless you'll promise not to try to escape."

She made no reply. "All right," he said, "ef you'd rather be tied." He came then and tied her hands behind her. Keeping one end of the rope in his own hand he lay down upon the dirt floor and was soon asleep. Diana sat with her back against the wall listening to the rain beating upon the roof and driving against the walls. The roof leaked badly in several places and the water that came through formed puddles on the floor which joined together into a little rivulet that wound to the doorway and disappeared beneath the door.

How hopeless! Diana stifled a sob. She was tired and hungry and weak from exhaustion. The frightful rain had cut off the frail vestige of a chance of rescue that there had been before. By now no man or beast could cross Salee's Flats. She knew one man who would try had he known of her predicament, but how was he to know of it — a hunted fugitive hiding in the mountains far to the north.

Realizing the necessity for haste if they were to cross the Flats before the wash became an impassable torrent, the three pursuers drove their tired horses onward at the top of their diminished speed. The race became at once a test for the survival of the fittest, and Blazes forged steadily farther and farther ahead of the other ponies. Long before Bull reached the Flats the rain was upon him, refreshing both horse and man, and Blazes, as though imbued with new life, increased the distance between himself and the two ponies now far behind. The driving rain was rapidly obliterating the trail that the man followed, yet he managed to cling to it to the very brink of the wash — to the very point where Colby and Diana had crossed, and there Bull drew rein to look down, scowling, upon a seething barrier of yellow water. Twenty feet wide it was and ten feet deep, swirling and boiling like a cauldron of hell. He eyed the greasy, muddy footing of the bank. Had it been firm and dry he had put Blazes to it for a jump, but he knew that it could not be done now, nor could he swim the horse. Even could the animal have made the crossing it could not have clambered out upon the top of that perpendicular, constantly caving wall, with the mighty current always dragging at it. But Bull was not hopeless—he was merely devising ways and means. Not for an instant had he considered the possibility of giving up the pursuit, or even of delaying it by waiting for the waters to recede. Taking his rope in his hand he dismounted and stepped close to the brink of the torrent, upon both sides of which grew numerous clumps of grease-wood. He seemed already to have formed a plan, for he drew one of his six-guns and hurled it across the wash. He followed it with the second gun and then with his heavy belt of cartridges. Then came his boots, one by one.

Shaking down the honda he swung a noose at the end of his rope, which, opening up, described a circle that seemed to revolve about his head at an angle of forty-five degrees with the ground, like a rakish halo—just for an instant, and then it rose and sailed gracefully across the new-born river to drop around a clump of grease-wood upon the opposite bank.

"Come here!" said Bull to Blazes, and the horse stepped to his side, close to the water's edge. "Stand!" commanded Bull, knowing that Blazes would stand where he was for hours, if necessary, until his master gave a new order.

Bull drew in his rope until it became taut and then he dragged heavily upon the grease-wood across the channel. It held despite his most strenuous efforts. He tied the loose end about his waist, stepped to the very edge of the water and leaped in.

Hal Colby awoke and looked about him. His eyes fell upon the girl sitting with her back against the wall across the room.

"Feelin' better?" he asked. "I am. Nothin' like sleep, onless it be grub."

She did not reply. He rose to his feet and approached her. "You're shore a sullen little devil, but I'll take that out o' you—a little lovin'll do that. Git up an' kiss me!"

"You unspeakable—THING! It would be an insult to a cur to call you that."

Colby laughed good-naturedly. "Ef you'd ruther have a bandit, I might turn one," he said, and again he laughed, this time at his own joke.

"If you are trying to suggest that I would prefer Bull, you are right. You may thank God that he is not here—but he will come—and you will pay."

"Well, you ain't got up and kissed me yet," said Colby. "Do you want me to yank you up? You got a lot to learn an' I'm the hombre what can learn you. I've hed a lot o' experience—I've tamed 'em before, as good as you. Tamed 'em an' made 'em like it. If it cain't be did one way it can another. Sometimes a quirt helps." He struck his chaps with the lash of the one he carried. "Git up, you!" He seized her by the arm and jerked her roughly to her feet. Again she struck him, and this time the man struck back—a stinging blow across her shoulders with the quirt. "I'll learn you!" he cried.

She tried to free herself, striking him repeatedly, but he held her off and lashed her cruelly, nor did he appear to care where the quirt fell.

The tumbling waters, engulfing Bull, rolled him over and over before, half drowned, his powerful strokes succeeded in raising his head above the surface. He had had no conception of the tremendous strength of the current. He was but as a bobbing bit of flotsam upon its surface. He could not stem it. He was helpless. The rope about his waist suddenly tautened and he was again dragged beneath the surface. He grasped it with his hands and tried to pull himself in toward shore, but the giant waters held him in their grip, dragging him downward, stronger by far than the strength of many men.

Suddenly the muddy flood spewed him to the surface once more—this time against the bank to which the opposite end of his rope was fastened and was dragging heavily upon its precarious anchor. He clutched at the slippery, red mud, clawing frantically for a hand-hold. The waters leaped upon him and beat him down, but still he fought on valiantly, not for his life but for the girl he loved.

and at last he won, dragging himself slowly out upon the bank. Almost exhausted he rose, staggering, to his feet and looked back across the torrent at Blazes.

"It ain't no use, boy," he said, with a shake of his head. "I was a-goin' to rope you an' drag you acrost, but it cain't be did. Now I reckon I'll hev to hoof it."

He sat down in the mud and pulled on his boots, gathered up his guns and belt, coiled his rope and turned his face southward. "Ef it takes a hundred years an' I hev to foller him plumb to hell," he muttered, "I'll git him!"

Still spent and blowing from his tremendous exertions against the flood, he staggered on through the sticky clay and the blinding rain, his head bent down against the storm. It was hard work, but never once did a thought of surrender enter his mind. He would find a ranch house somewhere and get a horse—he might even come upon some range stock. He had his lariat and there was a bare chance that he might get close enough to an animal to rope it. But he must have a horse! He felt helpless—entirely impotent—without one.

Imagine yourself thrust into a cold and unfriendly world, if you are a man, without a pocket knife, a bunch of keys, a handkerchief, money, or a pair of shoes and you will be able to appreciate how a cowboy feels without a horse.

Thus, buffeted by the storm, he shouldered on

until suddenly there loomed almost directly in his path the outlines of an adobe house. Fortune smiled upon him! Here he would find a horse! He stepped to the door and was about to knock when he heard the voice of a woman crying out in protestation and pain. Then he flung the door wide and stepped into the interior. Colby, holding Diana's wrist, was twisting it in an excess of rage, for she had struck him and repulsed him until the last vestige of his thin veneer of manhood had fallen from him, leaving exposed the raw, primordial beast.

He saw Bull the instant that the latter opened the door and swinging the girl in front of him reached for a gun. Diana, too, saw the figure in the doorway. A great wave of joy swept through her, and then she saw Colby's gun flash from its holster and knew that Bull could not shoot because of fear of hitting her; but she did not know Bull as well as she thought she knew him, and similarly was Colby deceived, for the man in the doorway fired from the hip the instant that Colby's gun was raised. The weapon fell from nerveless fingers, the grasp upon Diana's wrist relaxed, and Hal Colby pitched forward upon his face, a bullet hole between his eyes.

Diana swayed for an instant, dazed by the wonder of her deliverance, and then as Bull stepped toward her she went to meet him and put her arms about his neck.

"Bull!" It was half a sob. The man took her in his arms.

"Diana!" The word carried all the reverence of a benediction.

Raising her face from his shoulder she pushed him away a little. "Bull," she said, "once you told me that you loved me. Tell me so again."

"'Love' don't tell the half of it, girl," he said, his voice husky with emotion.

"Oh, Bull," she cried, "I have been such a fool. I love you! I have always loved you, but I did not know it until that night—the night they came after you at the West Ranch."

"But you couldn't love me, Diana, thinkin' I was The Black Coyote!"

"I don't care, Bull, what you are. All I care or know is that you are my man. We will go away together and start over again—will you, Bull, for my sake?"

And then he told her that he didn't have to go away—told her who The Black Coyote had been.

"Why, he even planted one o' the bullion sacks under my bed-roll at The West Ranch to prove I was the right hombre," said Bull. "Saw a sack o' dust I brung from Idaho, an' he tried to make 'em think it was yours. He used to send me off alone the days he was a-goin' to hold up the stage, so's when the time was ripe he could throw suspicion on me. He shore was a clever feller, Hal was."

"But the day Mack was wounded?" she asked. "We saw you coming in from the north and there was blood on your shirt."

"I got in a brush with Apaches up Cottonwood, me an' Gregorio, an' I got scratched. 'Twasn't nothin'."

"And to think that all the time he was professing friendship for you he was trying to make me believe that you were The Black Coyote," cried Diana. "He was worse than Mr. Corson and I thought him about the wickedest man I had ever known."

"We gotta think about gittin' back an' havin' a friendly pow-wow with thet there Corson gent," said Bull. "By golly, the sun's out! Everything's happy, Diana, now thet you're safe."

They walked to the doorway. The rain had stopped as suddenly as it had begun, and now the fierce sun blazed down upon the steaming mud.

"Where's your horses?" asked Bull.

"In a shed behind the house."

"Good! We'll start along. They's a bridge twenty-five miles below here ef I ain't mistaken. I think I know this here shack. I was down this way two year ago."

"But what about him?" She nodded back toward the body of Colby.

"He kin rot here fer all I care," said Bull, bitterly—"a-hurtin' you! God, I wisht he had nine lives like a cat, so's I could kill him a few more times."

She closed the door behind them. "We'll have to notify Gum Smith, so they can send down and bury him."

"Gum Smith won't never get the chanct," he said.

They walked to the shed and he saddled the two horses, rested now and refreshed a little by the past hours of relief from the heat, and after they had mounted and ridden half way to the wash they saw the figures of two men upon the opposite bank.

"Texas Pete and Shorty," he told her. They recognized the girl and Bull and whooped and shouted in the exuberance of youth and joy.

It was a hard ride to the bridge through the heavy mud, but it was made at last and then the four joined upon the same side and set out toward home, picking up Idaho en route, still weak, but able to sit a horse.

It was two days later before they rode into the Bar Y ranch yard, where they were met with wild acclaim by Willie, Wong and the men's cook.

"Where's Corson?" demanded Bull.

"The whole bunch has gone to town to close the deal. They was some hitch the other day. Wong said he heard 'em talkin'. Corson wouldn't take nothin' but gold an' Wainright had to send up to Aldea fer it. They say it's comin' in on today's stage."

"I'm goin' to town," announced Bull.

"So am I," said Diana.

"We'll all go," said Shorty.

"Git us up some fresh horses, Willie," said Texas Pete. Then he turned to Diana. "You ain't said yit thet I ain't foreman no more." They both smiled.

"Not yet, Pete. I'll have to talk it over with Bull," said Diana.

Remounted, they galloped off toward Hendersville—all but Idaho. Him they left behind, much to his disgust, for he needed rest.

They reached town half an hour after the stage had pulled in and, entering The Donovan House, found Corson, Lillian Manill, the two Wainrights, together with the attorney from Aldea and Gum Smith.

At sight of Bull, Gum Smith leaped to his feet. "Yo-all's undeh arrest!" he squealed.

"What fer?" asked Bull.

"Fer robbin' the United States Mail, thet's what fer."

"Hold your horses, Gum," admonished Bull, "I ain't quite ready fer you yet. I craves conversation with these here dudes fust." He turned to the elder Wainright. "You was honin' to pay a hundred and twenty-five thousand dollars to this here dude fer the Bar Y?"

"'Tain't none o' yore business," snapped Wainright.

Bull laid a hand upon the butt of one of his guns.

"Does I hev to run you out o' Hendersville to git a civil answer?" he demanded.

Wainright paled. "I've paid already, an' the Bar Y's mine," he answered, surlily.

"You've ben stung. Them two's crooks. The girl ain't no relation to Miss Henders' uncle an' we got the papers to prove it. We got the will, too, thet this skunk tried to git hold of an' destroy. Leastwise Miss Henders had 'em, but she sent 'em to Kansas City before Corson could git holt of 'em. Texas Pete, here, took 'em to Aldea. That's why you didn't find 'em in the office, Corson, when you robbed the safe. Wong saw you and told us about it just before we left the ranch today. All you got was the copies she made. I don't wonder you wanted gold from Wainright."

"He's lyin," cried Corson to Wainright. "Do you believe what a fellow like he is says? Why, he'll be in a federal penitentiary inside another month for robbing the mail. There isn't a jury on earth would take his word for anything."

"I ain't there yit an' no more I don't expect to be," said Bull.

"Yo-all's undeh arrest, jes the same, right now," cried Gum Smith, "an' Ah warns yo to come along peacable-like with me."

"Now I'm comin' to you, Gum," said Bull. "You better beat it, Gum. You ain't wuth shootin', with catridges the price they be," he continued. "Gregorio has told me the whole story. He's goin' straight now an' he wants to square himself. He's writ out an' signed a confession thet's goin' to make this climate bad fer your rheumatism."

"Gregorio's a dirty, lyin' greaser," screamed Gum. "They won't no one bulieve him neither. They ain't no one got the goods on me."

"No," said Bull, "but you have. Nearly every ounce of thet gold — except what you an' Colby spent an' what little you giv Gregorio's buried underneath the floor of the back room o' your saloon, an' me an' Pete an' Shorty's right here to see thet no hombre don't git it what don't belong to it."

Gum Smith paled. "'Tain't so! It's a damn lie!"

"Thet's the second time I ben called a liar in five minutes," said Bull. "I ain't did nothin' 'cause they's ladies present, but I'm goin' to send 'em outen the room in a minute an' then we'll talk about thet — ef you're still here. I'd advise you not to be, though. Wainright, I seen your buckboard tied out in front here. By crowdin' it'll hold five — meanin' you, thet ornery lookin' dude son o' yourn, Corson, Miss Manill an' Gum. You all be in it an' hittin' the trail north fer tother side o' the hill inside o' five minutes or me an' the boys is goin' to start shootin'. On the way, Wainright, you an' Corson kin settle thet little matter o' the hundred an' twenty-five thousand. Ef you kin git it back from him 'tain't nothin' to me, but ef you don't you deserve to lose it, fer you're jest as big a thief as he is, only not quite so bright in the head. Now git, an' git damn pronto!" His voice had suddenly changed from mocking irony to grim earnestness. It was a savage voice that uttered the final command. Gum Smith was the first out of the room. He was followed by the others. "See 'em to the edge of town, boys, an' see that they don't linger," said Bull to Shorty an' Texas Pete.

"Oh, mamma!" exclaimed Shorty. "Lead me to them funny pants!"

Bull turned to the attorney from Aldea. "I ain't got no proof thet you were in on this deal," he said; "so you kin wait an' go in on the stage to-morrer."

"Thanks," said the attorney. "No, I thought it a perfectly legitimate transaction; but I am glad they called me down, for now perhaps I can transact some real business for some other clients of mine. I had not been aware that the Bar Y was for sale, or I had been over here before. I represent a large syndicate of eastern packers whom I know would be interested in this property, and if Miss Henders will make me a proposition I shall be glad to transmit it to them—you will find them very different people to deal with than these others seem to have been."

"I thank you," said Diana, "but the Bar Y is not for sale. We are going to run the ranch together, aren't we, Bull?"

"You bet we are," he replied.

Mary Donovan burst from an inner room at the moment. "Bliss me heart!" she exclaimed. "An' I niver knew you was here 'til this very minute, an' I heard what yese jest said, Diana Henders, an' I'm not after bein' such a fool that I don't know what yese means. It makes me that happy, God bless ye! I must be after runnin' in an' tellin' me ould man—he'll be that glad, he will."

"Your old man!" exclaimed Diana.

"Sure now," said Mary Donovan, blushing, "didn't yese know 'at me an' Bob was married the day before yisterday? Shure they had to shoot him before I c'd git him. He niver was much, an' havin' a bullet hole clean through him don't make him no better, but thin he's a man, an' a poor one's better than none at all."